The razor continued to swirl, to attack in a thousand places at once, like being in the midst of a swarm of stinging bees. Wisely, Frank kicked under the man's swing and another slash opened the skin on the top of his hand, slice just like that. He kicked again into the man's stomach, harder than a mule, then again, lower, down in there, the son-of-a-bitch, and again in there. Blood all over now, his hands and arms red. The man crouched, holding one arm over his aches while the sharecropper moved in with a deft step, grabbed an arm but took a deep cut along the thigh, opening it up to the gristle. He managed to grab the arm, the arm with the razor, and hoisted his knee and cracked the man's arm over it at the elbow, snapping it once, twice, until a bluish-white bone leaped out on the side, peeking through the dark skin. The stranger's eyes rolled back in his head, then he crashed to the floor.

hot snake nights

cole riley

an original holloway house edition

**HOLLOWAY HOUSE PUBLISHING COMPANY
LOS ANGELES, CALIFORNIA**

A Holloway House Original Edition

HOT SNAKE NIGHTS

All rights reserved under International and Pan-American Copyright Conventions. Without limiting rights under the copyright reserved above, no part of this publication may be reproduced, stored in or introduced into a retrieval system, or transmitted, in any form, or by an means (electronic, mechanical, photocopying, recording, or otherwise), without the prior written permission of the publisher of this book. Published in the United Sates by Holloway House Publishing Group of Los Angeles, California. This is a work of fiction. Names, characters, places and incidents are either the product of the author's imagination or used fictitiously. Any resemblance to actual events or locales or persons, living or dead, is entirely coincidental. ISBN 0-87067-891-4 Copyright 1985 by Robert Fleming.

Printed in the United States of America

Sale of this book without a front cover may be unauthorized. If this book is without a cover, it may have been reported to the publisher as "unsold or destroyed" and neither the author or the publisher have received payment for it.

ISBN O-87067-891-4

COVER AND BOOK DESIGN BY **JESSE DENA**
COVER PHOTOGRAPHS: FARM SECURITY ADMINISTRATION

*For
Soledad
who made this book possible . . .*

hot snake nights

*"Hellbound on my trail,
hellbound on my trail."*
--Blues song by Robert Johnson
Summer, 1937

*"Evil comes forth when we seek to maim
ourselves and our loved ones.*
Doc "Haphazard" Finley
New Years Eve, 1961

Part One

THE ONLY CLUB

Chapter 1

The train went across a long bridge into cotton country. Overhead, the moon was glistening yellow, full, and Frank Boles looked down into his hands at the church fan advertising a funeral home in the next county. Two little black girls, grade school age, smiled back at him from the face of the fan. He was riding in the Jim Crow car for colored, occasionally glancing out into the night sky.

Across from him, an old woman sat with her gnarled, wrinkled hands folded in her lap. He could not stop staring at her, watching her put talcum powder on her small, withered bird neck. She was all dressed in black, with no hat or veil, and a gift-wrapped box on the seat beside her. It was wrapped, strangely enough, in Christmas paper, even though it was the middle of March.

This woman was an agent of Evil, the messenger of forbidden deeds, secret rites and rituals. Evil was a living spiritual being or at least that is what he wanted to believe. It was the middle of March, his father was dead and buried. He wondered for a second if this woman could have saved his sick Papa with her mumbo-jumbo if he had known her spirit name, if he had known her price. It was mournful, this whole business of his dead father. Buried in Arkansas. Whoever Frank Boles was, he was no longer himself. This was the saddest part.

Yes Lord, he thought, there was enough sadness to go around these days, especially in Mississippi. He slumped in his seat and nodded, letting sleep take him away from the bad memories and regret. Hours later, the porter shook him, telling the yawning man that his stop was coming up. Walking along the deserted highway, he suddenly remembered he was alone, dangerously alone, and hastened his steps.

He was relatively safe since this was one of the new highways with electric light. He kept walking homeward. For some reason, he had stood on the platform for several minutes after the train pulled out of the station. Probably because of his father, dead and buried in Arkansas.

In another hour he was home in the beaverboard shack. He let himself in and the door slammed shut with a loud, quick bang. Sweat ran down his face and soaked his shirt between his shoulders, leaving a dark stain. He walked over to the washbasin, filled it with cool pump water and splashed it on his face.

"Did they put him away nice?"

His wife was not the prettiest woman to look at and he could have done much better in that area. She was stout, had thick black hair, strong features and a worried expression. They had been married for sixteen years. Married to this girl from Louisiana. Mary.

Clarksdale wasn't that far away. He was thinking about this when she repeated her question.

12

"Yessuh, they put him away real fine," he said, lighting a cigarette. "A minister friend he knew in Little Rock said words over him and then we all went out to the graveyard. That's where the tears always come, at the graveyard."

"I had a bad dream last night," she said, her lips trembling. ". . . A real bad dream . . . so real."

"Must have been something you ate. You didn't eat over at your sister's again?"

"No. That gal ain't never home. She's messing with some new mechanic that just moved on the Victoria Plantation."

"That's one hot-tailed gal," he chuckled. "Tell me about this dream you had."

She walked away from him but he followed her, getting her in a bearhug, holding her tight against him. She lowered her eyes and smiled as he kissed her on the lips.

"I won't tell nobody, Mary. Come on now."

She looked blank for a moment, then pushed him away from her. "This dream really scared me, scared me to death. Somethin' real bad is going to happen. I know it."

He took a deep drag from his cigarette and flicked the ash into his palm. "That's crazy talk there. I'm the one that should be plumb crazy. Damn, my father's just died."

"When we going to move, Frank?" Mary asked this with a sneer in her voice. He didn't answer so she asked him again, swatting a fly with a roll of balled up newspaper to make her point. She wanted an answer.

A truck horn sounded in the distance, much like a moan, as the two of them stood silently, caught up in their own inner thoughts.

"Something's still bothering me," she said. "It's the boy, Little Frank. I don't know how to say it, other than he is getting worser and worser." She was sobbing now, tears on the back of her hands. "I's worried about him. He ain't normal, ain't never been normal. Look at me. I's all broke out from

13

bad nerves, worrying about that boy."

"What's matter with you?" He stared at the rash, a blotch of fine bumps, on her usually smooth face.

"I's scared. Something bad is gonna happen right here in this house. I know it, I feel it." She looked first at him and then at her hands again. Slowly she put her head down on the table and cried until no more tears came. All the while, he rubbed her neck and shoulders softly.

After a few minutes of this, she was restless, edgy. He had never seen her like this. For the longest time, she watched the floor, as if she was seeing something odd. Something that held her transfixed. Then her eyes widened, swelling in their reddened lids with a gaze of increasing terror.

He was quiet and so was she. Her breath became labored, short and tight. Her mouth drew back and he could hear the scream coming long before he heard it. This was serious. He held her and said soothingly that he was there and everything would be alright. What was it? What made her like this? What did she know that she wasn't saying?

"We have to do something about Little Frank," she said, almost in a whisper. She sighed deeply once. Her eyes were full of dread again. She squeezed them shut. Her words were blocked, she couldn't speak. She was fighting against something down in her to get them out. "He ... he ... had one of the ... one of the other kids ... by ... by the throat. He ... he wanted to kill ... I saw it. I saw it with my own eyes."

Finally she became relaxed after she said it. He lit another cigarette, arched an eyebrow and puffed it while he watched her.

"Am I goin' crazy?" she asked.

"Naw, naw ... I know. I think you are tired and a person'll say anything when she is tired."

Mary reflected for a moment. "Mebbe I shouldn't have said

nothing to you 'bout it. You got enough on your mind with your Papa dying and all. I didn't mean to put no more worry on you. I really didn't."

"How long . . . he been acting up?" Frank interrupted.

"For quite awhile, especially while you was gone." Suddenly she thought of something else. "Frank, can't nobody say I didn't do right by him. I treated him jes' like the others. No different."

"Nobody is going to say that. You've been a good mama to him."

"Then what's wrong with him? Tell me that. What's wrong? He's dangerous, really dangerous."

"Maybe you are making more of this than you should," Frank said coolly, his face racked with concern.

"You understand so little. Mens."

"What should I understand, Mary? I know that boy inside and out. He is my son. My flesh and blood. He is slow in the head but he ain't going to hurt nobody. I know that much."

She wore a pained expression on her face. "He is too strong for me to handle. I couldn't get him to come out from under the bed yesterday. Then he gave that crazy look of his and showed his teeth at me. Then he come out when he was good and ready. He started turning around and around in circles like he do sometimes and wouldn't stop. I don't understand him at all. Lord, he's getting real bad."

"When we going to move, Frank?" Mary asked again. She wanted to hear a date, a definite date.

"Soon, real soon," he answered. He shrugged his broad shoulders, his John Henry workman's shoulders, as Mary's sister called them, and told her not to let him forget Mister Wiley's food bill next Friday. His children were safe in their beds, at home. They had to be inside when dark came, because the white folks had been raising hell since two boys from the Wright Plantation robbed that dime store in Memphis and shot a young white girl. They were crazy mad because the murdered girl was with child, in her sixth month.

"There is always some devilment going," she said. "Soon as they get growed up some, I'm gone send them North to Aunt Pearl. I want grandchildren and that ain't guaranteed down here."

"What's this 'bout the kids right now? What's on your mind?"

"Nothing really. Just a feeling I had."

After a deep breath, she said, "You said that last year . . . soon . . . real soon. Give me a time so I can have something to hope for. I can't stand it like this, not knowing anything. Tell me anything, lie. You can lie. Can't you?"

He smirked, then mumbled under his breath. Aloud he said: "Don't mess with me, not like I feel today. Shut your damn mouth! Don't let me have to tell you again. I don't want to hear nothing else 'bout leaving." He was sure he would hit her if he didn't go outside, so he pushed past her and went out.

Chapter 2

He looked toward his spanking new outhouse and recalled its stink which was always strongest in the summer. The odor was almost hidden by the soil, almost.

His wife plopped into one of the chairs near the front door of their shack. She felt depressed from looking at the place, a junkpile on blocks. However, the children did give her some comfort. All nine of them: Teenie, Mance, Bue, Dit, Bracey, Buddy, Jake, Lincoln, and Little Frank. Lincoln was the lap baby. Often people passing on the highway stopped to take pictures of their shack, slipping the children cash to pose near a tractor or a ditch.

Frank walked over to one of the children. "Teenie, where's your mama, gal?" The little girl put one arm around his waist and pointed with the other to the door.

He heard his wife's voice coming from the other room. "Frank, is that you? Always sneaking up on me. You gone

17

have to talk to that boy that is courting Bue. That buck sniffing around here too much. I don't want no foolishness out them two." She slipped by him in a quick movement to the outside to hang up some wet clothes.

"What he do?" Frank asked.

"Well, the boy won't go home," she said. "While you was gone, he was around here every night. He is up to no good. All they do is whisper and carry on. Twice I caught them all hugged up."

He placed more wood in the stove, keeping clear of the flames, and turned to her. "I'll talk to the boy's papa. Got enough mouths in this house, can't afford no more." He wiped his hot hands on his overalls to cool them.

"Mister Jesse come by while you was gone. Told him you was away on business. He said you owed some money so you better see him."

He looked down and smiled. "I'll go and see that peckerwood before suppertime. Be back." As he left to cross the yard, the children hung on him, some trailed behind him. Teenie and Bue waved at him from a small rise near the trees and stood talking among themselves. Glumly, he walked away, out over the fields in the high grass. The children watched his head bob with each of his long strides.

When he arrived at the big house, he sent one of the foremen, Possum Higgs, to get Mister Jesse. His eyes shadowed the white man until he disappeared into one of the barns. Soon Mister Jesse came out of the barn, a cane knife in his hand, and walked toward Frank and past him into the house without any type of greeting. After another five or ten minutes, the white man emerged and took a position on the porch, standing and looking down at Frank. There was not a speck of dirt or grease on his khaki work clothes anywhere.

"You stepped away for a minute there, eh Frank boy?" Mister Jesse asked, forcing air into his fat jowls. The man was at least seventy pounds overweight.

"Yessuh. Had business in town for a day or so."

"Boy, look like you gone have another fine crop. And you been workin real good with the men in the fields. Member I asked you about Coleman, told you to tell him to shape up."

"Yessuh." He said it with a sense of submission.

"That nigger don't look like he want to work," the boss man said, chewing his wad of Red Man and spitting into the dust. "That nigger's crop always bad and short. Borrowing all the time. Ain't doing nothing. What's wrong with him? You my ears amongst those niggers. What's wrong with the boy?"

"I don't know. He don't talk much. I can't speak on what he got in his mind."

"Watch your mouth, boy," Mister Jesse warned. "Now he made a deal with me just like you other boys did and he ain't doing his part. Want you to pep him up, Frank boy. You one of my best boys, depending on you." With that, Mister Jesse reached over and patted Frank on the head, like you would do with a puppy, or better yet, a small child.

Frank hesitated. "But sir, I told you . . . I can't make them mens mind me."

Mister Jesse mumbled something to Possum Higgs about monkey trials and nigger-lovers. "Boy, you back talking me? You do what I tell you and no lip."

"Mister Jesse I had a bad time myself this year," Frank said, lowering his eyes. "Land ain't as good as it used to be. You seen the rains we had. Then the cold, ground cold plumb through March. Bad cold spell. Mens can't make no weather, that's God's work."

The boss man turned to Higgs and sneered, "Bring me my cow-hide. This boy needs an ass whupping."

"No suh." Frank made it real lowly, pure nigger.

He glared at the black man. "Nigger, the land must be

worked. Work harder. You get behind them, eh Frank boy?" His words were said with a smile that could have started a brushfire. No more back-talk, nigger.

Once dismissed, Frank hastened his pace toward home. The sky was clouded over, like more rain. Damn that white man, he thought. Sometimes those fool peckerwoods could make you mad, you just wanted to kill one of them. In the hollow, he saw his boy, Buddy, sitting on a stump. Alone. The boy heard him at the very last second and he jumped with surprise. They both laughed and looked at the sky, talking about how bad it was. The dark clouds.

His father dug at him, slapping the boy on his back. "What devilment you out here conjuring up?" The boy's face carried a strange burden, wrinkles of deep thought furrowed his brow.

Buddy dropped his head and spoke. "Papa, will I be exactly like you when I finish growing? I told Jake I would be and he say naw. I say he was wrong because we was from the same blood and got to end up the same way. He say naw, we all different stocks like some horses from the same mama and papa is fast and slow. What you say, papa?"

His eyes rose and met his father's. The trees behind them slanted under a gentle gust of wind, almost as if they were listening in.

"Both of you is right," the father smiled. "All of us is different and same. But more different than same. That's why we got different names, because all of us is different. We the same because we's all peoples. Member when we was by that magic man friend of Ted Taylor's papa. Member that? We was over at his house that night and he made a bunch of different gloves come out of one glove. They's all different, but they's all gloves. Just different gloves and they's all come out the same hand. God made me and your mama and we made all you all." He was proud of his example, the wise father speaketh.

Buddy smiled. "That's why our second name's the same."
His father slapped at a mosquito near his ear and nodded.

Frank returned to the point. "Boy, I ain't no model. You
gone have to live your own life, your own way. Don't worry
about it none. You'll do a good job when you have to."

Damn the boy's time, he thought. Ask more questions than
a crow's got feathers. But that's good, means he got some
sense. He guided the boy off the stump, together they made
a new path through the high grass, with the green blades dropping behind them like they were swimming a cut through lake
water. Overhead, patches of sky began peeping through the
clouds until the dark puffs broke up their meeting to congre-
gate somewhere else.

"Papa, when Big Pa died, did you cry?"

"What you think? Believe this ... I didn't laugh."

Still walking homeward. Suddenly Frank asked, "What you
know 'bout this boy messing with Bue?" He glanced down
at the boy trying to match his long steps. Again the sound
of the grass under their feet and the rustle of weeds and their
stickers. Valiantly, the boy's voice fought with the grass stalks'
song so the father's tenor talk rang out alone.

"He touched her."

"Feeling her up, huh?"

"Jes' touched her and kissed her on the face."

"Yeah, go on. And don't tell your mama none of this here."

"Some of the Smith boys say she fast-tailed and will lay
down with anybody."

"Is she fast? She ain't messing with a heap of boys, is she?"

"Naw papa, she only mess with one boy. And she jes' hug
him a lot. Nothin' more than that, papa."

"You sure?"

"Yeah."

"Well, let them talk. Don't worry 'bout what them other

21

boys say about her if it ain't true. They mad cause they don't know nothing for sure."

The dust yard added their footsteps to the ones it had already collected. Frank smiled again at his son, wiped his feet on a bunch of rags at the door and the boy did likewise. Supper was ready.

Instantly Bue and Teenie pulled the boy's arm and yanked him into a corner, whispering. Asking him rapid questions. Their mother called to her family over the fingers of the food aroma, the come and the get of it. Pretending not to hear, Frank scrubbed his hands in the basin and listened to Bue ask Billy; ". . . did he ask you about that?" He decided he would speak to her after the others had gone to bed. After he finished eating, he'd speak to the boy and his father. When everyone washed up, they ate their supper. Two chickens and sidemeat, brown gravy, cornbread, peas and rice. The gravy vanished and Mary went to the sack of flour to get a handful to make some more.

She eyed her man shoveling food into his mouth. Tonight after they were in bed, she would put the question of Little Frank to his father. Once again. Something was wrong with him, something in his head. Maybe the doctor should check him again, maybe blood was not getting to somewhere in there.

Chapter 3

That evening Frank talked to his daughter about her young man and the limits of their relationship. Her large, brown eyes grew mean when he told her to watch her step. Occasionally, she would roll her eyes, fold her arms over her budding breasts, clucking her tongue as though she was disgusted with this kind of talk. He held her arm so tight that the blood went around the area where he gripped. Angrily, she straightened up a bit and pierced his face with a stare.

"You's only fourteen," he said, controlling himself. "You must think you're grown. Until you get seventeen or eighteen, you do what I tell you and not before."

"I's fourteen goin' on fifteen."

"Keep that boy away from here when I's not here," he snapped at her. "Hear me? What I say, gal?"

"We ain't doing nothing wrong," she frowned when she said it. "He ain't done nothing not proper. We wasn't doing nothing, daddy." A plea in her reply but an edge of stubborn pride there too.

"Did he touched you under your clothes?"

"Naw. He's a nice boy."

"Do his folks know all of this is going on?"

"What, papa?"

"You and him, playing with fire. Do they know? Has he taken you to meet his peoples?"

"Not yet."

He was pulling up a chair, indicating the worse of the confrontation was over. "I don't want no funny stuff out of you two and make sure it stays that way. You know what I mean. Now you know you are too old for me to give you a whupping like the others. But if you act like a child, I'll treat you like one. Hear?"

"Yessuh. I'll be good."

He smiled at her slyly, then held her close, her head under his arm like birds sometimes do their young. "You part of me, gal," he said gently. "Don't shame the ones who love you. You love your old papa, right?" She was blushing, snickering with her hand to her mouth.

"Have you been giving your mama a hand with the chores around here? She looks awfully tired."

"Yessuh."

He tickled her. "You didn't answer my question. Do you love your papa?"

"Yessuh, you know I do, daddy."

Feeling that he had done his duty, Frank slipped into his heavy coat for the brisk night air and set out for the boy's house to convey the same message. In five minutes, there were denials, threats and other harsh words in the boy's house. The boy pleaded not guilty, while his father added that the young girls around there got real fast quick and the boys were no match for them if they wanted something in them. The wrong thing to say to a man like Frank, devoted father and family man. He looked the man over with a cold, terrible eye, wondering if he should kick his ass for a remark like that. Then he asked him to step outside and Ted's father hesitated because he knew Frank's reputation for acting a fool, wanting to fight all the time at the drop of a hat. Once they were standing in the front of the house, Frank laid into the man something fierce, cussing and pointing his thick finger in the man's chest. Capping it off with steel-coated threats and a snarl. He walked away, the man watching his back, then Frank stopped and pointed at him once, something amounting to "don't let me have to come over here again with this mess, won't be no talk." A mule coughed hard from back of a shed somewhere.

Frank's wife waited at the front door. The chill of the evening air made her pull her tattered wool sweater over her bare shoulders. She pondered how to tell him again about Little Frank, the child had his name but he was nothing like him. Nothing but a lot of trouble. Slow in the head. Worrysome. Soon be twelve, more like a baby by the way he thought. She didn't want to burden Frank with so much all at once. Still something had to be said. Mary prepared the children for bed, taking the dirty clothes off the smaller ones and wiping their noses. The older children helped somewhat, especially with her dragging around like she was. She had her mind set. He must be told. Mary looked at her flock, at the chain they had weaved, some weak links and some strong links. Lord knowed she loved them all, but Little Frank wasn't like the rest of them, he took so much out of her. Drained her. It was enough worrying about the lap baby, Lincoln. If Little Frank was not so ugly in his looks, white lady in Natchez said he was a Mongoloid; she could never tell her husband that . . . yet she knowed he felt the same way. Funny but the boy didn't look like anyone she knowed among her peoples, and from what she saw of Frank's peoples, the boy was a foreigner, a freak of Nature. She loved him anyway, a mother's caring. It was hard sometimes but she did. After the children were settled, she sat on the bed, composed her thoughts, picked out all the right keys to make her words hit their mark. None would be wasted.

Just then it came to her. When Little Frank was born, there were problems right after her water broke. The inside pressures under her swollen stomach, the ones that made her hunch up, bend and churn. At last a feeling of pinpricks and then hot knives shot all over her. So she moaned and moved, shifting her wet thighs with the pain. Always happened the same way, she remembered herself at the time, you remember the first time and the last one, maybe one or two in between but not all of them. Not the actual birth. Only the one that is going on right now. That tearing pain, ooooh Lord. Someone, probably Miz Blanche, said the baby was stuck sideways or breech or something, and the cord knotted around his neck. Finally the cord was cut and tied, the baby washed down in warm water, slime wiped off its face. Her Frank was there somewhere; she could feel him, feel his presence. Voices all around her. Put on some more water. Make haste! Put a move on. Mary, how you feel, gal? The dull ache and the weakness. Pretty rough this time, huh? Yes, it's a boy! Good God, Frank gone smile himself to death standing over there. What lungs! That shore is a strange cry like he's hurt. Big one too. Look like Frank, just like you Frank. She felt Frank's hand on her face, rough and full of callouses. Then the midwife's voice. That's one proud nigger tonight, grinning from ear to ear. The baby made a few faces, opened one eye to check things out. Mary smiled with some effort and then it wailed again, face all twisted up. Voices. Frank's first. How much you think it weigh, Coreen? Then the midwife again. Big baby, about ten or eleven pounds. A real horse. They took the baby from her, began greasing it up. She could feel the hands on her stomach, pressing, pressing, the afterbirth oozing out onto her legs. Onto her tired legs. She laughed as she thought that she must have a door down there as big as her children be.

As she was going to lay down, she spied one of Mance's feet sticking out from under the covers. He rolled in his sleep, talking to himself. She projected her voice like an auctioner; it turned the corner.

"Mance, look at them feets," she yelled. "How rusty they looks. Boy, if you don't get up and wash them, I'm gone put trails on your behind." She heard his feeble answer from the other room, heard him hit the floor and later his hands wringing the water out of a rag in the basin. His shadow, caught by the glow of the lamp, played on the wall.

"Rinse that rag out before you put it up too. You hear me boy."

"Yessum."

Mary closed her eyes for a minute, letting her mind and body get in step. Finally, she drew herself erect, shed her clothes and slid under the giant warm hand of the quilt. She dozed off until the weight of her husband's body on the mattress brought her back. He smelled husky. She liked how he smelled in the pitch black room.

"Woman, what's this about Little Frank?" He asked it with a sigh tone. Mary launched into how she had to chase him every night to force the boy to come home, how he punched the girls and always in the wrong places, how he threatened the older boys with anything he could pick up, and how he didn't obey. He didn't mind no matter how much she hit him. He was mean, had an evil streak in him. The boy wanted to hurt somebody and would one day unless they put a stop to it right now. Her husband's attitude said he didn't want to talk about the boy, not really. But she had to tell him. This was the only time she could corner him.

"I knowed he was headstrong," Frank said angrily. His wife leaned on his massive shoulder while he dealt with the issue inside.

"It's like he locked up in himself, can't talk to nobody," Mary continued. "Jes' make noise. Sometimes he act like he don't hear me, Frank. He bites himself, took a big hunk out his arm the other day. You seed where I wrapped him there?" She waited for his answer, some indication he was listening to her.

It came. "Uh-huh." Then silence again.

She was pouring it on now. "I caught him outside beating his head against a tree like something in his head was pestering him. Driving him crazy. Did it one day until he was out cold. Scared me half to death. He still messes on himself as big as he is. Eleven years old and he still can't dress himself, even though he is almost grown. He jes' hold himself and rock, sit off from the others. Everybody was cryin when Miz Allen told us 'bout Deacon New passing, he come laughing. Like some kind of beast, laughing low in his throat. You know, the boy has a devil in him."

Frank replied quick, "Ain't no devil in him. There might be something wrong with his head though. Saw a radio like that once, couldn't hold no station long. That's how he is."

"You ain't heard half of it," her voice came weakly but tinged with sarcasm. "Frank, sometimes he jes' stares at his hands, jes' stare like he ain't never seed them before. He jumps up and down on the bed or hide under the covers and rock. Other times, he runs in a circle and shrieks. Get mad as a kicked dog if I don't feed him before the others."

"What else he do?" asked Frank, wondering where he was during all of this.

"He snatches their food out of their plates. It's tiresome keeping them off him. Sometimes they act like they may hurt him, do him harm. He thinks they playing with him. Then he fall out in laughter on the ground, rubbing his face in the dirt."

"He hurt anybody?" asked Frank calmly.

"No, but he will. You watch and see. He's too big. He's dangerous, gone hurt one of these girls here. He hit Teenie hard in her belly. How I knowed because I seed her throwing up beside the house."

Frank moved into another position, on his side. "He don't do nothing when I's 'round here."

"Mebbe he's afraid of you. I don't know. Shoot, even Otis noticed something funny with him. What we gone do, Frank?"

"Hmmmm. Mebbe I'll take him in hand. See what I can do with him. Give him some work around the house here. He'll carry his share and it'll make a man out of him."

She wanted to hear his answer to this one. "Are you going to keep him from gettin' violent?"

Frank dismissed the query. "Whup his ass, that's all."

Seeing that she was not getting through, Mary turned over in bed and laid still without shutting her eyes. Her husband couldn't understand this mood. Why was she acting like this? He had listened to what she said. Damn, the boy seemed to be fairly normal for what was wrong with him and that was not their fault. They just had to live with it.

"Frank . . . member Elsie? The thin girl who used to live with the Palmers. She married and moved to Flint, Michigan. Anyway, she sent me two boxes of clothes. Ain't seed them yet, so I don't know what we got. Recall Captain Dodge, he worked on the Red Rooster place for years. They found him dead yesterday in a gulley, head bashed in."

"Oh yeah."

She adjusted the flame of the lamp, lower. "Nobody cared for him no how. He bore watching. He had two faces, one face for us and one face for them. Sometimes he even had two for us. Yeah, he probably went too far and it caught up with him. Sheriff ain't doing too much cause he was colored."

"That's how that peckerwood would like me to be," Frank added. "But I won't have no parts of it. No sir."

"Honey, water coming through the roof in three places."

"Get it tomorrow," said Frank, sounding as if he was almost asleep.

She nudged him in the side. "Ellis was by to see you while you was gone." He stirred a bit.

"He saw me leavin' so why did he come by?" There was smoke and fire in his ears and throat. His wife quickly replied that Ellis left right away, as soon as he saw Frank was not at home. This calmed Frank down.

Mary returned to Little Frank's behavior, for one more try. "That boy has an evil streak in him. Today he jes' stare and stare at me like he was thinking 'bout killing me or somethin'."

Frank dropped his arm over her, touching her breast lightly, where she could barely feel it. They heard a noise in the room. What was that? There, there it was again. Frank moved his hand around on the table until he located the lamp. He turned it up. There! It was Little Frank, standing still, his eyes set on them as though they were food. Mary jumped in surprise at the presence of madness in the boy's expression. Shaking his head, her husband pulled himself out of bed and guided the boy to the other room, back to his pallet.

30

Chapter 4

Saturday afternoon in July. The children went outdoors, longing to run and play in the tall, sticky grass in the woods. Jake fell, bouncing heavily on his side, and his knee had a deep bruise from the hard impact. He rubbed it, thinking it hurt to fall. Hurt bad. The others, Mance, Dit and Teenie, were sprinting toward the road with a cloud of dust pursuing them.

Heels hitting the back of his legs, Jake struck out after them, yelling for a halt in the action. They stopped to let him catch up. Mance announced to his playmates that he was the wind and made the appropriate sounds.

Dit did headstands. The rest watched, cheering him on.

The sweat on their bare arms and faces attracted flies and they shooed them away with big sweeps of their hands. Anyone could tell these children were family. Everything about them seemed alike; the circle motion of their heads, round faces, flared nostrils and wiry bodies that could bend back double. The infamous feet with the bulb heels. The copper color of their skin shone in the bright sunlight and held a ray of its own.

Then they started throwing rocks at each other. Finally, Mance got one in the small of his back and began crying, exclaiming that he would tell Daddy. He needed comfort so the group gathered around him, patting him to break the sobs.

"I should tell on y'all," Mance said matter-of-factly. His sobbing would not let him speak properly.

"You a sissy." Dit's voice was harsh, full of spite.

The image of his father came into his head, big and powerful, and he realized he couldn't tattle on them for playing too rough. His father didn't like crybabies at all.

"Naw, I won't put y'all in no trouble. Let's do something else." Mance understood diplomacy quite well.

"LAST TAG!" Jake assumed command.

Everybody ran in different directions, off the road, through the brush, down the side of the levee and over the ditch into the field. Jake was it, waving his arms, and he ran after Teenie. She went up a tall pine tree as though she had claws for hands, much too high for him to get her, up in the small branches. He shook a small fist at her, daring her to come within reach. Enjoying her triumph, Teenie giggled and threw twigs down on her pursuer, mocking his futile efforts to lure her into his grasp.

"Come and git me, you big monkey," she shouted.

He tried to climb after her, the branches squeaked under his weight, warning of possible tragedy if he continued in his attempt. Realizing he had little chance of catching Teenie, Jake glanced around from his vantage point for the rest of them.

"Fraidy cat, fraidy cat!" Teenie teased from her secure perch as Jake descended, seeking other prey.

"Too dumb, too slow." Two child voices taunted the unlucky boy.

He tagged Mance making a break across the gulley, then burst into a loud, long laugh and stepped back. Mance dived and tagged him before he could react. They walked alongside each other, boasting about hand speed, tagging the other back and forth. In the end, Jake ducked, his head almost tucked between his knees, and Mance missed. He was on the heels of his fleeing brother, Dit, when Mance recovered. But Dit ran from Jake, thinking he was still "it."

"I'm not it no more," Jake pleaded.

"You better not be," Dit replied, slowing down.

The two boys watched defiantly as Mance gained on them. Just as he was within range, they divided and before he could decide which one he wanted, they were out of reach. At the bend of the road, Teenie danced in the middle of a dust cloud, shaking her little body, singsonging Mance's name. He started after her and she blazed away. Unfortunately, her older brother tripped on a discarded branch, in stride, and down he went.

Teenie laughed until her chest hurt, sharp needles of pain and she had to stop.

"You gone git it now, Teenie. You asking for it and you gone git it." Mance hollered at her, limping on the injured limb.

"Awright, who's the clumsy one now?" Jake had the last guffaw, recalling his brother's jokes about his earlier spill.

The only thing that broke up the comedy was the arrival of Bue's boyfriend, Ted, walking along the road, coming toward them. The lanky young man stopped picking his nose, looked at Mance sprawled in the dirt and laughed. His dog stood at his side, sniffing the fallen boy's outstretched leg. The smelly mongrel did not like the children since they teased it every chance they got. Naturally, the dog never forgot them. It circled them, stalking. The dog growled at Mance, bared

33

its fangs and the boy, frightened, quickly got to his feet. As a defense, Teenie and Jake held rocks at the ready and Mance lifted his hand to throw.

"Don't hit my dog, you burrheads!" protested the dog's owner. However, the children paid no attention to him, keeping their arms cocked.

"Or what?" Jake snarled, acting mannish.

"Or I'll beat your ass for you, that's what! Get outa my way. Ain't got no time for no kids." He pushed Jake in the chest and the boy landed in the spot where Mance's imprint was still visible.

"Dirty dog!" Teenie hurled her rock and hit the animal in the neck. It yelped in pain, recoiled and started after her. Her example inspired the others to throw their rocks, but the dog, on the run, caused them to miss. Without hesitation, Teenie went up a tree, only pausing to shout at the disgusted dog that barked violently at her. She made funny faces at it.

Dit came from the other side of the road. "Call your hound off my sister, Mister Bigshot." The dog's master smirked, then whistled for his pet and they trotted off, disappearing from view around the bend. Satisfied that the animal was gone, Teenie climbed down from her haven, giggling in high tones as usual.

"Anybody hurt?"

"Naw, that dumb dog couldn't bite hisself," said Mance. Everyone laughed.

"What Bue sees in that nigger, I don't know," added Jake, feeling on his previously wounded knee.

Teenie joked, "He look like his dog to me." It got a laugh. Suddenly Mance tagged Teenie, who tagged Dit, who tagged Jake, who tagged Mance.

"Shoot, he have to lick all of us," remarked Dit, who was tagged by Mance while the rest spread out.

They grew tired of chasing each other, the tag game, but

34

there was still energy to burn. Jake started an argument over who was the fastest and Dit yelled he was, while Teenie, the smallest of the lot, hollered she could beat both of them. Mance could beat no one so he appointed himself judge. They knew from past races who was the fastest; Dit was first, Jake second and Teenie a step behind him. After the race, they sat on a fallen tree at the side of the road, panting, thinking what to do next.

Now Teenie dashed over the gulley into the high grass, the others followed and she dropped down, where they couldn't see her. Dit's voice boomed out calling her name. Up she shot, running. Then down again. Down in the grass, Teenie laid perfectly still, listening to them draw closer, closer. Up again, run a bit, then down. This was a new game, her game and she liked it, because she had the upper hand. After a few minutes, she popped up on the road behind them, yelling and waving her tiny arms. The boys ran after her. With that wild run of hers, Teenie took off down the road.

The little girl jumped over the ditch again into the grass, but where she landed, there was a caterpillar. She waved the others to her, keeping her large brown eyes glued on the insect crawling on a leaf in her hand. Curious, the boys gathered around. She bluffed Mance as if she was going to throw it on him and he stepped back, holding his hand over his face. Dit grabbed the leaf, turned it upside down yet the caterpillar held on. During all of this, Jake wandered away from the group, exploring for himself.

"Come here, y'all! Look!" He cried out, standing near a large anthill.

They ran over to him; Dit still carrying the leaf with the caterpillar and Teenie walking behind the boys, sulking. The anthill was enormous, swarming with a hoard of ants, all scurrying about rapidly. Jake was quick to point out the ones with wings, the ones toting eggs and others carting pieces of what appeared to him to be dead ants.

"I hear they just like peoples," explained Jake. "Some of them work, some of them just lay around and guard the hill. Mister Beauford told me once that some ants went crazy in some place and started eating up the peoples and stuff. Run the folks all out their houses."

"Aw, you telling a tale. You oughta stop." Mance wasn't buying any of that.

"Uh-huh. They did too."

Teenie looked him in the eye and asked, "How you know he wasn't fooling you? Ain't no ant gone swallow peoples!" She gave him a wave of his hand, the dismissal gesture of a queen.

Jake had to make them believe. "Hey Dit, put that bug on this hill and watch what they do to it."

Dit smiled and glanced around at the crew, pivoting his body to theatrically acknowledge the smiles of agreement from the rest. Once the caterpillar was placed on the hill, the ants quickly surrounded it, cutting off its route of escape. Then they swarmed over it. It wiggled but couldn't get away.

It would take more than that to convince Teenie. "Just because they get on it, don't mean they gone eat it, fools," she said. She stood with her back to the boys, hands on her hips.

"I ain't no fool," Jake said, moving toward the girl as though he would hit her.

"I still don't see them eating him up," Teenie informed them. "We'll miss supper out here messing around with a big old bug. Naw, them little things can't get no peoples down their mouths. Too little."

Jake shrugged his shoulders and said, "Don't put me in it. I was saying what I heard Mister Beauford say." Indeed the caterpillar was covered with ants, its green and yellow length barely visible underneath their furious onslaught, but

36

they didn't seem to be eating the insect.

"Mebbe they ain't hungry," Dit conceded.

"If they's eating him, they's taking mighty small bites because you sure can't see them," joked Teenie.

Her words hurt Jake's feelings and Dit sensed it, placing his arm around him. They began walking away, talking between themselves. When Jake looked over his shoulder, Teenie stuck her tongue out at him and giggled.

Soon Dit stopped in his tracks, holding up one hand. "Shhhhh, I think I hear something, voices."

The group caught up with him in a fast trot. Dit motioned for them to be quiet, placing a hand to his lips and they eased up to the sounds. He assumed command now, raising his hand once more in the style of a cavalry man in the old wild west. They crawled closer to the noises, very cautious and careful not to let the weeds give them away. This was real adventure. They became rocks and listened; soon two people came walking into view.

"Why must I do anything more than a kiss?" A feminine voice sounded gently in the stillness.

Two people. One was Bue's boyfriend, Ted, and the other was their sister, their older sister. The children smiled among themselves, this should be good.

"If you love me like you say, you'd prove it," Ted explained.

"Suppose I get big with a baby, what are you gone to do then?" Bue asked.

"I'll do what's right, give the baby a name. We don't want anybody saying you had a bastard."

For the first time, she realized that she was afraid. Ted was asking a lot of her, asking her to do something that could ruin both of their lives. He had a mean face, the face of a man who held a grudge or had a score to settle. Sometimes she felt he hated women by what he said about marriage or children. He also had cold eyes, steel gray from his white planter father's bloodline, the man his black father worked for at the Webb Plantation.

"What are you so afraid about?" her suitor asked, pulling her down beside him in the grass.

"Can't you behave yourself for one minute, always something," Bue said. "Be sweet, don't ruin our time together. I get tired of wrestling with you. Be nice."

He did not reply.

Concealed in the grass, the children were getting an earful, until Teenie whispered that they should jump Ted and give her a chance to run away. Jake said she didn't look as if she wanted to escape and the others laughed quietly, except Teenie who thought her big sister was in danger.

Meanwhile Ted continued to stare at Bue as though he had something important, desperately important, to tell her but couldn't find the exact words to do it. He touched the inside of her thighs with his index finger, sliding it upward to her breasts, where the finger blossomed into a hand covering the one closest to him.

At first their voices were low, conspiratorial, then they became loud enough for the eavesdropping children to hear. Bue allowed her beau's hand to caress her nipples a moment more, enjoying the easy circular patterns of his touch on her soft brown skin, then she laid on her back. They heard her say she didn't like a common nigger, no trash. She wanted to do stuff with her life, go places and do new things. Her boy friend was gazing at her body lustily, agitated and having a very difficult time breathing. In fact, the children could hear him from where they were hiding.

"You know I's the best one in these parts for you, darling," said Ted, in a voice loaded with sugar. "You must believe that, that I wants you and needs you awful bad. You done mess with my mind." He poured it on, yet Bue gave no response.

"Like caramel candy." He ran his hand over her rump and she shivered.

"You know I needs you, so bad, awful bad." His hands became daring, seeking to explore other frontiers, wantonly probing. She shook her head and clamped down on his feelers with one of her own.

"Aw, come on gal," he protested. "You got to see I's telling the truth. Don't make me suffer, please." He twisted his face in mock agony.

"So this is all you want," Bue said, unbuttoning her blouse and exposing her big tan breasts in the sunlight.

"Lemme kiss 'em," Ted panted. "Aw please . . ."

"Naw, we gotta talk. This ain't no easy pleasure here." Bue was continuing to hold his hands. He could have taken her by force, big farm boy that he was, but he decided to play along.

"How are you gone take care of me, my needs?" She watched him while his mouth formed the best lie it could. "Ted, you ain't working. Are you?"

From their hiding place, the children smiled at the drama and laughed into their palms.

"You my job," Ted sweet talked. "I'll make you my job, my lifetime job. I knows you wants something better than this way, this farm and dirt way. I knowed that when I first seed you, knowed you's quality." He scooted closer, within range of her breasts. There was very little resistance in her. She no longer pushed him away.

"You needs a real job. Mebbe Daddy can find something for you. He wouldn't mind doing that."

"That sounds mighty fine as long as I have you."

Her voice was velvety now. "You must love me a little bit." Ted nodded, grinning as he leaned to kiss her lips.

He was about to kiss her again when he pulled her legs apart and slid her panties to her ankles. She asked him not to hurt her, to be gentle. He was all thumbs, pawing her buttocks in an effort to remove her gingham dress. His huge right hand gripped her long jet black hair and his left held her flat, so all his weight could go into the opening thrust, Cruel but necessary because he figured the first time would be rough for her. Bue yelled in pain and struggled, trying to get away but he was already inside her. He rotated his hips, driving deeper, harder and harder. She suddenly burst into tears, kicking at him, shouting that's enough. He was lost to her, into the heat of the act, lifting her legs so he could go even deeper. She bit his hand and tore at his hair while he humped her faster. Ohh-ohhhhh, he moaned into her ear, ohhh I's got to pull out-t-t ... ohhh. He rolled off of her, the come spurting from him, splattering on her belly and thighs.

"You bastard, you sweet yellow bastard." Bue snickered bitterly.

"Did you like it? Did you enjoy the fuck I put on you? It didn't hurt too much, did it?"

"Don't make it sound vulgar. We didn't fuck, we made love. And yeah, it did hurt, hurt like hell but I's sure it'll hurt less the next time." Bue fixed her hair over her ears.

Something in the weeds caught his attention and he peered in that direction. His dog, which the children did not see when they came up, now appeared from nowhere and walked toward them, growling under his breath. Thinking quickly, Teenie found a rock and hurled it at the animal, hitting it in the head. It yelped in pain. The dog didn't run after them. Ted would have chased them but Bue was holding his arm. He jerked against her to pull free, cursing them.

Teenie jumped to her feet, cupped her hands around her mouth and shouted in sing-song:

"Dog face, dog face
ugliest face around this place!
dog face, dog face

40

ugliest face around this place!"

Goddamn," Ted cursed. "I'll break their necks!"

"Did they see us? Do you think they saw anything?"

"Naw, I don't think they'll talk if they did. Don't worry, Bue."

The children hightailed it to the bog, where the tall cattails and thickets grew, where the long creepers hung down from the trees. Their favorite game was crossing the bog on a giant cypress tree that had fallen during a storm. In their minds, it was a bridge, a highway over the brown murky water underneath. Their father warned them too many times not to play here because one of them could get hurt, but who could resist such excitement, such fantasy. So they continued to come back, to walk the tree, to cross their secret bridge.

"I's first," Jake said proudly. "I's the pioneer."

The others disagreed, quarrelling about who would go first, about who was the trailblazer. Mance, the practical one, went to the edge and looked down, then shook his head. He would go last, which was what he usually said. Bravely, Jake balanced on the tree, quite shaky at first, with one foot up in the air. Gradually he found the knack of it, arms outstretched like a tightrope walker in the circus, and walked on across without any further problems.

"I don't want to go across anymore," Dit said. "I have to tell Papa on Bue. She gone get herself in real trouble."

"Leave her alone," Jake answered back harshly. "She knows what she's doing. Next one across. Don't be afraid. Teenie, you got so much mouth, why don't you go next?"

Warily, Mance sat down on a stump and watched. Sometimes he didn't go across if he didn't feel lucky. Today was one of those days. He didn't trust it.

"I's still gone tell on her, letting that dog face do that to her. Whew, Papa'll kill her when he finds out."

"I said forget it. Let her dig her own grave. You ain't got

nothing to do with what she do. Nothing."

Surprisingly, Dit went next, making it look more difficult than it was. The tree was mossy, slippery in spots where the bark had worn off. But he did a little number, threatening to lose his balance and fall, stumbling for show. All the while he imitated a noise somewhere between a car and an airplane. Arms akimbo and rocking unsteadily as if he needed help, quick. Then Teenie sprang forward, bouncing, right on his heels. She made a monkey cry, jumped slightly and Dit, who was already clowning, lurched backward. It was for real this time. Mance stood up, his mouth open in horror. The tree rolled, throwing them both and propelling a screaming Teenie into the slimy water. However, Dit managed to grab onto the tree and hold on, with his legs dangling in the air. Straining to the point where his muscles ached, he hoisted himself up to safety.

Jake panicked, yelling and running in every direction. He didn't know what to do. In shock, Mance scooted out on the tree to see if he could help Dit reach her. All of the boys were crying mute tears of disbelief and horror; they must save her, their little sister. Teenie was going to die if they didn't get her out of the swirling water. Jake, angered by their helplessness, tore a branch from a nearby tree, stripped it of its leaves, and passed it to Dit, who could almost reach her but not quite. Under the water, the soft, hungry mud tugged, grabbed at Teenie's feet and she screamed shrilly, her arms darted about in frenzied movements, out of control. Silently, the boys looked on, mouths agape and hopeless. Everything was too short. They couldn't reach her. Any one of them would have gladly given his life to save her but to watch her die, die like this. The more she struggled, the faster she was going down. The little girl looked up at her brothers as if she did not understand what was going on; tears shining on her cheeks. Mance wanted to run for home. When he got to the other side across the fallen tree, Jake wouldn't let him go, saying that it would be too late.

Suddenly remembering Bue and her young beau, Mance jerked free and ran off to get them. The muck was swallowing Teenie. Her tiny arms thrashed the grimy water, her frail tiny arms. She screamed and screamed, fighting it as the soft riverbed tried to suck her under. It made a noise, a hideous noise like the earth did when it took gulps of water and air, only louder. The water was up to her neck, climbing. Dit was still trying to get her hands, reaching to get just one of them, with the gritty water and mud surging around the lower half of her face. Her eyes bulged in absolute fear.

When Mance located Bue and Ted, he was so out of breath that they had to wait for what he had to say. Once informed, they ran as fast as they could toward the tragedy, pushing their way through the thickets and briars, making their own shortcut. As they arrived, they saw where she went down. Sorrow and grief. Jake cried on Mance's shoulder, squinting his red eyes and Dit sat on the ground as an Indian might do, covering his face. Little circles and bubbles could be seen on the top of the filthy water where she went down. Finally Bue collapsed in sadness, bawling like a soiled baby, and her boyfriend held her against him when her legs weakened.

Chapter 5

Frank Boles took a long time with his mourning, fretting over the loss of his youngest girl and how her body was never found. He was beyond consolation and his work seemed to reflect that his mind was no longer in it. So one day he left the plantation and hitchhiked to Clarksdale to look up a good-time gal he had met there some time back.

When he arrived, Adele's girl friend, Nette, was looking through some photographs her cousins had taken during a recent family reunion in Florida with their newly purchased Kodak. The camera produced remarkably clear pictures, the variety with chewed edges. She heard his footsteps on the stairs, sounding as if someone dropped a brick, picked it up and dropped it again. Curious, she turned her face toward the door. Quickly and almost without thinking, Nette placed the pictures on a nearby dresser drawer and she raised her long brown arms over her big bosom to fidget with her hair.

Frank met Nette four years ago at a house party given by a carnival man he knew from Itta Bena. He thought she was one of the prettiest women he had ever laid eyes on. Eagerly, he knocked once hard. She opened the door a crack to see who it was, and upon seeing, then drew back in mock surprise.

"Well, well," she said. "How you doing, Country?"

"Okay, could be better," he said in a rush of words. "I hope—" His voice choked off in a sob.

She stepped around him to get a closer look at his face where she saw lines of tension forming. Finally she spoke: "What's a matter, baby? You look bad. Have a sitdown."

Nette waved him to the bed, smiling sympathetically, but Frank chose a chair instead.

Only after ten minutes had passed did he notice that she was sitting naked on the bed; her reddish hair in tight curls close to her head and in direct contrast to the black triangle of her pubic hair between her sagging thighs. Her body had seen better days and was now on the decline. A thick torso, wide ass and short, hairy legs. Her feet were abnormally large, boats, and ashy at the ankles and heels. But she was mighty pretty to him.

"You a real pistol for sure," said Frank, sitting slumped in the chair with his head in his hands.

She switched her fat rump over to the closet, bent over to look into a box, and chose a dress. Aware of his red, swollen eyes on her, she turned it around and placed the revealing bit of fabric against her.

"My baby girl died last Saturday."

Lost in her own thoughts, Nette made a grunt for a reply, like so what.

"Hurt me bad, sure did," he told her. "The wife and the other chillun hurt the same way. Hate that she left so young, never had a chance to see life. It bad to lose them when you see the promise in them."

Frank sat down in the chair and a tear surfaced in one eye but he got it with a quick hand. Silent, Nette sat again on the bed, lifting one hefty leg to put on her underclothes. "You never told me you's a married man, Country. Never would have guessed." Her first lie of the afternoon.

"We never talked."

"Yeah," she chuckled. "That's true. It was all business that night. So that's why you shot out of here like a nigger with Red Devil Lye in his draws. A wife and kids, Lawd have mercy." Her rough hands were on her breasts, those over-filled teats, doing something. Frank had his eyes on them.

"Uh-huh, didn't want no stir at the nest," said Frank, chopping off the remark as if she should ignore it, which she did.

"How your little one die?" She put the light blue dress in front of her again and looked at herself in the mirror.

"Suckhole ate her up." A tear again. Again he timed his hand perfectly.

"Too bad. I guess it's hard to lose them. How many you got?" She pivoted to regard him, staring here, then there.

"Had nine . . . counting Teenie." Frank felt the burden of grief sinking further on him, the dead weight of it. Maybe a joke would be good about now. Something to take his mind off his child's death. He wondered if he had come for sympathy or loving, most likely both. Seemed like he was getting neither one. Strange woman, this Nette. Miss Big Chest herself. Heart like glass.

"There's a bottle behind the chester drawer, yonder, in a bag. Keeps it hid. Lotta fools come through here." A pause. Then she asked: "What was she like, your little one?" Nette played with a tube of bright red lipstick on her lips, painting them larger and juicy, opening them as though she was taking something into them. She was used to indulging people in their private games, their little fantasies. Sure this farmer was a sap, but there was something about him that she liked more than most.

Nette watched him kneel down and run his hand behind the piece of furniture. He wanted a drink bad. Probably as much she did.

Frank talked up to her, with his hand still searching underneath the dresser, gathering cobwebs. "Teenie was a sweet thing. Like to raise a fuss all the time, didn't take no truck with the stuff girls usually like. She was like me. Had a heap of fire in her, a born hellraiser . . ." He trailed off when the memory of her became too much for him, became too vivid. The bottle, now in his hand, went bottom up. His throat jerked as the liquid slid down. His Adam's apple bobbed in a furious rhythm.

"Country, I have a little girl myself," she said lazily. "She lives in Magnolia with my aunt. I would have liked to have some more but I never met no man worth having them for. Besides, if I fell in love with every man that's done laid on me . . . I wouldn't make a living."

He picked his nose. "This ain't no type of life for nobody, going man to man. Ain't you ever wanted better?"

"Yes and naw."

Frank flipped the bottle again, long, and handed it to her. "Hunh?"

"I hadn't figgered on this for no lifetime thing. Know what I says? Just a short spell. I don't feel like an easy woman. Naw, I can take care of myself. Do I look like a pushover?"

"Naw, not at all."

He stretched out in the chair, feeling woozy from the liquor on an empty stomach, and propped his feet on the bedrail.

Nette turned coyly to him and gave him her full profile, jutting out her chest some.

"Naw," lied Frank, keeping his gaze on her rear.

"Shit, I do as I please," she said after awhile. "Damn.

Know what I mean? Them wives do the same as me. They do it for you niggers to keep you. I get mines upfront, beforehand, with no ties to it."

"You got a heart of glass."

She laughed harshly and said: "It's still about having us women gapping our legs for your pleasure. I knows this much about you bastards and that is that your brains are between your legs. And that's what keeps our race down. You mens spend all your time chasing tail."

"And the white man don't do that?"

"I don't care about them peckerwoods. That's your problem too, matching everything you do with white folks. We ain't white, ain't never gone be white."

"You dumb whore!"

"Naw, you got it wrong. A whore, your black ass!"

Following that outburst, he ambled a few uncertain steps to the bed and sat on it. The bottle had very little blood left. The woman would not stop jawing, he thought.

"Country, you get tired of that same old stuff at home, eh?" Nette asked snidely. She picked crudely at her fingernails, then stopped to make a face in the mirror, checking the damage in wrinkles.

"Sometimes."

"Husbands always say that. What's so damned different about this one here? You think it's lined with velvet. This pussy look just like the one your wife got and it probably has the same amount of time left on it too."

Frank was not concerned with what she was talking about. Instead, he wondered how she operated. "You keep the money you make for yourself?"

"Hell yeah," she snarled. "I wouldn't do it otherwise. I used to give it away when I worked in a few other places, at a few places here and there. Me and that girl you met at Matt's, Adele. Now we're on our own. Yeah, sure is."

"Does your partner think like you?"

"My husband would have asked some dumb shit like that. He was just like you, used up. Burned out. Some other womens had had him before I got hold to him so there wasn't much left. He wasn't worth a damn."

"I don't want to hear you talk down some man I don't know," he said, blinking.

"Wait, lemme finish," she snapped angrily. "I waited on him hand and foot, washed his dirty draws and crusty socks. He smelt like something dead. I was really afraid of him then, crazy jealous he was. He caught me washing some stains out my panties after being out with a man-friend of his. I had to move, got hot around there. Too hot for me. I went off with some friends of my aunt, the one that got my little girl. Then I met this man named McBride. Damn, he had some bone on him. I sure miss that. Anyway, I went off with him and lived with him for a spell. Then he put me down for this young girl and I went from him to another man, a milkman."

He snickered to himself and gave her the bottle. It had been a little over half full when he got it, but now there was just a few sips left. "I don't want to hear this bullshit."

Like a true lush, Nette killed it in two gulps, enjoying the burn of it. He could tell she was no stranger to liquor; the gal took to it like a fish to water.

"Then I came back up this way," she said, watching him peering at her fleshy legs from the bed.

"You worked in some houses. How was it?" He asked her this to keep her talking.

"Why you want to know? You working for somebody, the law maybe?" Nette stood back and hacked him up with her eyes.

"Naw, just curious."

"One thing I learned is never let a nigger know too much about you. Ain't safe."

"What was it like, working in them houses?"

"You don't stop, do you?" She examined him in the mirror, contemplating his motives. He seemed harmless, but you could never tell about the bastards. Their price was so low. But one for two bits.

"You don't think much of Negro mens, do you?"

"Any colored woman with common sense don't. I ain't worried about y'all. You too much trouble. Too much heartpain for me."

He noticed how her tight dress puckered in between her legs when she put it on, that mound between her thighs.

He sidestepped her remark and asked his question again. Ignoring him, she took that dress back off over her head and then her underclothes. The kitchen window was open, the curtains blowing, and he thought how good the breeze must feel on her bare skin. She bent over, with her naked ass to him.

"Them houses, them houses," she said, putting aside the clothes. "You suckers always want to know other folks' business, always want to hear what happen but never want to live through it yourselves. That's peoples for you. Them houses. It was work. Damn, I couldn't work the streets, not me. I like the music, like at Matt's some nights. All the hollering. The girls sizing the mens up for trade. The action. I worked this joint awhile back. Wasn't bad. Nigger named Fred Peel owned it. Those were some good times. Had a girlfriend named Beenita. Hair all plastered to her head, smoked the weed all the time. We did some crazy stunts together. Went all over getting into devilment." Now it was her turn to be engulfed by a memory. Her eyes fogged over with a pleasant gaze and she was standing there with a look on her face as though Beenita was in the room.

"What happened to the gal?"

"She got shot, killed."

51

"Must have rolled some stud."

"Naw, you don't know what you talking about. Nigger killed her because she wouldn't let him have none. Told him nice but he got crazy, slapped her. She spit in his face. I recall it plain as day. He pulled his pistol and shot her twice."

"Damn."

"Yeah. See what I mean about y'all."

"That was him. He ain't me."

"Shot her dead, for nothing." Nette was slowly shaking her head still, yet thinking about Beenita.

Shifting his weight, Frank scooted his body on the bed, and interrupted her thoughts. "Most girls that do what you do look like goats in the face. I don't like them like that, I like them to look like you. Like them nice looking where they'd melt if you touch them."

"See what I mean about y'all."

"What now?"

"I just spoke on it."

"What, woman?"

She was mad now; her voice became serious, cold. "Damn sex struck niggers. A woman can make y'all do near anything she want, made you do damn near anything to yourself. All for that pocket between her legs. Shit, most womens are good actors anyhow."

"What you mean? You know they likes it as much as mens do."

"Mebbe so," she said confidently. "But womens got to act because y'all don't be doing nothing but hitting it like a lick and a promise. We got to make y'all feel like y'all doing a good job." She was holding one leg out at a time; hold it out, then curve it back under as if she was going to kick. First one leg, then the other. He guessed it was some kind of exercise or other.

"You crazy as hell, you know that?" Frank said to her as

she finally sat on the bed with her back to him.

"Do you ever dream?" She asked from far off in her head somewhere. "I . . . used to have dreams of a woman making love to me. It's always the same dream, in one of those brass beds white womens have, plenty room, and the full moon can be seen through the window. Outside the ground looks real, grainy and a purple color. There is a smell of bodies, sweat and animal sex. This woman gets on top of me but I can barely feel her weight . . ."

"I don't need to hear this about you and some make-believe woman rolling on some bed and nothing going in. I hate bull-daggers."

She was saying: ". . . Her mouth covers mine like she's hungry, pressing her lips hard against mine, and soon I can't breathe. Her fingers touch the part of my leg where it flows into your hips, lightly though. I know what she wants. I tell myself that I'm not like her, not a woman who sleeps with other womens. All the while, her lips slide along my neck, brushing my throat, making me wet and suddenly the edge of her tongue darts over the soft skin between my thighs, up to my shoulders and a wildness goes through me like I don't know what I'll do soon . . ."

"So what if you wants to have some gal eat you, I don't care to hear about that filth."

"Listen," she went on, grabbing the back of her neck. "A woman is making love to me and I like it and I shouldn't. I turn my head back and forth, no you dyke, no. Down between my legs, down there. My fingers stroke her nipples, so sweet woman, a woman like me. After this, how can I ever let another man touch me? No matter how huge, how deep he goes. A woman can make me come, not a man, not a dick. Her fingers move inside me and my head swells as if it will burst. We come together with me whispering her name. I can't even get up when she leaves, my legs are too weak and then I wake up. Crazy, ain't it?"

"Why you so bitter?" asked Frank. "I believe men done kick the shit out your heart, and you can't feel no more."

"Thank you, Clark Gable." She lit a cigarette and winked at him.

"I mean it. You sick and don't know it. You all dried up inside like a prune."

Nette looked at his eyes and wondered what was going on behind them. How could she explain anything to this hick without him jumping to some judgment of her.

"I was married once to a nigger just like you," she said after a fit of coughing. "He didn't know what to do with it when he got it. All talk, no action."

Frank laughed aloud. "All mens know what to do with it when they get the chance. Mebbe your old man was queer or something."

"Naw. I thought you'd say that."

"I used to beg him to take me to bed," she said, her lower lip quivering. "I begged him. He liked that part but he never satisfied me. I hated it when he touched me."

He smiled at her. "You ain't never had a real man. That is what you need."

"That ain't what I need. Damn mens don't know shit about females. Not a thing."

"Your Mama probably turned you against mens at an early age. By God, I hope none of my girl chillun end up like that."

"My Mama!" she chortled. "I saw Mama twice while I was growing up and the last time she was all stretched out in a coffin. She had nothing to do with me. I wanted to be like my Papa."

"You probably wanted a privates too. Mebbe you wanted to be a man and hated your Mama. So now you go around, turning womens into something that'll hurt them, make them suffer."

"I can't stand making love with a man anymore."

He was quiet, watching her.

"Are you scared I might take her away from you? If you the big stud you supposed to be, you have nothing to worry about."

In his head, he was walking toward her, three steps to stand in front of her, then he raised his hand and knocked her down. His hand would leave a mark on her light yellow cheek and after that, he would grab her by the neck and squeeze.

Instead he patted his breast pocket for his cigarettes and said, "You sick. I thought you said that was just a dream. You didn't say it was real."

"Suppose it is real," she said, smiling wickedly.

"You sick," he kept repeating.

"Suppose it is real, suppose I know her body like I know mine. Suppose she likes womens too."

"You stinking bitch," he snarled in disgust.

When he met Adele that first time, her beauty struck him as highly unusual for this area; women like this were more common in New Orleans or Atlanta. What was she doing here in Clarksdale? Was she like Nette? That day, she said hello to him, showing a few teeth, and then she went on about her business. When he saw her later that night, she was on a street downtown, talking with two men he didn't know. He glanced in the other direction to seem nonchalant and when he looked back that way, she was now smiling at him. She had to say no. He would take her in his arms. She would lean on him, huddled against him and he would kiss her. Four years and she was still a mystery to him.

"Don't believe any of it," she laughed. "I was just teasing. It was a joke. Laugh."

He didn't say nothing. The cigarette he held was burning his fingers, hissing as it sizzled his skin.

"Are you mad at me?"

"Hell yeah," he answered sourly. He flipped over on his belly, gripping the bedrails with his hands and pressing his face against them. Like a convict. Nette lifted her legs up over him, straddled him.

"You all tight," she said. "Why don't you pull off some of that stuff you got on? Let me see if I can help some." She bent over from that split position and kissed him in the curve of his back. Afterwards, there was a small, wet spot. He didn't feel it.

She felt him stand up, the bed lighten and the springs sigh as he walked away. Then she heard the bolt sound on the door.

"A plumb fool," she mumbled to herself. "A dumb hick fool."

Chapter 6

Frank waited on the street near Adele's house, pacing and smoking cigarette after cigarette. He was extremely tired, especially after spending the night on the dangerous streets of Clarksdale and soon he found himself walking in that direction. Quite the stalker, he went up the stairs, quietly, a few steps at a time. No one was around yet, he was careful not to make a sound and disturb anyone.

The door was ajar, a thin ribbon of yellow light was visible, and through the opening he saw two young black women were on the bed, their naked bodies entwined in torrid lovemaking. One looked familiar but he couldn't be sure. They were totally lost in themselves and their raunchy act; one woman laid on the bed with her legs spread wide and the other one moved on top on her, cupping one red-hot breast in one hand and licking it wantonly. Frank stood there transfixed. The woman he thought he knew moaned lightly and closed her eyes, enjoying her seduction. He watched them intently as the aggressor's tongue floated over the taut mound of her belly to rest inside the throbbing pink cave of her lover's womanhood. Before long, her partner squealed in utter delight and locked her long legs around her seducer's tawny head, bucking up and down in a steady, molten climax. Yes, he was right: it was Nette with the wife of a deacon of a local Pentacostal church. If her old man saw this, he'd kill her for sure and the white folks probably wouldn't have done a damn thing about it, given the situation.

Just as silent as before, he went back down the steps, lit another cigarette and sat on the last one. Later, the deacon's wife came down, looking worn out, and stepped over him to make her way across the street. She never looked back once, hurrying in a flurry of movement as if to make an important appointment. A short time afterwards, Adele walked up, carrying a hat box. She showed no surprise at seeing him there.

Often, he wondered how she could be so interested in him when she could have had anyone she wanted. She was very beautiful and everyone said so. He was lonely, for the most part, and maybe he wanted to be. He liked sadness in a perverse way and he could be very intense about it. Teenie's death gave him the perfect opportunity to wallow in its savage sweetness, to drink without conscience and to feel sorry for himself without remorse. Now, Adele was facing him, smiling that quick, bright smile of hers, and he gallantly took the box from her.

"How long have you been waiting?" she asked. "Why didn't you go upstairs and wait inside?"

"I just came up. It ain't been long." He lied miserably.

"You don't look so good," Adele said with concern. "What's wrong? Are you sick?"

A large sedan went east on the street, with a small Confederate flag attached to its antenna, and a group of rowdy white boys yelled from its windows at the black people walking along the curb. They ignored the insults, keeping their eyes downcast, and continued on their way. Adele and Frank watched them for an instant, then went up the stairs, talking about the lynching of Emmitt Till, a young black boy from Chicago who had been killed and thrown into the river with his head bashed in.

Once inside, Frank hoisted his leg and removed his boot, rubbing his cramped toes. Unfortunately his sweaty feet smelled a bit, a tart odor, and Nette teased him about it by pinching her nose. She walked over to a long, brown coat laying across a straight-back chair, reached into a pocket and produced a pack of Camels. The woman offered him one as she shook a stick out. Frank said, no thanks, but he grabbed the matches from her and lit her cigarette. This made her smile and she said something vaguely about manners.

"Adele, I forgot to tell you but Country came here yesterday looking for you," said Nette, taking a deep drag on the cigarette. He watched it turn to ash, and fall on the light blue dress she was wearing, the one she had modeled for him the day before.

Meanwhile, Adele smiled like a Cheshire cat and wiggled her nose, sniffing. The aroma of sex was still in the room. "Sugar, I's glad you came back," she told Frank, putting the hat box on a table on a corner of the bed. She gave him an inviting wink while Nette's back was turned, or at least he interpreted it that way.

He was beaming and totally forgot about Nette. To keep him earnest, Nette glared at him in the mirror, then she strutted in front of him, cutting off his view. "Country, what your wife do when you be gone?" she asked, crossing her arms beneath her breasts.

Angered, Frank sat up stiff and regarded her coldly. He

didn't like low blows or signifying at all. "None of your damn business, that's what!"

"Aw, don't be so touchy, just teasing," said Nette in baby doll talk, wearing her most innocent little girl face. She leaned over to kiss him on the cheek, making a smooch sound, but he jerked away, so her lips missed his face.

"You married, big man?" asked Adele.

"Sometimes when the mood strikes me."

There was silence for a time. He remarked that it was a beautiful day, not addressing anyone in particular. He wanted to forget about Nette's wisecrack. No one answered. Instead, Nette was staring at them from the other room, where she stood, applying baby powder to her sweating underarms.

He was going to say something else, something to lighten the mood, but Nette interrupted him. "I'd keep my eye on that Negro there. He's got nine kids, nine and he spends his time out in the streets chasing tail." In turning away from Nette and her venom, he suddenly caught Adele's gaze. She was propped against the wall on the far side of the room, smoking a cigarette, alone.

He noticed she was making her way toward him, with something obviously on her mind. She sighed and looked at him there, at his in-seam. He felt uncomfortable at first, then he didn't give a damn.

"Eight kids now. One died a few days ago."

Nette moved to a position right behind Adele, resting her right hand on the younger woman's tanned shoulder which was bare and gleaming with sweat from the heat. The dress Adele wore fit her like a second skin, white, with a full skirt and a tapered waist. Her roommate saw Frank's eyes following her hand and she placed it around Adele's narrow waist.

"Ain't she pretty?" asked Nette condescendingly. "But you shouldn't be worrying about her, you should be worrying about your wife back at home with all that idle time."

He had never given the question any real thought before: What was his wife doing while he was away? He reasoned women were not like men, they didn't mind being left alone. "My wife's got enough to do with all the little ones," the farmer said. "They keeps her plenty busy, you better believe that."

"That's in the day, what about at night?" asked Nette quickly.

Frank approached Adele who remained still, standing obediently as if awaiting an order from her military superior. She didn't move a muscle, she just trembled slightly when Nette lifted the young woman's chin and caressed her face.

"You can have Adele, if you want," Nette smirked. The lesbian seemed so sure of herself and the mysterious spell she held over Adele. He could not stand to be in the same room with her. Until now, he believed he could establish some type of intimate relationship with the attractive woman, this Adele, but that feeling was rapidly vanishing.

"Where's the bottle?" Adele asked Nette. "You know, the one from yesterday." Her roommate was silent, continuing to massage the younger woman's smooth neck.

After several moments of eerie quiet, Nette wandered toward the kitchen and before her exit, she issued a command in a calm, low, masculine voice. "Adele, talk to him for awhile. I will be in the kitchen here, fixing something for us to eat."

Not finished with her show of power, she went on in a cruel, hard tone of voice which was accompanied by a look of disdain. That was for Frank's benefit. "She likes doing as she is told. It makes her feel good. She needs someone like me to keep her in line, isn't that so, my pretty baby?"

There was no reply. Adele lowered her beautiful green eyes submissively and continued to stand motionless, her arms hanging lifeless at her sides. Then her mistress was gone, off to her chores.

"Why do you let her talk to you like that?" asked Frank. "What has happened to you? What does she have on you to make you act like this, Adele? Tell me."

"I can't talk now," she answered with a weak smile. "I could get in real trouble then."

Gently, he put his right arm protectively around Adele and she recoiled, pulling away. He wondered what kind of life had she gotten into?

"Are you her lover?" he asked all in one breath. "Do you sleep with her?"

Then a silence, pure and crystal.

"She's been good to me," she finally said. "I need her but she is not my lover. A person can possess your body and still not be your lover. I could never return the type of love she desires, woman-love. She's a whore and I'm a failed school-teacher. I'm being punished for failing in life. I went crazy for awhile and she took care of me."

He asked, "Ain't this your house? So why don't you put the slut out?"

"I can't, Frank. She pays the rent. I lost my job and I can't pay the rent. I need her."

"If you want, I can set things right," he suggested, balling up his large, calloused hand into an enormous fist.

Adele raised her lovely face, shook her head, with her eyes brimming with fear. He was sure that she was not telling him everything. Suddenly her expression changed drastically and she whispered softly that evil Nette was coming back. He looked her over again. Her skirt perfectly displayed her round, appealing hips and the fine curve of her waist. She was ex- cellently proportioned in every aspect, from her beautiful face to her small feet. Never had he seen eyes reflecting such sur- render and terror, absolute fright. She seemed to be the model victim, the vestal virgin awaiting the supreme sacrifice.

62

Nette returned, the arrival of the Plague. She turned a chair around and sat with her legs over it like a jockey. Her voice carried an ironic edge. "What lies you been telling this farmer? You tell him how good I been to you? A mother to you? Come here to me."

Adele did as she was told, begging softly. "Don't . . . don't . . . don't hurt me. I didn't say anything bad." She moaned a little and bit her lower lip in tearful anticipation.

Vexed, Frank narrowed his eyes. He felt genuine hatred for the older woman and her evil game of master and slave. For him, it was really sad since he thought blacks should have no need for such antics with the scourge of Jim Crow going in full swing. We should not be abusing each other, he mused as the two women talked among themselves.

"I didn't hurt her," assured Nette, smiling innocently. Her face was completely serene, full of tenderness. The two women smiled at each other for a time and then the older woman announced in a loving voice he had never heard before: "Honey, go to the kitchen and tend the chicken. Don't let it burn. Country, go home."

As Frank prepared to leave, Adele waved frantically to him from the kitchen and the farmer told her friend that he wanted to tell her something. Adele didn't say a word when he entered the kitchen. She just stared at him, straight in the eyes. He waited while she wrote down an address. She whispered tomorrow at sunset. Frank folded the slip of paper with the address into a wad and shoved it into his pocket.

Chapter 7

Where time seemed to race by before, now it crept. Frank became restless, waiting in the strange room at the colored hotel. It had been a good hour since he sent that gap-toothed boy to deliver a message to Adele, asking her to make haste. He needed to see her desperately, to talk to her without the wily lesbian being present. All he needed was a little time alone with Adele, just a little while. She was worth waiting for, worth any risk.

He didn't want to lay down yet. Frank pulled up the small dining table, slid it to the wall, positioned his chair under it, and laid his weary head across his folded arms on the ceramic tabletop. The noisy turn of the doorknob made him stir. Even in the shadows, he could see the beauty of this woman, Adele. She wore a long, lavender cotton dress and it was simply lovely, that lavender against those pretty brown legs. She was slightly out of breath from the climb up the stairs

65

past the reeking drunks and busy harlots with their nervous customers.

"Frank, I came as soon . . . as soon as I could, but I won't be able to stay long," Adele said. She paused in the doorway to assure him that she meant what she said.

His entire body wanted to pull her into it, to be one with her, whether she struggled or not. If what his Papa said about finding the right gal was true, the one right gal in the world, here she was. But she belonged to someone else and so did he. He had to be the only man she wanted or loved, the man that all men added up to. To him, she was the best of all women, the point at the top of the rise, at the peak of the mountain beyond the clouds.

He kissed her once and held her tight. He decided that one kiss would be enough for now, for he didn't want to ruin the precious moment of their first time together alone in years because of animal lust.

Her thin waist was in his hands and his lips met the soft down of her skin. A beam of something akin to lightning bound them together until Adele finally moved away, smoothing her dress.

"This ain't real, Frank," she said. "It's our bodies talking to us. It can't change anything for us. We both in a bad fix."

"I know it won't. Do you know I had my heart set on seeing you? Don't hurt me too. First, Teenie dies and now this." There were cracks in his words, cracks that let her know he was not playacting.

Adele studied his broad face, the way he stood, so proud. The way he used his hands while talking, the strange light in his eyes that would come and go, the hardness of his farmer's body. She studied, she looked, but she did not approach.

"You got a woman waiting for you right now. That could be me. I can't take the chance on you leaving me when you get tired of me. At least Nette . . ."

"Don't mention that she-he around me. I have heard enough about her to last me a lifetime, damn bulldagger."

"Nette is not a woman to be played with," she said with a somber face. "She could make things rough for both of us. All the riff-raff in this town know her and a plenty of them would do anything for her. She once told me if I ever left her, she'd come and get me. I believe her."

"You scared of her?"

She looked at him with bewilderment. "You really don't understand any of this? You just think you can come here and take me off with you without any trouble. It's not that easy. It's never that easy."

"But I's talking about us, you and me . . ."

"I am too. I'm thinking about your wife and the children. I just think if she was me and I had all those children, waiting for you to come back when you get good and ready. No, Frank. You want me today and it'll be another one tomorrow. Then somebody different the day after that. I know about men like you, Frank. Most women do but they never say anything."

He pleaded with her. "Naw . . . naw, darling. I would never do that with you. You special to me, real special."

"I can't leave Nette for you, not for you," she said firmly. "Not now or ever."

"But you didn't kiss me like that. You kiss me like you still care."

She didn't answer him immediately. Her hand moved across his thick hair, stopping at his broad nose. "Yes, sure I care, probably will for a long time because we had something nice back then. I will never forget that. I can't run out on Nette after all she's done for me. I can't. Yes, she's cruel at times but I can live with that."

"I had babies before and you loved me then," he whined.

"That was then and this is now."

He saw everything he really wanted to know on her face; all the answers were there yet he pretended to not know them. "To hell with that. I's talking about now."

"You really don't understand anything, do you?"

"You ain't talking to some damn kid. I ain't no fool even if I ain't had the book learning you got."

"Frank, I didn't say you was. Did I?"

"Hush, listen here," Frank said, impatient. "So you gone punish me for making a mistake. I do things my own way, by myself, in my own time. I's a one-type. I works for what I get."

"You ain't no different from nobody else. Dammit, I wish I had money for all the niggers that have run that line on me, about how different they were, how they this and how they that."

"What you know about anything? You have all you want, a chance to go North and do whatever you want. I can't do that."

"You're nothing but a farmer," she said simply. "A good one but still a farmer."

"So that makes you better than me, huh? Just because I's a sharecropper."

"Please, Frank, please don't."

"You don't know how I feels about you. You can't tell me I don't love you. I don't care about this other hogwash you talking, I don't care."

She was becoming angry now. "You got less brains than I thought you had. Listen to me, Frank."

"Spit out the real reason, the real truth," he snapped. "I bet you a pussy licker too like your friend back there."

"You're hearing the truth and you know it. You don't care about nobody but yourself. You want to live those lies you tell yourself." She scooted a chair to the wall and sat with

68

a portion of her back to Frank, preferring not to look him in the face.

He waited all this time for her and she talks to him like this. He wanted to slap the taste out of her mouth. "Sure, sure," he said with sarcasm.

"The way you think, you wouldn't know it if you hurt somebody or not," she countered. "You would make it right in your own head." The longer the conversation lasted, the more Adele realized what it was that kept her from reaching out to Frank. She suddenly realized how shallow and selfish this man was. The truth of her realization hurt her more deeply than anything he could have done to her physically.

Frank watched her stare at her legs as if they would turn into clothespins before too long. "Aw woman, that bulldyke got your mind all messed up," he retorted. "Shit, the day womens rule the world, that'll be it 'cause you womens are too wrapped up in your feelings. You can't sit down and hash a thing out like a man. That's why the Good Book say womens and children supposed to obey mens."

"Thought you didn't put too much stock in the Bible. That's what you told me."

"Parts of it alright, I guess."

A laugh came from somewhere down inside her, a mocking laugh. It had a forced ring to it. "Frank, the world isn't as dangerous as you think, you can come out now."

What could he do now? He mumbled to himself, ". . . ain't no future in a sharecropper, huh?" Aloud, he said, "So, this is it then. We're finished, just like that?"

Adele nodded a yes.

He gave her a quizzical look, then grimaced and dropped himself on the hard hotel bed, with a defeated face. Holding her dress to keep it from riding up her shapely brown legs, Adele sat beside him. He thought he heard someone coming up the steps, maybe not. Maybe it was all in his head.

"I don't hate you, just some of your ways," explained Adele. "I know you mean well." She felt herself decide that she did not want to crush or destroy him, only to give him the reason why there was nothing there between them any longer. She wanted him to know that.

"Why didn't you tell me about the gal before now?" he asked her, thinking what would she do if he hopped on her and kissed her. His hand lay in waiting by her leg, for the ambush.

"Who? Nette?"

"Yeah, that bitch!"

"You know the answer to that. What good would it have done?"

There was nothing he could say after that. His hand fell back on his thigh, a retreat of sorts.

"Frank, you mad?"

He lied, not to appear weak. "Naw."

"What about your wife?" she asked, prying. "How is she taking the little girl's death?" Stretching out her legs on the bed, Adele avoided his stare and talked in the direction of her feet. "Shouldn't you be there with her now? This is probably a very bad time for her."

He didn't like what she was trying to say, damn her. Why bring his wife into this? He attempted to defend why he'd left her. "I couldn't stand all that crying and mess. The kids walking around with long faces so I had to see you before you left or something."

"That's a lie, Frank. You had forgotten all about me. See what I mean about you?"

"I just had to get away, couldn't stand it around there," he began to explain. "That crying and all. It was too much for me."

"They cried because they loved her. Didn't you love her? She was your child."

"Yeah, I loved her but a man can't spend all his time crying. I had to get away from there to clear my head."

"Glad I ain't married to you."

"What you say?"

She ignored him again. He was trying to listen to what he thought was someone outside of their room.

Yes, there was that sound again, right outside the door. Who was it? Lord, don't let it be Nette for his sake. Suddenly, there was a loud crash at the door and it gave way, flew open immediately. It happened with such speed that neither Adele and Frank could react. A man that Adele recognized instantly as a stooge of Nette's stepped into the room, saying: "You filthy bitch! Up with this bastard after all she's done for you. I's glad that she let me follow you. Damn your asses to hell!"

Both Frank and Adele shouted it wasn't like that, no, not like it looked, not at all. Their hands were in front of them, to shield them from whatever he had in mind, no, not like that at all. He had to listen to them. Frank saw the man's arm whip, they backed off the bed, a snapping sound, in his hand was a long, gleaming pearl-handled straight razor, double-edged. Frank bumped into Adele in his effort to get to his feet, her body hitting the floor and going up the wall like water backwards. The stranger raised his arm and swung the razor in a quick series of moves, sideswipes, he meant to cut somebody, up and across. Its sharpness made a deadly swishing sound as it cleaved the air.

"Nigger, you a dead man," the man snarled, then shouted and charged Frank, screaming like a crazed person. Out of control. Razor moving in wild arcs, slashes. Frank caught one across his shirt, opening it with a low noise, a red line appearing on his chest, hands and arms in front of him to block, one more slash, then another, he wanted to cover his face, goddamn the man's mad, cuts through the skin. The flesh was hacked to the bone, the wounds lined with red, then filled with blood to pour off in drops and splotches to the floor and to the walls when he jerked his arms around to catch the sharp bite of the steel edge. His shirt clung to the bloody areas on his arms and chest and the entire time Adele screaming innocence in his ear, that she would be spared, yet the man still yelled and cut at them, his low voice laughing into their faces. The razor continued to swirl, to attack in a thousand places at once, like being in the midst of a swarm of stinging bees. Wisely, Frank kicked under the man's swing and another slash opened the skin on the top of his hand, slice just like that. He kicked again into the man's stomach, harder than a mule, then again, lower, down in there, the son-of-a-bitch, and again in there. Blood all over now, his hands and arms red. The man crouched, holding one arm over his aches while the sharecropper moved in with a deft step, grabbed an arm but took a deep cut along the thigh, opening it up to the gristle. He managed to grab the arm, the arm with the razor, and hoisted his knee and cracked the man's arm over it at the elbow, snapping it once, twice, until a bluish-white bone leaped out on the side, peeking through the dark skin. The stranger's eyes rolled back in his head, then he crashed to the floor. Frank felt faint too, from the loss of blood. It covered his pants and shirt, what was left of them; his arms, chest, and one hand, his left. He touched his face with his good hand, no damage there. Adele was hysterical, still screaming and he pivoted and slapped the shit out of her. Cuts all over him and she carrying on like that. Not a damn scratch on her.

Chapter 8

Before passing out, he heard someone crying, at least he thought he did, and it wasn't Adele. He couldn't seem to wake up, his body didn't obey. Get up now, no response. He couldn't move it, couldn't sit up. It was much like the feeling when your arm falls asleep from poor circulation, pins and needles all over. Oh Lord, what's happening here?

He felt arms pick him up like a limp rag doll, his legs dangling and head bobbing toward the ground, leaking blood from a slash along the right cheekbone. He tried to cry out, to call to those around him. But nothing came out of his mouth. He was terrified since all he could do was lie there and pray. Two men carried him to the home of a friend of Adele's, a carpenter, and they waited for the doctor who also doubled as a dentist. He could hear them talking about him through the fog that had wrapped itself around his head, choking him somewhat, as he heard the carpenter say he was

73

dying. He's lost too much blood, the man said.

Sweat rolled off of him, a disturbing buzzing sound hit him right between the eyes, pulling him very rapidly through a long, dark tunnel. He fought against the magnetic sensation, the invisible suction that appeared to be extracting his spirit from its prison of flesh, and slowly the shell fell away in the distance. He saw it all. It was happening so quickly. He laughed as a giddy sensation went through him, it made him float, a being of light. Ahead loomed another bright collection of light and beyond it came the music of souls adrift. And it was real. When his mind quieted, he could feel the presence of others around him, theirs was a talk without words, a language of peace and joy. One big smile. Then a rushing sound like a hurricane filled his head, a strong wind and he saw his sliced body stretched out in mid-air. Sailing above the ground or floor and suddenly he was no longer afraid of anything. Let it come. The darkness became a strange one, everything so quiet and peaceful. Below was a sheet of glass, a long sheet of clear glass, silvery in a way though, with arms and hands reaching up from it. It was an odd forest in all shades and tones of gray. He could still see that light and somehow he followed it. He must be dead or something. He couldn't tell anybody about this when and if he got back. Nobody. Everything he had thought or had done that was wrong went past him in a flash, like on one of those conveyor belts the cotton bales rode on. When he returned, he would do a lot with his life, that's for sure. The image of being drawn toward the light on a warm current washing around his ankles took possession of him; green and yellow birds with long beaks flew past his eyes, past him over the valley of glass into the light, dogs bark from somewhere in the distance, the light rose higher and the birds changed direction, something burned in his throat, a noise, akin to the hum of bees, trailed by bubbles which gave a vague heat, then rays of golden flame, but still no creatures with wings. That's what he wanted to see. Nothing less.

A dingy carpet of bleached bones was now underneath him, covered with a thick red fungus. It stuck to his legs and his feet, and he got on his knees to look at it more closely. Now he was frozen in that position, and then he saw Adele and Nette come out of a mist, not seeing him there. Nette told Adele to hurry up, she didn't have all fucking day. Adele was bending over, mouth open, in a submissive pose before her mistress. There was the harsh sound of a slap, and Adele fell flat on her soft stomach, her butt arched up, full and plump. Only Nette had anything on, real tight pants made out of a slick material, with a big bulge in the wrong place. She was beyond his view for a moment, only for a moment, and finally he could see that her breasts were quite small, mannish, the titties of a carnival fat man. Nothing like a woman's tits should be. The lesbian stripped with precision, shedding the pants to reveal the same thing he had in his pants. Only hers was animal size, and his eyes bulged. Anyway, none of this was right, especially when Adele looked at the thing, rubbed the head of it between her fingers, smiled wantonly and licked her lips. That wasn't like her to do that. Nette said something about not needing men no how, they could stay away from them without any regret, they could satisfy themselves. She mounted his woman and started pumping between her legs, while Adele moved against her in a circular motion. He wanted to believe that she was enjoying this against her will. Nette stopped quickly, pulled herself out of her writhing lover, pointed her gigantic man-root at him and whispered evilly, "You're next, farmer. I got a surprise for you." She was stroking the big thing with both hands, aiming it ... like a gun. He couldn't look anymore. He was helpless to do anything but look. An enormous scream gathered at the rear of his throat, gaining steam and force, then it burst forth.

He heard voices in the background, in the room over him.
Someone said he really wants to live and a voice like Adele's
answered that he was a strong man. He took a breath, shallow
and labored, then another. He was starting to come back, he
could feel it.

Chapter 9

Frank was asleep now, the real crisis had passed three days after the assault. Worried, Adele felt too agitated to sleep, so she sat in a chair beside the wounded sharecropper's bed. Everyone knew about the incident, that big row at the colored hotel, but none had placed them at this address. Clarksdale would laugh a long time over this stupid affair, even though very few had the real story on it. She stood up slowly, careful not to awaken him.

No rug covered the dark wood floor and the curtains were made of Quality Flour sacks. The room was furnished with one other bed, a table covered with tools, piles of various sized nails and two claw hammers. There was a battered bureau for the carpenter's wardrobe and two overcoats hung on a nail along the wall near the front door. She found her pack of cigarettes among the clutter on the table and got one out. As she turned toward the bed she noticed that Frank had kicked the covers away from him. He was on his side, sleeping soundly, his face in an angry frown. She put the blankets over him again, tucking the corners under his body. She loved him in an offbeat way, almost. The notion that she owed him something bothered her, nagged her and she wished it would go away. She thought about his fight with the stranger and what that really meant. His bravery was something she couldn't ignore. She knew he needed her now and that awakened a tenderness inside her for him. Her hearing about his work in the fields made her realize he was worn out in spirit, beaten down and the little girl's death brought everything to a head. She couldn't abandon him now, not with him like this. Flat on his back, laid up in his sick bed. Besides, there was no going back to Nette. That was out of the question after the fight at the hotel.

In a half hour, he yawned and tried to sit up. He didn't have the strength, so she placed a couple of pillows under his head. His skin was ashy, pale and wet with sweat. Yet, he didn't have a fever. Pain showed in his eyes, even though he made an attempt to pretend he was much better.

"How are you feeling?" she asked him.

"I'll live, I guess," he joked without a smile. "That guy went to town on me, didn't he?"

Adele grinned and said, "He sure did. Boy, you had us all scared you weren't going to make it there for awhile. Are you in a lot of pain?"

"Hell yes. Why did she do this?"

She pursed her lips, narrowed her eyes at him, thought it over and said, "She did it because she loves me and she didn't want me to leave her. You are lucky to be alive. If she would have had things her way, we'd be putting you in the ground now."

"Did she want to kill you too?" he asked.

She studied his face and the cheek wound before answer-

78

ing. "Yes."

"Tough woman," he said. "Give me a smoke."

Reluctantly she gave him a cigarette, held a lighted match under it and watched him bring it to his lips with his good hand. He winced as he did it.

The way she looked at him was so loving and full of concern. He felt moved to new feelings he had never known before, not even with his wife. She loved him after all and the bloody fight had made certain of that.

He looked at her, waiting for her to say something. She was restless, unsure about what to do with her hands. They shared a tense moment of silence just gazing into each other's eyes. He was hurting again from the numerous cuts all over his body. Some of them were irritating him by itching and he couldn't scratch them.

He seemed thoughtful, on the verge of tears. "I really ruined things for you. You was alright before I came along. I don't know why you even stay around here to help me. I don't deserve it."

"Frank, things could be worse. We could be both dead. Do you know that?" She was almost crying. His sadness was getting to her.

"How do I repay . . . you for doing this?" he asked, very quietly.

Adele tried to convince him of her sincerity. "I don't want anything from you. Just get well and stop worrying so much. If I ever want something, I'll ask for it. You can believe that."

He was starting to cry lightly, his large body shivering under the blankets, tears running down his bruised face. This went on for a long time. He made an effort to speak and again the tears came. It hurt her to see him in such a state. Men never cried like this, so openly. She was touched by his tears, his despair, his emptiness.

She sat in the chair once more, leaning over to him. She

managed to take his head in her arms and held him against her chest. He yielded to her kindness and smiled as she kissed his red, swollen eyes.

"I didn't mean to do that. I shouldn't be crying like I just went to a funeral, crying for no reason at all."

Adele shook her head. "It's good to cry. People rarely cry for nothing. You needed to do that. When is the last time you cried? I bet you can't remember when."

He rubbed his lower lip with a thick forefinger and said calmly, "Crying's a waste of time." Then he told her about a time when he was a young boy walking home from the company store with a paper sack of groceries. A group of four older boys chased him through the woods, threatening to beat him up. Along the way, he tripped headlong, spilling out the bag's precious contents but he jumped up in fear and left them. It never occurred to him that his father would see him running like a coward, chased home by the toughs without his groceries. His Papa stepped back inside the house, pushed him out and locked the door. Frank got two ass whippings that day; one from the big boys and another from his father for running home like a coward and for crying like a sissy. He never forgot that lesson.

Adele stared at him for a moment. "Your father was cruel. What did he think that would prove? How could he just lock you outside to take a beating like that?"

"He was trying to make a man out of me." He grinned wolfishly. "And that's what he did."

She put her mouth fully on his. "He made a Frankenstein monster, he created a madman. That's what he did."

He sounded hurt and bitter. "Naw, the white folks did that part. He was trying to get me ready for them and Mississippi white folks are among the worse. I's serious as a stroke."

"Hush," she said playfully. She rubbed her nose against his. "Thank you for saving me from that evil witch, Nette.

If all of this had never happened, I'd never known how sick she really is. She doesn't know how to love, not even herself. Let alone someone else."

"I love you," he said.

Adele played the dumb blonde role, putting her hands into the prayer position. "Oh, my hero. You've come through evil villains, trigger-happy sheriffs, big rats, forest fires and across the hot desert to save me from my life of sin."

"What's a vill-lane?"

She corrected him. "Villain. A bad guy. Edward G. Robinson, Paul Muni, George Raft, Humphrey Bogart. Like those guys."

Frank smiled at her innocently and politely asked, "Who are all them people you named? Do they live around here? Mebbe they run some juke joints or something."

She gave him a devilish look to see if he was joking and belly-laughed. "I forgot. The colored show around here doesn't show much of anything. They're movie stars, fool. You know, Hollywood."

With that, they burst into chuckles, until he asked her to let him get some sleep. He needed so much of it to get his strength back. Nothing would ever take the scars of that day away. Even Adele's love could not do that.

Chapter 10

People recognized Adele every night that she prowled the main streets of Clarksdale. She went out just before midnight, walking the streets in an attempt to clear her head. In a way, she hoped she would run into Nette and she knew that meant another fight. The picture of the stranger, sprawled on the floor with his eyes rolled back in his head, stayed with her. She couldn't shake it. Her heart always beat quickly whenever the scene came to her.

The main thing she recalled about that night was Frank, his hair a mess, trying to hold himself up. He had grabbed her hand and stumbled toward the door. He was dripping with blood. As he shut off the light, he looked at the fallen stranger, still out, laying doubled up, with a purple foam on his lips. Then it was dark inside the room, no sound but their breathing. He listened for noises coming from outside the door, somebody on the stairs. Just to be safe. All of the fight was out of him. He couldn't go at it again. He then opened the door quickly and looked out. There was no one on the stairs. He snatched her by the hand and started running to no place in particular. Over his shoulder, he yelled where could they hide? She answered him while fighting for breath and they changed directions.

They were the center of attention on the streets as people tried to figure what kind of accident they had been involved in. He was real weak and twice he fell down from exhaustion, only his will kept him coming. It was a heroic effort and she couldn't forget any of it.

"Hold on Frank, hold on," she said.

"Okay darling," he was talking through a mist.

She fought with the keys, trying to find the right one, but her hands were trembling too much. The door finally swung open. But she had not opened it, the carpenter's daughter had. The girl's eyes searched their faces with a desperation, then they saw her father. Otis, the carpenter, didn't say a word as he unbuttoned Frank's blood-soaked shirt to get at the wounds. His daughter returned with a bowl of water, touched Otis' arm and backed away. In her hand was something wrapped in a towel. Frank was feeling the razor tracks on his chest with his unmarked hand, some had dried and some others were still bleeding. It was the same story concerning his arms, where the blade had traveled up and down their length, and in his maimed hand, where deep cuts throbbed in the palm. The sharecropper said he had to smile when he thought about seeing the man's bone pop through the skin, looking like a big chicken bone. Everyone laughed after that.

What was Adele Hudson doing in a situation like this? That was the first question she recalled asking herself. Working rapidly, Otis and his daughter dabbed at the slashes with damp cloths, cleaning and dressing them with salve. The carpenter's daughter, Theda they later found was her name, watched

Frank intently. He winced when Otis hit a stinging spot.

After they got him cleaned up, he was assisted to a chair. He seemed uneasy because of the way Theda looked at him. When he tried to get to his feet, he collapsed back into the chair. He tried again and his arms went around her shoulders. Otis stood nearby, in case he was needed. The little girl ran off into another room. Everyone knew she was probably crying. What a night that was!

Chapter 11

From the tiny window near his bed, Frank could watch a group of white schoolboys standing before a new building being constructed, observing the black workmen hustling to and fro with long beams of fresh timber under their arms. Some laborers beat the wooden ribs together with hammer and nail for the skin to be fit over. He saw the well-dressed supervisor chew them out, poking his finger in the faces of a couple of the men.

Sadly, he glanced around the house. He missed his wife and the young ones, and most definitely he missed the food she cooked: highly seasoned black-eyed peas, fluffy wild rice, honey baked sweet potatoes, hot cornbread, and spice laden collard greens with a hint of salt pork in them. The family would sit around the big table and the forks hit the plates solidly, with a musical regularity. Very little talk would pass among the eager diners. His wife enjoyed the spectacle of witnessing the disappearance of the food, none wasted or picked over. Frank sometimes held a rib aloft, with the sizzling sauce dripping between his fingers as he crunched the meat with energetic jaws.

Those thoughts vanished quickly when he imagined Mister Jesse, the plantation foreman, scouring the countryside in search of him. That bullwhip would be tucked neatly under one armpit, ready for use. Even at settlement time, he intimidated the pickers coming to the big house to get their cash share of a year's wages, all that would remain after debts. The lanky foreman, the stereotypical redneck, watched each sack being lifted and checked the metal hook as it was put through the drawstring. He fixed the weight, pushing it by the notch on the scale. When the sack and the weight balanced, Mister Jesse read off the weight figure and made a notation in his book.

"It look heavier that that, suh." Frank kept his eyes toward the ground whenever he spoke to the white man.

"What you say, boy?"

"Nothin' suh. You right. That suits me fine."

Always eating crow, always. During one of his trips to the market after his recovery, he ran into Mister Jesse and two of his assistants getting out of their pickup truck near his destination. The horn honked twice, but Frank continued walking. Finally he stopped and crossed the street to the truck.

There were newly purchased tools in the back seat, along with a bag of canned beers, pig skins in a plastic wrapper, and three apples. The white men were sweating off their weight and the truck seemed like an oven inside. He stood near the passenger's door, out of reach.

The foreman ceased chewing tobacco. "Nigger, whar you been?"

"I moved out for a while," said Frank truthfully.

"Who tole you to leave? Did you have my permission?"

"Naw suh." Frank was very humble, almost pathetic.

"Come closer, nigger," the foreman said angrily. "Ain't I always treated you fair. Ain't I? Right, I have. Treated you better than some of the others. I thought you was more like us. But you let me down. You let me down, Frank boy. I's very disappointed in you. You got lazy on me. No-count. Why?"

Frank looked down at the curb. "It's private, Mister Jesse, suh. Home trouble."

The three white men laughed. Mister Jesse moved within reach of Frank. "What's this I hear about you and your wife?"

More white people were standing around now and some had their dogs, their nigger hunting dogs, along. All this Frank digested in a glance. But he was not in the mood for this kind of talk coming from Mister Jesse or not.

"Ain't none of your business, suh," he told the white man.

"What you say to me, coon?" his boss shouted.

He stood his ground, looking the white men in their faces. "I say we ain't together no more. Another man in there on the job now."

That humored Mister Jesse, who cackled until he fell against one of his assistants, now standing beside him.

"Niggers," he joked. "I don't understand you people for the life of me. I'll be dog. What y'all do, pass your women around among your friends?" The assistants endorsed the wisecrack with a hearty chuckle.

"Suh," Frank pleaded humbly, his gaze dropped. "Please don't make me talk about it. It's between me and my wife. Not here in front of all these folks."

"Shit, ain't nothing you got private!" the foreman snapped. "Especially your woman. This is 1956 and ain't a nigger in this country that can tell a white man what he can and cannot do. Remember that, black boy. Shit, you bastards come to me for food, don't you? Don't you? You come to me for work and jobs, don't you? You come to me for money, don't you? So don't tell me nothing about you got anything private. You a nigger and you work for me. I own your black ass, get that? Understand? If I wanted to know everything in your thick burrhead, you better tell me. Understand, boy?"

He understood the white man in a way many black folks didn't. Last year when the NAACP petitioned the Clarksdale city council for the right to eat and drink anywhere, the whites laughed themselves into cramps. Many of the whites were talking about two famous boys from the area, Faulkner and Tennessee Williams, yet they didn't say much about the countless bodies being fished out of the Mississippi River. Almost daily. A black man's life was and is cheap, he thought.

"I's unnerstand, boss," he said it in true darky talk and the white men smiled. This boy knew his place after all.

Mister Jesse pushed him back and took out a hankie. "And don't be breathing in my face when I's talking to you, nigger. What's wrong with you?"

"Yessuh," said Frank excitedly. Mister Jesse had never spoke to him like this before. This was somebody else. He had always figured if he minded his own business, there would never be any trouble for him. It didn't work that way. Mister Jesse smacked him in the face. His head went back with the blow but he kept his feet. The assistants laughed rudely and the boss smacked him again, openhanded, like he was a woman.

The circle of men closed around him, cutting off effective escape route. "Boy, you forget where you are sometimes. Don't you?"

Holding his face, Frank said a no sir and turned to go.

They made a joke among them, then the foreman reached over with his hand, rubbed it roughly across the black man's cheek, as though the color would come off. He pinched it, his dirt-caked fingernails biting the skin with the coldness of scissors cutting flesh.

"Not so fast," the foreman said, putting more pressure into his grip. "Don't ever walk away from me as long as you live. You stand still when I talk to you."

"I was jes tryin' to keep from leavin' my home for good," he appealed. "Suh, my wife don't want me no more. Another man's been foolin' 'round with her. That's 'bout it, suh. Home trouble like I said 'fore."

"Have you lost your mind, nigger?" the foreman was saying to him as he placed his hands around Frank's throat. "Now, you didn't tell me what you doing up here, away from where you supposed to be."

Frank thought quick. "Seeing somebody about help for my sick boy, Little Frank."

"Damn it, you lying. You been away from home too long to be doing that. Thought you could lie to me. You ain't living with your family no more. Don't lie to me, coon." He stung Frank across the mouth with another slap. Frank tasted blood.

"You are messing with my crop, my money," the white man continued. "I can't have that. Understand? You work just like everybody else."

Real casual. "Yessuh."

"What? What do you understand, darkie?"

Frank corrected his erect profile accordingly and recited the right words with the vigor of a well-worn Easter speech. "I's understand I's messing with your money, suh."

He recalled a time when talk was flying hard and heavy from near Drew, Mississippi. According to word of mouth, one of the big white men in the county was the cause of it. It seems his wife loved dark meat and often cruised the side roads in search of it. Frank knew her well. She had made a play for him once but he politely declined. But many would take her, take the risk and ravage her thick pink body, leaving her sprawled, spent on the back seat of her long, bottle-green Buick Roadmaster. Others were not so lucky and got caught. The youngest Yancey boy, a fine looking lad, was one of them. He was often spotted walking around in town, mumbling to no one in particular, with a vacant look in his eyes. Women whispered among themselves about the waste of such a handsome young man, cut to a stub. One chilly morning, the Yancey boy dressed himself in one of his mama's tattered dresses, painted his lips red with rouge and put a bonnet on his head. After careful planning, he fired his father's .44 into his face, all because of his nub, his manhood cruelly trimmed by nightriders.

Another slap almost ripped his head off. As soon as the bossman told him to have his black nigger ass back in the field at sunup tomorrow and added get out of his sight, Frank ran all the way home. The place was empty. There was nobody in it at all until a drunken Adele staggered into it after midnight and he didn't ask any questions. He had been crying earlier.

Part Two

NORMAL
UNDER THE
CIRCUMSTANCES

Chapter 12

Mary Thomas sat with her neighbor, Beneather Reed, in the two rockers on the porch, watching the children at play in the dust. Her neighbor was known for her ability to gossip, to twist the truth from a story, and her knack to blow anything out of proportion. She only came around when she needed something new to talk about. The woman could meddle in other people's affairs, run off at the mouth, but she was good company when there was no one else to talk with. And there was no one else to talk with, especially since Frank had gone away. Still, Mary knew anything she said to this fat woman would be spread as soon as she left the yard, and in twenty different versions.

"Hush gal, lemme tell you," Beneather was saying, laughing. "Don't let no man see you soft or it's over. You can't let no man make a fool out of you."

Mary gave no response, kept on rocking and watching the

young eyes.

"Mary, I knows about chirren," Beneather lamented. "Yes Lawd, had two myself. They dead on me. Shoot, them mens use them babies to tie you down and keep from doing things."

Mary was somewhat taken aback by her tone of voice, because it seemed to have honest affection in it. She felt free to speak her mind, well almost. "Babies or no. Besides, it ain't the children gettin me down, it's him hisself. He don't bit more love me than the man in the moon, but I gots too much time in him and these kids to go off and do something foolish. Know what I mean?"

"Kids just tie you down."

"Yessir."

"Frank don't beat you, do he?"

"No, gal, just leave me all time by my lonesome," said Mary, shaking her head. "Sometimes don't see him for months. That's worse than a whupping. And these children is a struggle, believe me."

Pausing to get her next question right, her friend shrugged. "Your family don't like him much, huh?"

"That's true sure nuff," Mary said with a chuckle. "Thinks he's a rambler. All my family against him, but he act like he don't care. He just take care of us and do his dirt when he want."

Beneather looked at her. "Well, I rules my man, keeps an edge on him. But too long a time done gone by for you to try and do something with this one here you got. Nothing gone change him if it in him to act a fool. Still, you try and keep a rein on his mind."

"One thing sure," Mary said, feeling her big stomach.

"What's that, gal?"

"I don't want no more children. Raising these here about to drive me crazy. Have them just to see them die. Lawd knows, when my Teenie left here, I thought I was about to follow her." Mary sagged in the chair. The girl's face was before her in the faces of the other little ones running in the yard.

"How did Frank take it, Teenie's death?"

"He go off by hisself and come back. His eyes look like he been crying. Frank loved that little one. She was just like him to the tee. Yes, it hurt him bad."

Beneather was shocked. "What you say?"

"Yeah, he did. When his uncle died, what really raised him, he acted the same way. The doctors had told Frank the man didn't have long to live. But it still busted him up."

Her nosy neighbors didn't think the big Negro had any feelings in him. "What did he do? Did he cry in front of you?"

"Frank was there when he died on them. He got real quiet. I was there, watching him. You could see by his face, there was pain in him someplace, but he was a man about it and kept it down. I didn't see him for nigh three weeks after that. When he come back, he was alright. Never spoke on it none since."

"When was the last time when you seed Emma?" asked Beneather.

"Ain't seed Emma in a spell," snorted Mary. "Since we had that last falling out. She used to come by regular, come and sit around. She brought me pies and things. I gived her fruit I put up. Then I come to notice how she'd look at Frank when she thought I wasn't looking. Look at him like he was a piece of cake. I caught her by herself, told her don't even darken my doorway. Naw, ain't none of that under my nose."

"Gal, you did right. You sure did right. What you gone do about that boy there?"

"Oh, Lil Frank. Don't rightly know."

"He don't look like he right in the head. Might mess around and hurt somebody. Watch what I say."

"I know, girl. He gittin worser. Nothing can be done. Ole

lady from up near Natchez come through here Friday week, say he got some new hant on him."

"A hant, where?"

"Up in his head. I knowed that before she told me. I try and keep an eye on him."

"What Frank say?" Beneather's eyes grew wide.

"He act like the boy's alright. But inside, he know Lil Frank ain't okay. Speck it hurt him too deep to say it to himself."

Beneather sighed, pursing her lips. "Hmmmmm. Day comin' when you might have to put that boy away somewhere. Maybe up in Memphis or over in Jackson. They's got places for his kind."

Mary's face saddened and she wiped her eyes. "I know, Beneather, but I just hate to see one of my own like that. Locked up like some dog or something." Mary raised her voice to Bue, who was not far away, trying to listen to what they were saying. "Go get the baby and bring him here to me. And bring his eats too." The girl ran into the house.

The baby possessed a stubborn streak second only to his father. Mary tried to get Lincoln to take some stew, to no avail. He would eat for a while, as fast as she could get it to his mouth. But as soon as he tired of the food, he would look about, then kick and cry, beating the air with his tiny arms. If she brought the spoon close, Lincoln wouldn't open his mouth or he would turn his head.

Beneather ignored the activity with the baby. "Mary, what you use on your face to keep it so clear?"

"Drink plenty of water and use lemon water on it. Keeps them bumps down."

"Uh-huh."

"Beneather, ain't you never wanted no more babies since your other two died?" Mary asked, holding the baby's mouth and shoveling in the spoon.

"Babies. I wanted them since and I tried to have them, too.

That's when I was younger. My womb must be made of glass, always dropped them early. Mens put their seed in there but it wouldn't stick. I can't complain. I done had a good life." The woman gazed off in space and let her face grow long.

Mary grinned. "I like them when they like this, small and helpless. They ain't no trouble then because they need you. I really can't kick about nothing. I likes carrying babies. You know, when they inside you and growing."

"Mens don't want no babies, though," Beneather said. "You know what they want. If they do have babies, they always want a man-child to carry on their name, so they can carry their head high and strut amongst the others. Shoot, you did Frank proud."

"Girl, don't let them tell you that lie. They likes them girl babies too, crazy about them girls. You watch a man with his girl baby. You'll see all over his face, just smiling and stuff. And fool thing about it, them girls be crazy about them mens too. I's seen Bue, Alice, and especially that Teenie go fool crazy over their papa many a day." They laughed on that for a few minutes.

"A lots of peoples can't handle the load babies put on them," added Mary. "They don't like knowing the young ones are depending on them and all. Shoot, know something, Mary? I never did miss that bleeding and them cramp pains no how." They clamped their mouths on that.

The women watched the younger Frank walking around and around a Chinaberry tree. Mary mused aloud, "Mebbe I looked too hard at a crazy person or something, reason why he like that. I was real careful where my mind was when I was carryin' him. Wanted Lil Frank to be something special. Turn out he plumb crazy. It ain't right for him to go through life like that." She was noticing the blank expression on the boy's face. Beneather saw it too but kept her mouth shut.

Then the visitor said, "Somebody might have done something to him while you weren't around. You know, when he was a baby and you didn't see it."

Mary turned to the woman and said harshly, "No, I looked after him special. Did all I could. I didn't do nothin' to rouse his nature when he was small. Nothin' like that. They say if you mess with a baby down there, that will mess him up. I fed him right, held him some."

Beneather shook her head in pity. "You got your hands full here, gal. Been to Pinetop with him?"

"Shoot yeah. Doctor up there told me I should have his manhood trimmed and his tonsils yanked out. This was when he was small. Say he would stop being like that. I think he was a jackleg, so I ain't been back since."

"How you take care of all of these others, work, clean house and watch him too?" Beneather asked the question in short breaths and sighed like she was helping Mary do it.

"Ain't easy. The older chirren help a lot. They watch him when I's busy. And see, he love the water and it take everybody to keep him from going off, gettin' drowned somewhere."

"Yeah, you probably took him to the wrong doctor up there. You should look into it again."

Mary gave her a tired look. "Still, much as I knows that, I hates to see him go off in them homes. Won't get the care we give him here. Probably lay around, mess on himself and not get cleaned. End up looking like a bag of bones, probably never come out of it. It's best he be around peoples, his peoples, so we can take care of him."

"He understand you when you talk to him?" asked Beneather.

"Yeah," Mary answered. "He knows what I say when I talk to him by how I works my voice. If I talk to him soft, he know that. If I holler at him, he know that too. No, he ain't no complete fool, but Lawd, he pretty close. Poor thing."

Lil Frank, across the yard, was engrossed in stomping in the head of his shadow.

"The problem could be in what you feed him," said Beneather, playing the role of detective. There weren't too many mysteries around her house, but there were plenty here.

"If that's the case, all my clan here would be mad because they all eats the same food. I hates to see him eat. He act like some animal and if you don't feed him first, before the others, he'll get it hisself. No table manners at all. Boy just eat with his hands, real terrible." She heard Beneather gasp. Mary moved her head so she could see Little Frank. All the while he was watching her from behind the tree with the blank look again.

"I never hear him say anything. Do he talk?"

Frank's wife replied, "Naw, he don't talk none. He make noises like a hissing or a growl. Sometimes he get mad and yell at the top of his voice until you look at him. I hope to God that he don't ever learn about no man and woman love, you know."

"You think he will?"

"Well, sometimes I catch him playing with hisself." Her words came out as if she was somewhere else in thought. And she was; her mind was seeing Buddy and Dit wrestling an ax from the mute to keep him from killing their old moo cow. The boys were locked in a violent struggle.

"Mary, this go on all day?"

She felt Beneather's eyes going from the antics of the boy to the spreading rivers of gray hair on her head. "Yessir, all day." Then she yelled to Dit to stop the boy from pulling his hair out.

Chapter 13

There was no one on the main highway or in the front yard when Frank came home. In her half-awakened state, his wife could still discern her man's weighty footsteps. He wobbled and stumbled through the doorway, but she still didn't stir. With a short groan, he eased himself into a chair.

"We have to talk." Mary was tearful yet controlled. Her husband started talking in his normal tone of voice, but she shushed him, telling him to lower the volume so he wouldn't wake the children.

"About what, woman?"

"We have to talk," insisted Mary. "This is becoming more than I can stand. You leave me right when I needs you most, right after Teenie dies. Lil Frank cutting up and Bue done gone boy crazy. I needs you here, not in town chasing tail."

He was ready to tell her the story he had rehearsed. For some reason, he couldn't bring himself to say it. He stuttered

103

and fumbled with the words.

"Don't lie to me, Frank." She was mad and she wanted him to know it.

Frank realized she was waiting to get him in bed where he could go nowhere, where he couldn't do anything but lay there and listen. She went into the kitchen and got herself a glass of pump water. It seemed no time passed before she slipped into bed beside him, with her butt to him. It was dark. The way she was breathing, quick and nervous, assured him what she had to say would not be the usual. She was really upset.

She asked coldly, "You ready to talk?"

"Go head on." He was waiting for this one. The last time it was about Little Frank; this time it would be about them, their future together. Maybe she heard some gossip. Something was bothering her.

"Frank. You asleep?"

"Naw, speak. I's tired."

"Frank, we ain't been honest 'bout us, 'bout how we living. We been lying 'bout everything. We just lying and lying. And we can't keep on doing that."

Yeah, she was mad alright. Something was bothering her and she meant to get it off her mind. He didn't know what the woman was talking about. He'd stayed out before and he never got none of this when he got home. Maybe Nette's warning was right.

"Honey, you upset," he said. "You about to blow up at me 'bout nothing. Why start a fight when everything's alright?" He was hoping for an easy out. She turned to face him in the bed. It didn't matter to him because of the darkness.

She wanted to punch him. "Frank, I ain't crazy. I got good sense. You don't want to look at what's going on, at what you been doing here lately, going off for days and forgetting us here. You away from here more than you home. I ask you to help me with Bue and Lil Frank. You don't. These chirren going wild. I can't make them mind by myself." She seemed like a dam about to burst.

"Er ... er ... er ..."

"Let me finish my say, Frank."

He countered, "You changed up on me. You needed me before, you and the chirren. You didn't act like this. Now you want to be the man, you want to be the head of the house while I's in it. I knowed it was tough on you while I was gone but I's back and it'll be different now."

"It ain't no different. While you was gone, I looked at myself, at how I was. I got tired of waiting on you, waiting on you to do things for me, for us. Tired of waiting period. I was lonesome. I needs a man I can count on. Not somebody who gone leave me the dirty work while he out good-timing it. Folks around here talk 'bout me like a dog."

"To hell with some peoples talking. They ain't feeding our family."

"Neither is you, Frank. Ain't hardly nothing in this house to eat. We living from hand to mouth. What you gone do, Frank? Let me know now. What is it gone be? You my man or not?"

He was stunned, shocked. She never talked like this before. Never. Not to him. Somebody put this mess in her head.

Frank sat up in the bed, shaking with anger and the pains in his head. A pounding headache that came on him suddenly and without warning. "Tell me this much," he snapped at her. "What do you mean by all this? Them stupid gals you talk with done put this fool idea in your mouth. They got you all hot to kick me out." He let the words echo around the room with a slight pause.

She sat up too. He felt the bed move.

"I hate it because you don't hear me," Mary said with bitterness. "I might as well be talking to that wall there. You don't ever think 'bout me stuck here. You don't ever think I might want a good time too. You don't care 'bout anybody in this house! You don't pay nobody here no attention."

In that instant, Mary wished she was stronger so she could whip his ass, punch him in the mouth. She was crying, mad and confused. He moved slowly toward her sobs, to touch her. She pulled back out of reach.

"You only thinks of yourself, only yourself," snarled his wife. "Only yourself and your pleasure."

He thought, I've heard that before. He was sick of those words. Hisself and his pleasure, shit.

Frank pondered over what she said, matched it with what Adele had told him earlier and concluded that they were right. He was selfish. But he must be the man of his house and he couldn't let her take over. That was for damn sure.

She hesitated, then said, "I love you, Frank, but I just have to tell you how I feels. I don't know how much more I can take. You acting like most menfolk do. You see what's happening and act like you don't know what you seeing. But you knows. I knows you know."

He listened, his mind working harder than usual. He was thinking about the Mary he met a long time ago, the way she was when he first met her. Young, sassy, full of life. He met her on the access road going toward Pinetop. One of the field hands was bothering her. Big, burly buck kept making her drop the load of groceries she was carrying. Teasing her. He recalled how he told the man to leave her be, to go on about his business. The man swung at him and he ducked. And he didn't miss with his fist and hit the man hard in the face and dropped him in a sitting position on the dirt road. Then the man ran off and Frank moved in. Mary smiled at him and he was hooked.

"We got chirren to raise, Frank," remarked Mary. "They needs both of us to raise them right, not one of us. I can't do it alone."

Frank wasn't listening. He shut her out. He was thinking what would have happened if he had stayed single.

He said, returning to the surface, "That's what womens are for, chirren. Mens can't bear babies. You all supposed to be the mamas."

"Oh, and what are you supposed to be? You act like you single while I stay around here and slave. I's supposed to take what you give out?"

"Yeah, that's right."

"Naw sir, naw." She was getting madder.

It was time for him to show her who the boss was. "Yeah, you right. Other womens treat their man right. You don't hear them giving their mens any lip."

Mary was silent. It was no use talking to him. He had rocks in his head for brains. "Put your mind on this here," she told him. "What you gone do if Bue gets knocked up by that boy and he don't marry her? She'll just be a burden around the house on us with another mouth to feed. And the older she get, the harder it'll be for her to get a decent man."

"Just throw her ass out," said Frank cruelly. "Throw her out, baby and all. That's all you can do."

"You don't mean that." She couldn't believe he said that.

"Yeah, I mean it. Throw her out of here. I warned her. I saw the boy and warned him too. That's all I can do. I can't follow her around holding her panties up and her legs together. I can't do it and I won't."

"Frank!!!"

Frank added, "I mean what I say." He sizzled inside. What did she mean 'what was she going to do while he was gone?' Shit, his wife just better wait until he gets back and better not ever, ever, let him find another man in his house jumping her behind his back. Not his wife. Better not.

In the morning he was gone. She didn't hear him leave in

the night. All of his things were gone with him. There was not a trace of him, except his pistol; as though the same breeze that brought him back to her had taken him away again.

Chapter 14

That next Monday was a day that Mary would not forget for a long time. In the clear blue sky above, there appeared a cluster of grim, ominous clouds, as if someone had reached into a traveling bag and had thrown them there. The rain, which followed, was a downpour. The small children were in the front yard playing, while the boys spied again on Bue and her boyfriend from an unseen vantage point. Everyone was soaked by the time they ran the distance to the chicken shack. Later, their mother sighed deeply and fixed up two hot bottles of castor oil for them. She sliced two lemons to give to each one a portion to squeeze into their mouths to kill the taste. As they undressed, a pile of wet clothes accumulated on the wood floor.

"Line up for your dose. Dit, get 'em in here." Mary located a rag to wrap around the warm bottles, preferring to pour rather than spoon the hot, slimy liquid.

"Mama, we ain't gotta take none, do we?" asked Mance.

"Mance, if you don't stop worrying me, I'll—"

Bue walked over to her mother, showed the whites of her eyes. "I ain't got no cold. See, my eyes are clear."

"I don't want to hear no mess out of you all," insisted their mother.

The clothes emitted a damp odor. Valiantly, Bue stepped up first, since she liked to get the dose over and done with. Her mother remembered Bue's affair with the no-count Taylor boy at the last moment and poured a little extra down her throat. Mary watched her daughter swallow it, then sent her on her way. Next, Dit and Jake.

"Mama, lemme git some water to go with it," Jake begged. His mother grabbed his arm and pulled him close. Thrust the lemon into his hand. "Open up, wider, wider," said Mary. "You kids act like this is the first time you took a laxative."

Jake stood in front of her for a time and shook in quick shivers as he tasted the oil going down. His mother moved him aside and asked for Dit. She had a hand on Buddy, the next victim.

Stalling for time, Buddy answered, "Last time I seed him was by the outhouse. He was going to pee." He was smiling but the smile left when she flipped his head back and laid a healthy dose on his tongue.

He grimaced and said, "That stuff's nasty."

She was running out of patience. "Swallow it, go head on now. Swallow it all. Don't hold it in your mouth either." Her hand put a lock on Dit's shoulder. "Stay here until I see you swallow it all."

The real chore would be to get Little Frank to take his dose and the boys struggled with the mute. She told them to bring him to her. The retarded boy fought, kicked and bit, even tried to gouge Buddy's eyes out. After a hearty effort, they pried the boy's mouth open and their mother got a big dose into him. The little ones were no trouble, not like him.

Later, Bue stood with her best girl friend, Joleen, looking out over the road, toward the fields, vast and green.

"I's going to see Ted and that's that," said Bue defiantly. "I ain't no child no more. I's a woman, feels like one."

"You gone mess yourself up fooling wit him," warned Joleen.

"Naw, I won't," said Bue. "I knows what I's doing."

Joleen laughed, tilted her head back. "You headed for trouble for sure. You knows that Ted Taylor don't mean you no good, not one bit. When he gits what he wants, he'll leave you high and dry. Watch and see."

Bue presented her back to her girl friend. "How do you know he ain't got it from me already? What do you say to that, Miz Goody-Goody?"

Joleen was astonished. "What are you saying? He didn't put it in you, did he?"

"Well, not quite but almost," Bue lied. "Girl, he kiss so good that it makes your head swim. Thought I would die, just die." Her face felt hot. Her Ted was quite the lover, sure was.

Joleen wore a puzzled expression. "But he ain't done nothing else, right?"

"Naw, not yet." She lied again.

"What you gone do if he give you a baby? Your papa will be crazy and Ted might git hurt."

"What he gone do if he ain't around?"

Her friend refused to accept that. "But he coming back and then he'll put Ted in his place."

Bue felt evil. "Shoot, he better be watching that Ellis. Notice how he and Mama gettin' more friendly? He brings her things, sits around talking. I don't like him none because I know what he's up to. If Papa don't watch out, he might try to move in."

111

"Girl, I don't like him either," agreed Alice. "He's trying to do Mama like he did Mildred but she don't see it. She act like she's trying to drive him off to make room for Fatso."

"Him who?"

"Papa, that's who."

The two girls stood silently, watching each other for a time. Then Bue said quietly, "I know, I know. That's how it look. That's why Papa don't come home and Beneather and Ellis working on her, done turned her against him. I can't be standing here talkin' to you, got to see my honey. We'll talk when I gets back."

Alice watched Bue walk toward the ditch and go across, into the field. She yelled at her and Bue stopped. If Alice cautioned her once more about the evils of men, she'd break her fool neck because, after all, there was nothing wicked about Ted, her darling Ted. Bue laughed loudly, tossed her hair and ran off to meet her lover. The ground was still wet from the short storm, the stickers and bushes bathed her legs as she ran. For an unknown reason, the air was quite pleasant, having that sweet, clean smell that comes after a rain.

In a few minutes, she was standing in the spot where they were supposed to meet. Assuming a sultry pose, Bue braced herself against a tall pine and waited. The sounds of footsteps, quick and sure, came from somewhere behind her. Instinctively, she knew it was him. Ted, her lover.

"How you doing today, Miz Pretty?" said Ted, holding out his hands.

Gingerly, Bue took them with hers, feeling as though she was a little girl. "Aw, Ted Taylor, your mouth is jes' full of flattery and lies but I likes it." Then she covered her mouth and giggled.

"I's glad you do, wit' your pretty self."

She pinched him lightly on the top of his chubby hands, maybe to relieve the growling beast in her stomach, for the

112

castor oil was making itself known. Ted backed her against the pine and kissed her full on the lips. The young girl moved in unison with him, then caught herself. She held him at arms' length to give her a chance to gather her wits, her girl friend's words still ringing in her ears.

"Guess what?" asked her beau. "Them folks in town all got your Papa's name in their mouths, talking 'bout him all over. They sayin' Ellis throwed him out his own house." He waited for his biting statement to hit the desired target and for her comment on it.

His sweetheart said it was a lie and turned her head in time to see a fat rabbit sniff the warm air and take four long hops into the brush again.

"I can see you don't want to talk 'bout it," said Ted, edging closer to her. "Let's talk 'bout us. Have you made up your mind 'bout you and me?" He saw that question put some life back into her. He continued, "Then you have thought 'bout it?" Bue nodded sheepishly and gave him her best show of teeth. Having him talk like this made her head catch fire. She loved him, loved him deeply. Maybe too much, she thought.

Ted felt she was ready to give herself to him again but didn't want to appear easy. He was too strong for her; his smooth, tight muscles wiggling in mock battle with her smaller arms. Bue made a move to run, he had her blocked and pushed her back fiercely with a shove that threw her off-balance. Lustful. She trembled as his hands went over her body.

"I love you, Ted," said Bue when the bright fire of passion permitted her to speak. "But I must go home now, my belly's rumbling and that castor oil's gone make me do something in a minute." They held each other briefly, clinging to every second, until she pushed free and ran back the way she had come, leaving him there to scratch his head in amazement.

Chapter 15

"Here come Ellis, Mama," announced Mance with disdain. The obese man disregarded the harsh look the boy gave him and handed him the melon and groceries he had brought for them. Dit helped his brother carry the load through the quiet house. At the back door, the older children sat in a flock with sad faces, showing their displeasure at his untimely visit.

Ellis asked, "Where your Mama, boy?" There was no quick reply and the children continued to sit with pained expressions, watching their hands. Sniffles. The mute, Little Frank, was sprawled behind them, rocking, a quilt over his head.

Another day of woe. Mary came from the back room, closed her eyes, wringing her hands. "When is that doctor gone get here? The boy will be dead before the fool comes. Holy Jesus, I can't lose another one." Tears moved slow in the creases by her nose toward her chin.

115

Placing his hands around her shoulders, Ellis put a touch of concern in his voice and asked, "What's wrong, Mary? Who sick?"

She gently shook her head. "It Jake. He jes' come in the house with a bad fever, fell out. An' he ain't come to yet. I's tried everythin' I could for him. Don't want give him too much medicine without knowin' what's ailing him. Sent Buddy for the doctor in Pinetop, should be here directly." Her brow was furrowed and Ellis saw she was on the verge of breaking down into tears again but she fought them back.

Ellis seemed worried. "This could be serious. Where Frank? He come home yet?" Some of the children rolled their eyes at him. This was no time for that, they said among themselves.

"I don't know where he is," said Mary, looking troubled. "Naw, I don't know where that fool is. Right now, I's thinkin' about that chile in there, whether he gone live or not. Don't say nothin' about Frank, hear me?" It was no occasion for romance or snide remarks about her absent husband.

Finally she gazed at him bitterly. Suddenly Buddy dashed into the room. He was out of breath but he managed to get the words out. "I told him Jake low sick. Doc say he be here as soon as he can. Don't move him, he say. I tole him that Jake was knocked out and his fever real high."

There was nothing anybody could do now but wait. Mary chased all of the children outdoors, giving them cookies to split among themselves. Buddy stayed with her to help out if he could. She stared at the door as the minutes passed, then hours. Around seven that evening, Mance ran to the front porch, nearly knocking over one of the rockers, yelling that the doctor was driving up.

A weather-beaten white man, in a black suit with his crumpled tie halfway down his chest, ambled in. Mary began explaining her son's illness. "He's in the back room there.

He awful sick."

"Where the other doctor, Doc Rodgers?" asked Ellis.

The man was too calm. "Doctor Rodgers is away at a convention up North and I'm filling in for him. Are you sure this is an emergency, Auntie? Could be a minor attack of sunstroke or a bad cold." Outside, the children were going over his car, looking in the windows, fingering the chrome.

"It bad or she wouldn't have sent for you," answered Ellis, a stern face on him.

Sounding official, the doctor said, "And you are the husband, the father of the child, I presume. Now . . ." His hands tinkered with something in his medical bag.

Ellis shook his head solemnly. "Naw, he's away on bizness in town. Should be back tonight sometime, suh. I's a friend of his'n." The fat man lied and Mary looked at him wistfully, thankful that he was there with her. At least she was not alone.

The doctor frowned while he straightened his tie. "Well, the fee is twenty-five dollahs for the visit. In advance, beforehand. Cash money. No credit. You know, it costs a lot of gas to come out here from where I live. I must be paid first, before I can administer any kind of service." Their mouths dropped in disbelief.

Where would they get that kind of money on the spur of the moment? Mister Jesse was away and wouldn't be back until the end of the week. That could be too late. But Mary bluffed, the only thing on her mind was her ailing boy and how he needed treatment now. "You will be paid, suh. Can't you jes' look at him an' see what wrong."

The doctor did not bat an eyelash. "No, I can't."

"Ellis, you got twenty-five dollahs 'til I gets some money from Mister Jesse?" asked Mary, her face ashen with panic.

Ellis put his hands in his pockets, knowing he didn't have a dime on him, and brought them out empty. She snapped at him, "When I needs money, you ain't got none. When I don't needs money, you flashin' it like it grow on trees." Her son was going to die, her second child lost this year.

She had a hex on her for sure, she thought while watching the doctor argue with Ellis over the money. Her papa told her when she was young that this life was the hardest for the poor and their family was among the poorest of the poor. Her father, born in the Delta, married a stringbean girl from Tallahassee, part Indian supposedly. Papa Charles, as he was called, loved the water, shrimp boats and traveling. For him, marriage was a casual affair. He loved the ladies and this caused Mary's mother untold suffering. Most of her papa's family, mixed blood Cajuns, lived in Louisiana, over near Milneburg. There were also a lot of Iberville Negroes in her clan. Papa Charles had worked with the Irish and German immigrants unloading ships in New Orleans. Just after he arrived in the Delta, Papa Charles was thrown under a tractor by a bunch of colored men playing around. Or so they said, she never believed the story at all. Nothing but bad luck, that's all she ever had.

She begged the doctor. "Please, suh, would you take my promise I will pay you when I gets the money tomorrow. My baby gone die if you don't help us. Please suh, please?" Her eyes were downcast, pleading with the man. Meanwhile Ellis, still with his pockets out, was throwing sharp looks at the doctor.

"I'm sorry," the doctor said with a note of finality. "I'm really sorry. I don't think I can accept that. Rules are that cash must be exchanged before I can do anything. We have expenses to be met so you must understand our position too. I want to help you but I can't. Understand that we must protect ourselves too." The man said it in much the way an eulogy is delivered.

In the background, Buddy nudged Mance and said, "He

gone let Jake die." Buddy noticed his brother was not particularly interested in what he was saying to him but in what was happening between the grownups.

"Protect!" Ellis yelled furiously. "Who protecting you right now? Huh? Tell me that." Mary pushed him away from the doctor, standing as a buffer between the two.

Bue cut her eyes at Ellis. "Shut up, fool. Let Mama handle it."

Her mother placed all of her emotions into what she had to say, into what she must say to the man. She would plead with him again and again until he understood. "Doctor, all I unnerstand is my boy is ailin' and needs care now. Sit down somewhere, Ellis. He's gots to know. Mister Whatever-your-name-is, my baby will die in there. Don't you unnerstand that? He gone die while we out there arguing over some damn money!"

The doctor wiped his brow with a handkerchief taken from a jacket pocket. "I want you to believe me when I say that I wish I could help you. I am a doctor. It is my job. I am just like anybody that works. Nobody works without getting paid for it. I must be paid for my services. I have to live too." The children moaned in chorus when he said it.

He glanced at Ellis balling up his fists as if he was going to strike the white man, an act of insanity in Mississippi. "This matter really doesn't concern you," the white man said calmly. "It's between the family and myself and you will not force me to do anything that I don't want to do, understand me well. I have nothing against you people, nothing. I always go out on a limb for the colored whenever I can but I've got to draw the line somewhere."

"You peckerwood—" muttered Ellis under his breath, the words barely audible.

"Why should I extend myself to someone with an attitude like yours?" The doctor narrowed his pale blue eyes and pointed at Ellis. "And watch those names, son. I think you're forgetting your place."

Ellis could barely hold back his anger. "So the boy is gone die, that's that." Frightened that things could get out of hand, Mary motioned to Buddy to take Ellis outside to cool off. Bue had left the action to look at her sick brother and returned with more bad news. "Mama, he looks worser. He's burnin' up."

"Mister Doctor, you got to do somethin' for 'im. Please, suh."

"There's nothing I can do. I believe I explained my position on the matter. I must go. I've got to make a few more stops before I turn in."

"You can't leave the child in this condition," screamed Ellis. "You can't. Ain't you got feelings?"

"I explained my policy. If it was not clear to you then I can go through it one more time for you."

Mary grabbed Ellis by the arm and guided him to the door. "Ellis, I said go outside. Lemme talk to 'im. You ain't doin' nothing but makin' things worse."

The doctor fingered his tie and turned to leave. "Maybe it's too late for me to do anything anyway. You should have taken the boy to the nearest colored hospital. I must go. There is nothing I can do here. I'm very sorry."

"How do you know? You ain't even looked at him!" Mary shrieked at his back while clutching Ellis around the stomach to keep him from jumping on the man.

From inside his car, the doctor remarked, "It's out of my hands. I suggest you take him to the hospital as I said earlier." Then he sped away. Mary covered her face with her hands and wept quietly. At her request, Buddy ran to get a neighbor, Sam Higgins, to drive them twenty miles to the nearest clinic. But Jake never regained consciousness and died on the way. No one was happier than Ellis. That night, he stayed with Mary under the guise of comfort in her moment of grief.

Chapter 16

Not very long after Jake's death, after a false sense of peace had returned to the house, Mary was changing Lincoln. He was wet. After drying him, she left him on the bed, on his back kicking. She went into the next room looking for a cloth to wash him with, and not finding one there, went outside to the clothesline.

Unseen, Little Frank stole into the room, placed an empty cast-iron skillet on the wood stove. Every so often, he looked in the direction of the door. There was no expression of any emotion on his face. The skillet was sizzling hot. He grabbed its handle, the heat burning his unprotected hand, hissing. With creeping steps, he entered the room where the baby was playing with his feet, walked over and stood for an instant. No one was in the house. He placed the glowing skillet calmly on the infant, holding it down and lifting it up, holding it down and lifting it up. The iron hissed again and again, frying the baby's tender flesh as he slid the skillet up and down the baby's body. The baby's shrill pain cry brought Mary running. She slapped the mute hard, in the face. He didn't move or make a sound. Instead he bared his teeth in a smile of sorts. The baby screamed and screamed.

Chapter 17

Just before nightfall, the children amused themselves with talk of the intense romance between Ellis and their mother. Mance, Dit and Buddy were sitting on buckets on the side of the shack. Overhead, the wind was still, but the summer heat was a killer again. The children were becoming accustomed to Ellis, his gifts for their mother and his nightly visits. Sometimes he would stay overnight, and lately, he would remain two or three days in a row. But never longer than that. Heat waves pushed past the children to where Mary stood on the porch, watching the baby walk. Lincoln had recovered remarkably well from the attack earlier in the day. The burns on his body were not as serious as they had first appeared. They were superficial but ugly to look at. The baby toddled a few unsteady feet, then fell, scooted backward, eased himself up again and staggered forward, then fell again. Mary smiled at his determination, while Ellis, standing behind her,

125

wrapped his arms around her waist.

"I sure hate to see that, don't you?" said Dit to no one in particular.

"Yeah," Mance said. "But I reckon Mama know what she doin'. She's grown an' Papa act like he don't care 'bout her or us."

"Buddy, tell him we seed him a few weeks back an' he ask about all us. Didn't he? We jus' didn't tell nobody. Tell Dit that we seed Papa."

"We did see Papa," agreed Buddy.

"Did you, for real? You ain't lyin' again."

Mance leaned back against the wall of the shack and smiled. The children observed a flock of crows land nearby, pecking in the dust. Dit scooped a handful of rocks and hurled them at the birds. He hit one in the side and the group took to the air, cawing loudly. For a moment, they circled above the shack, calling to each other, then they flew toward the river.

"We seed Papa at Otis' house," admitted Buddy, slapping his knee. "He was there visitin'. I don't recall if he say he would be there now. That was a while back."

"An' you jes' now tellin' us."

"I want to see him come back an' whup the hell out Ellis," Dit drawled with a touch of revenge. "I hate that tater-haid."

Dit stared solemnly at his brother. "Buddy, you better not let Mama hear you call him that."

Now one or two of the crows returned, swooping low, falling into a carefree glide over their heads. A rooster in the yard stopped its arrogant strut, spread its wings and looked skyward. Calmly, Buddy passed his hand over his hair and his lips narrowed to a line. He nudged his older brother on the arm and said, "Aw Dit, you 'fraid of evahthin'."

"You better be 'fraid of Ejay," taunted Dit, putting his fist against Buddy's cheek. "He say he gone whup your butt."

"That sissy couldn't whup Lincoln. He a lotta mouth, jes'

like you. Probably said that 'cause he had a gang of boys wit him."

Mance nodded at Buddy. "You can't whup him."

"Whup him and you too."

Buddy rose quickly and swung his arms in a move to overcome boredom. Any kind of movement was better than just sitting around. "You think Ellis gone move in?" No one answered; it was something none of them wanted to think about, his taking their father's place. Buddy removed his dirty undershirt and said, "He's been real nice to Mama, buying her stuff. Bet he moves in 'fore fall sets in. Watch and see."

"Mama ain't that dumb," Dit said defensively.

"What you know 'bout anythin'?"

Mance shrugged his shoulders. "Mama seems to like Ellis. I don't know why but she do."

"I can't stand the rings of fat around his neck," said Buddy, turning his eyes to the road in the distance. "A fat tater-haid. That's a good name for him."

Mance cleared his throat and spat in the dust. "I heard him tell Jack Smoot that he buried some money once at his place and later he couldn't find it. Real dumb."

"Aw, you tellin' a tale now."

"Naw, naw, I heard him say it. I did."

"Papa got to come back," said Dit bitterly. "He got to. This fool gone mess up things around here where they won't nevah be the same. He ain't good for Mama or us."

For several minutes, the brothers neither budged or said a word.

"Why won't Papa come home?" Buddy finally asked.

"I don't know," answered Dit. "Next time Mance goes to see him, have him take you along and you can ask Papa yourself."

"Dit, you talk too much," said Mance, folding his arms. "If I was older, I'd punch you."

127

"You gone do what, Mance?" Dit asked. "Don't mess wit me. Nigger, I'll slap you bald-haided. If you was older, you would be half daid if you kept actin' crazy."

"You need help. You worse off than Lil Frank." Mance knew Dit wished he could hurt their father, hurt him for going off and leaving them alone. He had watched his older brother change over the past weeks from a friendly, joking boy to a sullen, angry stranger. Dit had harsh words for everybody now, including their mother. No one knew what to say to him anymore.

"You talkin' trash, lil boy," threatened Dit. He grabbed his brother's thin arm, a hard grip that pained to the bone. He bent the arm slowly until Mance cried out, then he let it go. Mance breathed easier.

"You bully," Mance sobbed. He covered his eyes with his hands. He wanted to make Dit feel guilty for what he had done. "You know what I saw last night?"

"What?" The other two looked at him, waiting.

"Ellis was tusslin' wit Mama, tryin' to kiss her. He kept tryin' but she pushed his hands away. He think he a big lover or somethin'."

"Shhhhhhh." Dit signaled for them to quiet down. He was listening to the conversation between his mother and Ellis on the porch. They were arguing about his father and whether she should let him come back when he decided to return.

"I hate that tater-haid," growled Mance. "I ever catch him wit his hands on Mama, I gone hurt him. Hurt him bad."

"What he do to Mama?"

Dit looked stonily into space. "Yeah, what he do to Mama?" He was smashing his fist into his open palm, harder and harder with each passing second, thinking of the fat man standing just a few feet from him.

"He tried to make Mama kiss him, but she wouldn't. Told him she didn't feel like it."

Buddy attempted to lighten the mood. "What you goin' to hurt Ellis with, Dit? Your bad breath?"

"Naw, wit yours." Dit asked what happened after she refused to kiss him. Did the fat man keep trying or what?

"He was tellin' her fibs 'bout how he love her. But she jes' laugh and tell him to shut up. Wonder what he after?"

Dit laughed rudely. "If it's what I think you're talking 'bout, he got that already."

"When?"

"Shut up," said Mance angrily. "You always talkin' 'bout stuff you don't even know. Mama wouldn't do nothin' like that wit Ellis. Too fat. He'd squash her wit that belly of his'n."

"What Mama say after he kept askin' her for it?"

"She jes' laugh a lot and listen to him lie. Boy, he sure can talk when he want somethin'. The lies were poppin' out so fast you could barely hear 'em all."

Buddy stood up and glanced around the side of the shack at the porch. "I hate to hear him talk. He always acts like he knows so damn much. They're still there, talkin' away."

"You said a bad word." Mance pointed at Buddy. "I's tellin'."

"How long did he stay last night?" Dit wanted to know everything so he could give his father a full report. All the facts at once. Maybe that would make him come home.

"It was real late, almost mornin'."

"Naw," Buddy disagreed. "It was not. Mama told him her haid hurt. She laid down and he sat in a chair next to her. You all was sleep but I seed it all. He tried to make her let him lay down wit her but she say naw and he left."

"Her haid probably did hurt," Dit said boldly. "All them lies he be tellin'." He sucked a bad tooth, allowing the sour taste of old blood and decay to come into his mouth. Afterwards, he spat between his feet. "Did he talk 'bout Lil Frank? He always do, you know."

129

"Ellis say Mama should put Lil Frank away in the crazy house or one of them places for retards," revealed Buddy. "They have a place like that up near Memphis."

"Papa will come back, you watch."

"I don't think so, I think he forgot us." Dit was certain that they would never see their father again. He believed his mother had something to do with his leaving, but he didn't know what.

"Mebbe he's 'fraid of Ellis."

"You better stop, Dit. Hit me again and I gone tell."

"Watch your mouth. Papa ain't 'fraid of no tater-haid. He'd beat that fat pig to a pork chop. Ellis too fat to put up a good fight. Jes' look at him."

"I caught Ellis lookin' at Bue puttin' on her clothes. Jes' staring. He was lookin' at her like he wanted to do somethin' bad to her." Mance always knew the sensational tidbits, all the dirt.

"I know," admitted Dit. "I seed him lookin' twice. He might try to mess wit her too if we ain't careful. If he do anythin' to her, we'll do somethin' to him."

"Did you tell Mama, Mance?"

Mance sat back on the bucket and chuckled. "Naw, he was lookin' so hard that Mama caught him. She say somethin' to him and he stopped."

The night came and went. The children always woke early but today they had waked earlier than usual with much excitement. They were planning to visit their father, a secret plan to get him back had been hatched yesterday and they were sworn to carry it out. But there were visitors before noon, Ellis and Beneather.

Both Ellis and his accomplice were wearing the same clothes they were wearing the last time the children saw them. Dit made certain that he commented on that to the others. Bue told him to stop making fun of Ellis. He seemed to be genuinely in love with their mother and that was more than she could say about their father. He didn't care or else he would be here right now, she reasoned. No one could argue with that.

"Mary, be nice and bring out my chair," asked Ellis. "And get me a cool glass of water too. Please ma'am."

"Okay Ellis." Mary disappeared into the house before they blinked.

Once she was gone, Beneather and Ellis began chatting about his control over the deserted woman in low tones of conspiracy. Playing the lover's role, Ellis opened a cigarette pack, tapped one out in her direction. But she refused it and he stuck one end of the Camel into his mouth.

"Ellis, you sure got her in line," joked Beneather. "You got her jes' like you like 'em. Silly womens. She wait on you hand and foot all the time?" Ellis didn't answer right away, choosing to deep-puff the Camel, long enough for the silence to signify something.

"What do you think?" Ellis said this as he stepped up on the porch and dropped into the rocker where Mary had been sitting earlier.

Mary came out with the requested chair, tripping a bit. Ellis, gallantly, stood but did not help her, instead he waited until she put the chair down. As soon as she had finished that task, he reminded her about the glass of water, adding how dry his throat was.

"Hold on, Ellis. I can't do but one thing at a time. My hands was full." Mary went back into the house and Beneather laughed cruelly into her hands, barely able to conceal her disdain for the Bowles woman. Mary Bowles was Ellis' puppet, that was for sure. Ellis sat down in his chair with the haughty air of royalty, arms folded on his chest.

Mary returned with a pitcher of cool water and glasses for everyone. So fast was the transformation of Beneather's facial expression that Mary never noticed the look of ridicule.

"Mary, I hate to keep at you, but could you get me a sammich to go with this," asked Ellis. "That sure would be nice after the long walk I had to get here. Please, thank you ma'am." Mary frowned, started to protest, then decided against it. Beneather did another silent laugh during her absence and the two schemers talked again, growing reckless with the long wait.

"She's 'bout as dull as her boy there," said Ellis, indicating Little Frank playing with a shovel and whacking his head with it. "I see how he got that way. That woman ain't got nothin' above her shoulders. Nothin' at all."

"You shouldn't talk 'bout her like that," teased his accomplice. "Ellis, you knows how she feels 'bout you."

"So what are you two talkin' 'bout?" Mary reappeared like a bubble bursting, and still she missed hearing their conversation. They were not foolish to talk loud enough that she might hear. Meanwhile Ellis attacked the sandwich viciously.

Mary wiped her forehead with her arm. While squeezing past Beneather, Mary made a face to her woman visitor to show she was on to Ellis' game but that she was humoring him. Men, after all, were big babies and they loved to be waited on. It made them feel important. Beneather smiled politely and watched Ellis eat.

"Is the sammich okay?" asked Mary, glancing at Ellis.

"It'll do," he replied.

Between his fourth and fifth bite, Ellis said, "Onliest thing, Mary sugar, it's hard for me to eat wit this coat in the way. I might get grease on it or something. Jes' put it inside the doorway, you don't have to git up and go all the way in. Please, baby."

Mary was about to sit anyway, to hell with Ellis and his requests. But Ellis was not having any hint of rebellion in front of Beneather so he made certain that Mary realized he wanted the coat moved as soon as possible. "Before you sit down, please honey."

Mary ran her shaking hand along her cheek, damn this man, and took the coat from Ellis. To finalize his show of authority, Ellis gave her a smack on the backside as she stepped around him to go inside. Mary kept her distance after the display, hating him for humiliating her with Beneather sitting there, watching. Not in front of her.

During this errand, they shared a quiet laugh. When Mary returned, Ellis sent her on six more, get this, get that, until Beneather had seen enough and decided to leave to spread the news. Yes, Ellis had Mary Boles jumping through hoops, just like he did Mildred when he was courting her. That man had a way with women, especially stupid women like Mary and Millie. Ellis was the Delta's answer to Cary Grant, a white movie star she saw one time in a picture at the old Dixie theatre.

Chapter 18

Bue waited for dark again, feeling the renewed urge to speak with her mother about her love for Ted. When the others were asleep, she lit a candle and went outdoors. She felt completely alone, but suddenly she was terrified of it. Her mother didn't seem aware of Ellis' attempts to seduce her, first with words, then with gifts. It was all confusing, her father gone, her mother love crazy for a fat man, and now pressure from Ted to run off with him to New York. Understandably, she was bewildered by her feelings, by what she heard in her head and by what her body told her. Was this how a woman felt? Are you a woman at fifteen? She realized she needed advice, maybe her mama could help her there.

A cough made Bue aware that she was not the only one who could not sleep. Her mother, dressed in a long slip, was facing away from her when she came into the room. Mary was greasing her scalp, parting her hair and plaiting it. Outside, the quarter moon made the dust look like fine sugar.

The girl walked to her mother, put her head on the older woman's shoulder.

"What's wrong? You sick?" Mary touched her child's forehead, back and under her neck.

"Naw, I was thinkin' 'bout things and couldn't sleep," Bue said, twisting her hands.

Her mother regarded her with a slight amusement. "What things, gal?"

"You know, Mama. Things." But couldn't come right out and say what she wanted to say, because her mother rarely talked about matters such as love, courting or marriage. She hoped she had caught her mother at a good time.

"What things, baby?" repeated her mother. "Ain't no foolishness, is it? It too late for that. I want to finish my head." Mary twisted the plaits with astonishing speed and a skill that could only have come with time. Nervous, Bue stuck her little finger in the hair grease, held it up and inspected it.

"Don't play wit that," said her mother in a low voice. "Cost money. Talk now or go to bed."

"When you know you ready to take a husband, Mama?" Bue spit out the question, quick, as though she was telling her mother about her first time with Ted in the field. Her mother sighed deeply and lowered her hands. It was Bue's time now. Time for her to ask the questions she had once asked her Mama when she was a girl. Mary prayed she would have better answers than the ones that her mother had had for her back then.

Mary laughed at her daughter. "How you know you a woman yet?"

Bue kept her eyes straight ahead, not looking at her mother. "I feels like one, Mama."

"And how is that?"

"Like I knows a woman must feel." Bue paused; she didn't

want to give herself away. "Like she would feel when she ain't a girl no more."

Her mother was silent while she pulled hair out of her comb. "You right 'bout that, child," she said. "A woman feels different from a girl. A woman got more duty on her than a girl. But womens is also different from mens, different by how they feels and thinks. We sometimes got to take low, act weaker, got to, got to 'cause some mens need a woman to be that way."

"Why, Mama?"

Mary was surprised at the ring of authority in her voice. " 'Cause mens are afraid of a woman with a strong will an' strong arms. You gots to be weak for the man to make him feel strong, especially when the man around other mens. All mens ain't like this but some are. If his woman act up then, the other mens would think he less than a man. Mens funny that way. An' you want your man to have respect so you be what he need you to be."

"All mens like that?"

"Naw, jes' the ones that ain't full mens yet," said her mother with a scornful smile. "They's the ones who needs that to make them feel like what they ain't. Unnerstand?"

"Uh-huh."

"Bue, I don't mind you courtin' this boy but I don't want to see you mess yourself up. You know what I mean?"

"Yessum."

"If a man smart, look right decent, thinks like you some, wants what you want an' treats you good . . . don't let him get away, 'cause them kind rare like hen's teeth."

"Uh-huh."

"One mo' thing," added Mary. "Nevah marry a man that thinks he pretty. Marry one uglier than you."

"Why?"

Mary looked into her eyes. " 'Cause pretty mens'll love

hisself an' won't have time for you. An' keep away from that needs a prop, liquor and the like. You don't want to spend your life toting somebody." Her right foot went to sleep and she shook it to get the blood circulating again.

The girl watched her mother intently, eager for the sage words, listening with great anticipation. Yet she marvelled in the fact that she was hearing these things from the woman who would never talk about anything but cooking and working in the field.

"Mama, where you learn all this?" asked Bue.

Her mother smiled knowingly. "Aw, I ain't so wise. My Mama told me a lot of what I's tellin' you an' some of it I learnt on my own from jes' livin'. Some of it, most of it, come from the Good Book. There are laws that's passed down to us. Get that Bible yonder an' bring it here." Bue followed her mother's direction and retrieved the Bible from where it lay among her sewing materials.

Her mother gave them reading lessons from that Bible on Sunday mornings since no church was in walking distance. Mary opened it to a passage and said, "Read the verses I got marked off."

Bue was about to start reading when her mother interrupted her. The reason for the break in the session was her mother's insistence to do this job right, to prepare her child as much as she could for what awaited her in the days ahead. Mary thought to herself, it is hard enough when you know most things about this life, but without anything, without any type of guidance, a person is lost. That was where the Bible came in.

"Think on this too," said her mother, touching her child's arm. "Make sure you like the man 'fore you give yourself to him. Then, make sure you knows his mind-set as best as you can, 'cause when the preacher say them words over y'all, that's it. You gotta be careful, gal, 'cause a man'll tell you he love you all day. Most of them be wastin' time by sayin' it. That's time when he could be doin' it, time he could be showing you by what he do. Yeah, be careful, Bue, 'cause if the wrong peoples get together . . . in the end there ain't much left of nair one of them. Both be ruint. Go head on an' read the book."

"Mama, you say nevah marry a pretty man," Bue said. "Is Papa a ugly man? Is that why you wit him?"

Her mother ignored her. "When you read, try to make your voice carry so I can hear you. Don't worry 'bout wakin' nobody up. They sleep like the dead." She slid a chair underneath herself and her daughter did the same, the book in her lap. The steady flame of the lamp made the room shadowy, transformed it into almost a holy place, a place in need of ritual.

"Even as Sarah obeyed Abra-ham, call him Lawd, whose daughters ye are, as long as ye do well an' are not afraid with any a-mazement. Likewise ye husbands . . ."

"Stop!" The Bible always managed to rouse her mother, make her excited with its tales of passion and discipline. Mary asked the girl where the verse was found and who wrote it.

"First Peter, third chapter, four to fifth verse."

Mary nodded slightly for her to continue. "Go head on, read the next one. Read where the paper's stickin' out. Any of them verses there."

"And Adam say this is bone of my bones and flesh of my flesh, she shall be called woman, 'cause she was taken out of man."

"Uh-huh. You understand that?"

Bue answered eagerly. "Yessum."

"Read the next one." Mary's voice was slightly shrill.

"A virtue-ous woman is a crown to her husband, but she that maketh him shamed is as rottenness in his bones."

The implication of the verse Bue read was not lost on Mary,

with its hint of adultery and infidelity. What surprised her was how easily her daughter had decided to make her point about a matter that she knew nothing about, a grown-up matter. How could this child understand what loneliness did to a woman and her resolve? Values and high morality often became warped on long, lonely nights and difficult days when a kind word and support were so desperately needed.

"You gots this one marked." Bue seemed determined to force her mother to see that her romance with Ellis was in violation of the Holy Scriptures. A sham.

"Read the one I have marked. Nothin' mo'."

Bue kept her gaze on the book in her lap. "Nevertheless, to avoid fornication . . . what's that? Forn-i-cation?"

"I'll tell you when you finish. Read."

". . . to avoid fornication, let every man have his own wife and let every woman have her own husband. That's you and Ellis, huh?" A wicked, impish smirk came to Bue's face as she glanced at her mother out of the corner of her eye.

"That's not what it say," Mary insisted. "Read the next one. Read . . . I knows . . . read First Corinthians, thirteen chapter, fourth to eighth verse. Skip to sixth."

"You said you was goin' to tell me what forn-i-cation was."

"In a minute," her mother said. "Read what I told you now. Don't worry me."

"Love endures long and is patient and kind. Love never is envy-ous or boils with jealousy, is not boastful or vain-gloryous, does not display itself . . ."

"Uh-huh."

Bue read on. "It is not conceited, arrogant . . . what's that? Arrogant."

"That's what Frank was," Mary retorted. "Arrogant."

"Was? He ain't dead, Mama."

"I don't know that. I ain't seen him or talked to him. Now hush an' read." She was fuming at her daughter's antics.

140

". . . arrogant or inflated. Love does not insist on its own rights or its own way, for it is not self-seeking . . . it is not touchy. Ellis is touchy, ain't he Mama?"

"Keep Ellis out of your mouth," Mary shouted. "Don't let me have to tell you again. Read."

". . . is not touchy or fretful or resentful."

Mary sighed warily and motioned for her to read the next underlined passage.

"Love bears up under anything and everything that comes, is ever ready to believe the best of every person, its hopes are fadeless under all circum . . . circum . . ." Bue waited for her mother to pronounce the word, and when she didn't, she thrust the Bible at her.

"Circumstances. Circumstances."

"What's that?" asked Bue.

"It mean anythin' that happens," answered her mother.

". . . circumstances. Read the eighth one too?"

"Naw, that's alright. Close it up now."

"Love . . . love . . ." Bue disobeyed her.

Her mother exploded in anger. "I said close it. You don't listen to me anymo'. Do you?"

"Let me read it, please Mama."

"Naw, close it."

"Love never fails . . ."

"What I tell you?" Mary asked with exaggerated politeness. "You gone read it anyhow. You better learn to mind me. You ain't grown yet!"

Mary frowned. ". . . never fades out or becomes obsolete . . . what does obsolete mean?"

"Don't know."

Just a little more and she was finished with the verse, the forbidden verse. " . . . obsolete or comes to an end," read Bue with a sense of finality.

Tears blurred Mary's vision for a time. "I asked you not

to read it. Why don't you listen to me? Why?"

"Why you cryin'?" Bue had not expected such a response.

Mary sat there rigidly as though she was paralyzed and stared unblinkingly at her daughter. She was thinking about Frank, the empty nights and the fat man that had come into their lives. "Give me my Bible an' go back to bed!"

"It say love never come to an end, then you didn't love Papa, huh? That's why Ellis around here so much, huh?" Suddenly Bue felt a hard, stinging slap on her cheek and it brought tears to her eyes.

For a time, Mary stood facing away from her sobbing child. "Go to bed," she said in a low voice. "Don't let me have to tell you again. I don't want to see your face no mo' tonight." Bue rose from her chair, carried it over to the wall, and left. Her mother watched her go, visibly shaken and on the verge of tears again. She felt horrible for hitting the girl like that. Silently, she remained near the doorway, listening to the song of the cicadas and wondering where Frank was and what he was doing now, right now.

Chapter 19

Bue was rubbing a damp cloth across her broad thighs, over the cheeks of her buttocks and between her legs. In the morning light, her unlined, youthful face almost appeared angelic. She stretched now, black tufts of hair showing in her armpits as the water ran down her long limbs. Busily washing herself, she did not look around since no one was inside the shack. They were out in the yard, preparing to head out to the field for the day's work. She made a face and leaned over the cracked porcelain basin which was filled with a half bar of soap and sudsy water. When she finished her bath, she walked to the trunk which held clothes for special occasions and pulled out her best dress, the white one, frilled, with blue flowers. She would wear it to the jubilee on Saturday. Everyone would be there. All of the young people from around would be sure to come. She was so excited since it would give her a chance to see her Ted.

She sang to herself while she looked at her nude body, proud of its youth. Her legs were still wet, below the knees. As she put her arm out for the cloth, a sensation of being watched went through her, of a presence in the room with her. From this impulse, Bue turned toward the door and there was Little Frank. His eyes were glued to her gleaming body. Turning away from his gaze, she stooped and picked up her robe, covering herself. The boy remained there, watching. The features of his mongoloid face became twisted as he saw his sister's naked body. In one sense, there was no noticeable difference in how he looked at her, except when she saw him shift his eyes away from her face to her breasts and below. What was he up to? What was he going to do to her? Panic, cold as a chill, crept through her. She talked softly, softly to him, asking him to leave the room until she finished washing and putting on her clothes, saying this in the sweetest voice she could muster up in her fear. She thought about pushing him out of the room but she was afraid to. She was becoming more and more terrified. She wondered what he would do if she screamed. Little Frank did not seem so little now. The thought of his strong arms and hands jerking her around, and God knows what else, made her feel ill. She continued talking to him, asking him to leave the room until she was through.

But he was stationary, watching with that expression, watching her, watching her body underneath the flimsy robe.

She felt an urge to run outside but she remembered that her body was barely concealed behind the robe and Ellis was out there. Any movement might set him off so she was afraid to reach for any other article of clothing. Soon Little Frank approached her, closer, closer, until his hands were inches from her. She gasped in fright. She was horror-striken to the extent that her body would not obey; frozen and speechless. Coldly, the mute tightened his powerful hands around the silky fabric of her robe, his eyes still on her in that strange way, raising it back away from her with a quick jerk. Then he looked long and hard at her body, in front. Instinctively, his hands were clutching the robe in such a way that Bue would be yanked off-balance if she resisted. He stared intently at her breasts and at the dark triangle between her legs. The madness was in his face.

Once satisfied, he left the room, without a sound. For several minutes after her brother was gone, Bue stayed motionless with the robe held in front of her, terrified, alone and trembling.

Chapter 20

A blood-red sun sank in the distance toward the river. Mary glanced away from its bright, dying glare, feeling the ache that pained her deep inside. Like a wound that would never heal. She had just talked to Bue about Little Frank and the bathing incident of the day before. She sensed something was troubling her oldest child, what it was she had no way of knowing. But she realized once the girl had her mind on a thing, that was that, no turning around. Bue was stubborn and secretive like her father. Mary would sit and listen to her all night long and when it was all over, still not know what the girl expected of her. There were also times when there was nothing said. Nothing, just silence. During all of these talks, Mary monitored her daughter for any indication of pregnancy since she knew the girl was undoubtedly allowing Ted to give her pleasure. Something she didn't like at all.

What could she do about Little Frank? How long would

it be before he injured one of the other children? She remembered when the boy overpowered Dit in the yard, jumping up and down on his stomach with his knees, his manic hands locked around his older brother's throat till he passed out. Had it not been for Buddy pulling the mute off the boy, he would have been killed. Just the thought of it left her weak. What would she do? At times, Little Frank acted as if he wanted to talk, making sounds that no one really understood, gesturing with his hands. He was trapped inside himself and for this reason, she felt a great deal of sympathy for him. There were other days when Little Frank would roll about on the wood floor, his eyes twisting wildly in their sockets and a soap suds foam would appear at his mouth. On these days, only Mary could come near him and often he would not eat or drink. If he was fed by force, he would become violent and vomit all that had gone down. Each time following these episodes, the boy began howling, pawing his head in torment, laughing crazily afterwards. During other fits, he would pass out, becoming rigid like a corpse.

Easter Sunday past, the mute and Buddy got into it, with Buddy winning in the end after he punched his brother in the mouth. Busted his lips, blood going everywhere. Since then, a change had taken place. Little Frank obeyed them, their every request. He was no trouble now. He would come into the house without a struggle, without any protest. At the table, he would do the best he could, eating almost politely, never throwing food around. In the day, if the others were away, the boy could be ordered to stay in one place and he would. No running off or starting a ruckus. No howling or growls. He was a new person, as if returned from a frame of mind he had grown bored with. But the difference, the sudden transformation, was unnerving, because everyone in the household knew it was not real. It was play-acting as Mary called it. So the family was on edge, waiting for something to happen.

Mary told Bue that she feared the boy was up to something and that his good behavior was due to this. Some evil scheme, some sinister plot. She also cautioned the children to stay out of his way since no one knew what was going on in his head.

After a year of Ellis slinking around their home, Mary was not too sure about him either. She did not trust him. It seemed as though her every attempt to drop her defenses was met by some fool deed on his part which brought them back. Talk was, from Beneather no less, that he was courting Mildred again, that the two of them had been seen in town together, meeting on the sly. On nights when Mary and Ellis found each other in need of affection, the doubts returned, along with memories of her wandering husband. When they loved, when they were good, Mary often imagined him to be someone else, without fail Frank. The strong and gentle Frank from before. The sex was better for her that way. But she never called him out of his name, never.

There were times, like last night, when she almost did it but she always caught herself, and the man was never the wiser. Ellis had the tendency to be more bossy than Frank ever could be, do this, do that. Hurry up. She could not help but compare the two; they were the only men she had ever known in an intimate way. He would sometimes say things regarding the children which forced her to roll her eyes at him in a display of disapproval. Or he would hint she should be glad to have him with all of the children she had, adding that no man outside of him, that no man in his right mind, would have anything to do with her.

If she went somewhere, he had to know where and with whom, or maybe it was about dinner or maybe she did not move the dust and dirt around enough to suit him. Or why did the children track mud in the house. There was always something to bother her about, to fuss about. A new life of heartache. Oh, how she missed Frank. He was never like this. The other thing that got her goat was that she could never make a decision on her own, never, about anything. She had to think about what Ellis would say. At least Frank let her have her way around the house, about certain family matters and sometimes about the children. But not Ellis.

If she stayed with him, stuck it out with him, she would never have a mind of her own. The man was worse than Frank, that worthless no-count husband of hers out there whoring around in the streets. She realized she had traded one tyrant for another one, one boss for another boss. The battle with Ellis was a hard one and it took everything she knew to show him that she was not an echo. To hell with his selfish ways. Get this, get that. Too much sugar, too much salt. That was why, when they loved, she could not permit him to have but so much of her. He got her body all right, but all he got was a shell of flesh.

The fight continued everytime friends came by, he felt he must insult her in front of them. Everything at her expense or at the expense of her children. To counter this, she began flirting with his men friends, giving them the eye to make him jealous. This surprised her because this was not like her. She never did this before. After this last time, the ugliness of what she was doing and what she was becoming hit her full blast and she stopped the flirting.

If Mary felt a brave streak in her, she would humiliate Ellis before his chums, because she knew his weakness about his weight. She would deliberately compare the men's sizes, their strength and tonnage. Ellis was fat, no doubt about it. He loved to eat. His weight was a real problem for her at night, sometimes taking more of her breath than his caresses. Squashing her. Furthermore, he could not endure like Frank, he was huffing and puffing in no time. Sometimes she feared for him, his heart. Still he bragged with the men about his sexual ability, his staying power. What a lover he was! How the women loved a big, soft man they could hold rather than a thin one with bones like daggers.

He even bragged to her. She promised herself one night that she would tell him the truth. One Tuesday evening, she almost did it as she told him something her mama once used on her papa: "I can look down longer than you can look up." It was true. Anyway, he got mad and slapped her so hard that she saw stars.

"You know you love your big daddy," he would always say. "You couldn't live without the sugar he give you. Could you? Ain't that so?" If she had told him the truth, they would have ended up fighting.

What Beneather had said Sunday before last, catching and holding a man two different things. No lie. Men, Mary said to herself, grow tired of you quick, real easy, especially when they become too familiar with your body. Once they know it, that's it. Then they need the young girls in town since there ain't nothing too much a woman getting on in age can do to make a decent wage except something against the law. And too, you can get too old to change your ways. She couldn't change nothing about herself. She could not change how many children she had and she definitely could not change the old shack and give it charm with the money she was making, which was barely enough to make ends meet.

On the nights Ellis stayed, she watched Ellis while he slept, his eyes closed tight, listening to his snoring. The thought often occurred to her about how long he would be around. When will he leave? There would be a new face, another face to grow used to and learn what he liked and didn't like. Another face, another body laying beside her. One after another. Maybe Ellis was right, who else would have her? A ready-made family and responsibility. She could not do that to the

151

children and she could not do it to herself. Even if it meant being by herself, being alone.

What now? What was left? Think on the old memories, the blessings she already received like she was old and ripe for the ground. Think on the children who lived and the ones who fell along the way. The good times between Frank and her, back then. But what about now? What would she do if Ellis left her?

Nothing was always no how. Everything she did would be gone one day, children included. Not much, if anything, would last. Yeah, they would grow up and leave her. She knew change well. She had seen how mens change up, like Frank. One minute he was a good provider, good father, good man. The next he was drinking and whoring. Change. Like Ellis and all the sweet lies he told her in the beginning. Change. Maybe she would change too, after all this mess, becoming something or somebody else. She didn't know what the future would mean. Change. Like a clean towel to a dirty towel. Change. Like a pan of cobbler to an empty pan. Change, change. Maybe the folks will say she was a good mother. Maybe not. In the end, who will say it and what will it matter anyway. Truth known, nobody will probably know anything about her or even care that she lived, except her children and that was not promised.

"Mama, why you cryin'?" asked Bue, noticing the tears on her mother's face. "What wrong?"

Mary breathed through lips barely parted in fatigue. "Nothin'. Nothin' at all." She paused and covered her face. "Jes' tired. I's human too, you know. Ain't made of rocks. Wear down sometimes." She said this with the drained feeling that filled her insides, while staring at her fingernails as if they would turn into claws.

"You sure, Mama?" Bue tried to get a good glimpse at her.

"I's sure." The words were mumbled.

"I loves you, Mama." Bue put her cheek against her mother's cheek, delivering a gentle peck to prove her affection. Mary saw the warm glow in her oldest child's eyes. That look was worth it all, sometimes.

"I worry 'bout you gal," Mary said. "An' them young bucks you talkin to. Don't get fast on me now."

"Mama, don't worry. I ain't doin' nothin'."

This is me right here, Mary thought. This is it. There ain't no new path I can take. The girl still had something on her mind. What now, Bue? Ellis did what? Oh Lord, what kind of man is this? Naw, he didn't. He tried to get you to drink some liquor with him, been looking at you funny again too. He's going too far, too far. Said you was teasing him by not doing what? Was you, baby? I didn't mean that really, it's just everything all jumbled.

What else? You told him to leave the house, never come back or you'd what? You watch your mouth, young lady. Did he touch you? You know what I mean? He didn't, good.

When did this happen? Uh-huh. What did he say? Yeah? He say he taking care of you and this family and he didn't want no mess. You better do what he say? That bastid! Excuse me, make me cuss. But he didn't touch you or nothin'. Did he? Good.

Mary slid her arms around her daughter and held her close. Said you was tryin' to come between us. Gal, he can't come between you an' me, we's family. He's the outsider. What else he say? Well, jes' go on an' remember what I told you 'bout that boy. Don't worry 'bout Ellis. I'll take care of him. Don't come in here after dark. I can't stand no more hurts.

Let me see what them boys into. They too quiet. Come here, Buddy, you an' Mance. Where Dit? Bet he up to no good. Jes' look at y'all. What happened you . . . your mouth an' knee. Fightin' again. Uh-huh. What did I tell y'all 'bout that? Get out of my sight. An' wash that knee off, boy. I'll

153

deal wit you later. Mance, stay here. What happened? Mance, you my eyes an' ears. Slow down. You talkin' too fast. The boys was fightin'. Why? Over what Ejay said 'bout Ellis. What did she say? Not 'bout Ellis. Yeah, I know that Ejay don't like Buddy 'cause of the way he carry hisself. Mance, don't worry 'bout that. People funny like that. Won't like you 'cause of your clothes, the way you look or the way you act. Don't worry none, they ignorant. So what happen? Ejay an' a gang of the boys. Did you help your brother? What did you do? You did what? You kicked him when he was down. Mance, mens don't fight like that. They use they fists. Go on an' finish tellin' me.

"Bue told me an' Dit that she was goin' to lie on Ellis so you would quit him," Mance tattled. "Told us that yesstidy." He was smiling the entire time, aiming to please.

"Why would she do a thing like that?"

Mance rocked on his heels. " 'Cause she don't like him. None of us do. He too fat, Mama. You knows he is."

"Hush up and get outside and play." Mary touched her hand to her forehead. "We'll talk more later on." The boy was out of the house in a flash. Why would the girl lie like that? Why?

154

Chapter 21

That evening, Ellis and Mary sat on the porch in the rockers, chatting about the future and the children. He put his rocker closer to hers, smiling lovingly as his hand travelled along her leg, over the roundness of her thigh.

"Mary your chillun are evil," Ellis said. "What's that oldest boy's name? Yeah, him. Buddy walked up to me on the road an' say I shouldn't be here when his papa ain't here, that he is comin' back. When they goin' to forget that man?"

"You can't expect them to forget their papa," answered Mary. "After all, it ain't been that long."

He raised his eyebrows. "It been long enough. Been more than a year. That ain't the half, then the boy balls up one of his fists, puts it in my face an' shakes it. I should have knocked him on his ass, acting that way after all I did for y'all."

"Ellis, he jes' a boy. You grown. You should know better

155

than to let him rile you like that. He don't mean nothin'. He jes' a child."

Ellis frowned and shook his head. "If he was a little older, I'd slap the livin' hell out of him. Child, shit. Better give me some respect or I will." He crossed his chunky, short legs and looked out toward the main road. "Know what I heard in town?"

"What do you hear now?" Mary didn't want to hear any more gossip but she decided to humor him.

"They say the Taylor boy puttin' out he done had your gal," he said, smiling wickedly. "Had her up in the woods a couple of times. What you gettin' mad 'bout? It natural. Gals gone do it. They love to lay on they backs an' let the boys ride 'em. Ain't knowed one yet that didn't."

"I don't want to hear no hear-say. That he-say an' she-say mess. Ellis, tell me the truth. Have you been tryin' to mess wit Bue any?"

He feigned disgust. "Hell naw. Where you come up wit somethin' like that? Naw ma'am, but I sure would like to mess wit you some."

"Don't talk to me like that," said Mary, with a sneer on her lips. "I ain't trash now. You ain't dealin' wit them hussies in town. And take your hands away."

"What's the matter wit you this evenin'?" pleaded Ellis. "What I do now? Huh?" He did not want o miss out tonight on some loving. Mildred had been stingy lately and he needed physical contact, bad.

"Mebbe later on?" Ellis grinned, hoping to prove himself harmless.

Her face expressed resentment. "I don't reckon so. I don't feel like that tonight. I needs somethin' else but I don't think you got it in you to give."

"What you talkin' 'bout now, woman? Must be thinkin' on that shiftless man of yours, Frank. Still thinkin' 'bout him.

156

How long will it be before you forget him an' go on livin'?"

Mary glanced at him, then she turned her back to him. The smell of the wood stove in action drifted out to her, causing her to tweak her nose. Why was this man in her life at all? He gave her no help at all with Little Frank and that child was her major worry and concern. She had tried every homemade remedy recommended to her: juice of the milkweek, bits of fingernails soaked in the extract of polk root, Jack of War tea boiling hot, pinch of alum in his food, steeped mullen leaves, three and four tablespoons of the cream of Tartar, ten cents worth of Jockey Club blown in the eyes, lavender tea to do harm to the evil spirit in the boy's body and High John the Conqueror. All of them and no effect.

She still watched him in silence. "I ain't never been wit any other man but you an' Frank. This here is all I got. My children an' my house. My happiness an' the happiness of my children is in your hands. Don't hurt me. Don't hurt us, Ellis."

Her pleas were touching, even to a hard hearted sort such as Ellis. She sounded so weak, so defenseless to him that he imagined he could get anything he wanted from her. The first part of his plan to take control of the Boles household was complete and her dependence on him, so he thought, was absolute. He felt arrogant, proud. Two women at his will. Both of them needing him and he, well, could give less than a damn about either one of them.

"Naw baby, you can trust me," he cooed at her.

Chapter 22

Little Frank walked quickly out of the yard, head down, then ran across the vast fields toward the main road. He did not turn his head when cars whizzed past, even when someone called to him. Another car, filled with whites, pulled up to the shoulder of the road near him and he heard one man whistle at him. That frightened him for some reason. He stepped up his pace, walking faster without looking back.

He was so far away from home, too far away, and there was nothing familiar about any of this. Suddenly, the car appeared again and cut swiftly across his path, blocking his escape. Two men leaped out of the sedan, staring hard at him. Hey nigger boy, don't run off. What did that mean? Words meant nothing to him, he thought while he tried to outdistance their threat. One of them grabbed his arm, glaring, and he yanked away. When he tried to speak to the man, nothing would come out but the barking and grunts. The man stood back now and laughed at him. They laughed at the thick line of drool that flowed from his big purple lips, over his square jaw, down his neck into his collar.

The driver of the car adjusted his cap and yelled to the others. "Let's go on to town. Them gals are waitin' for mah kisses. We ain't got no time fuh some niggah moron."

He stopped when he saw one of his corn-fed buddies put his hand in his coat pocket and bring out a pistol. Little Frank flinched as the men held him still. He shuddered in anticipation of what these strangers might do to him, strange people, strange place. Tears flooded his eyes. He stared at the men through tears, smiling sadly. An empty, stupid smile.

"Nobody'll know if we rough the boy up a little," one man said, waving a piece of chain. "The nigger's a mute, can't say nothin' or tell no tales." The men laughed at the thought of easy fun at the black boy's expense.

The shortest man shoved the boy to the ground, where he could kick him without too much trouble. A couple good ones to the ribs. The man with the gun knelt over him from behind, laughing wildly, putting the weapon near the boy's temple. Little Frank showed no fear. He grinned at the strangers. That angered them more, making them a bit more daring.

"The niggah thinks we foolin'," said the gunman in a rush of words. "We serious, you darky bastid!" The seriousness of it did not strike home with the mute, even when he heard the click of the trigger. The chamber was empty, but the men were surprised at the boy's coolness. He grinned at them, not saying anything, not one plea for mercy. The gunman lowered the pistol to the boy's mouth and Little Frank opened it wider to accommodate the gun barrel. The men looked at each other in wonder, shaking their heads in amazement. The boy was a real fool, with grits between the ears for brains. At the last instant, the gunman moved the pistol away from the boy's gaping mouth, just inches from the lips and fired a single shot into the air.

The unexpected sound of the speeding bullet zipping across Little Frank's face sent him scrambling toward the woods, on his knees. He growled at the men, the sound deep in his throat. He had words for them, his words, but his lips hung slack.

"Shit," the driver said, folding his arms. He walked over to the boy, who was still grinning. "Let the boy be."

That was when somebody hit the mute on the head and a bright light flashed before his eyes. He woke up later on the road with a sharp pain over his forehead and a warm stickiness along the left side of his face. Blood. He felt a similar sensation in his right leg, like hot water running to his foot, so he sat quietly. The men were gone.

He had trouble breathing, blood in his mouth. He recalled the gun barrel between his lips, that feeling of metal and flesh and an urge to suck it. He limped along the road, trying to ignore the pain behind his eyes. He felt weak and slightly dizzy. He turned into a dirt road leading from the main route, following it for a time. Where was he now? Where was everybody? He found a grassy spot beneath a magnolia tree and lay down and watched the powder-blue sky.

He heard a noise, growling in his stomach. His head became hot, the blood pouring inside somewhere, and he closed his eyes. Tight, tighter. The ache was bigger than ever and he covered his ears with his hands. Then Little Frank became aware of voices near the access road, sounded like two of them, a Mama and a Daddy voice. He ducked down into the high grass, watching them talking among themselves. He loved to watch their lips move, to imagine what they could be saying to each other, whatever the words meant. He listened closely until it began to bore him, their talking. The man pressed the woman against him. They were talking low now and he strained to hear what they said. The man and the woman stayed that way, arms wrapped around the other, and he thought of his sister, Bue.

"I ain't nevah felt like this before," the woman said, sliding her arms around her lover's broad neck.

"Look at the boy," her beau said, pointing at Little Frank hiding by the tree. "He has blood on 'im. Hey, ain't that the Boles boy, the crazy one."

"Shouldn't we take 'im home?" the woman whispered. "I knows he won't know the way back, besides he might be hurt bad."

The man helped him to his feet and the couple took him to a pickup truck that had been parked farther down the road. The boy was no problem. He was glad to be among kind faces for once. The man lit a cigarette and gave it to his girl friend, who stuck it to her full lips. She smiled at the man. The boy watched them intently, only stopping when the man turned on the radio. Music, any kind of music, always made him feel better, made him happy. He hummed to himself, grinning to his new friends, and rocked to the beat.

"I want to puff on that stick some," the man said, reaching for the cigarette. "He like music. How 'bout that?"

The woman dabbed at the wounds on his face with a lace handkerchief and gently pushed his head back so his nose would stop bleeding. It would not, so she started to panic.

"He should be seed by a doctor," she said with alarm in her words. "He could be bleeding inside his haid."

"Are you crazy too?" The man was angry with her. Little Frank could hear it in his voice as he saw the cigarette smoke eddie from the man's nostrils. The truck bounced over the ruts in the road, sometimes hitting its bottom on the ground, sending its occupants off the seat. The boy loved it and howled each time it happened. His friends stopped talking aloud and whispered to each other.

162

"We ain't leavin' 'im out here," the woman said, stroking the boy's bruised cheek. "We can't. If we stop at Jather's papa's house, mebbe they know what to do 'bout 'im."

The boy sensed they were talking about him and leaned forward, listening. His nose wouldn't stop bleeding. It was getting on the woman's dress and her beau frowned at him. He was lost temporarily in his own world, waving his hands in front of his eyes, moving his fingers. Little Frank stopped the behavior as swiftly as he had started it, stopped to watch them watch him. He thought about banging his head on the metal dashboard of the truck.

"This boy's folks should be horsewhipped for lettin' 'im run off by hisself," the woman complained.

"What's the matter, sweetheart?"

She took a deep breath before speaking. "He's so pitiful. I feel sorry for 'im. He's got to go through his whole life like that. A complete fool."

Her lover switched into another gear to help the coughing truck take a small hill. "Darling, I's shore glad it's him that way an' not me. That's how you got to look at things. Anyone but not me."

The woman looked off, at the passing woods and cars, then touched her wet eyes with the bloodied lace. She ignored much of what the man was saying. "Yeah. Okay. Anything you say, Bob. I can't wait till we have our younguns."

"What does that mean? Can't wait till we have our younguns. What you saying, gal? Don't mess wit me. Not ovah some half-wit fool kid."

"Gawd," the woman said. "Ain't you got a heart?"

Her man cut her off. "Naw." Although the couple ceased talking for the ride's duration, the boy entertained himself by biting his arm. His new friends got out, shouted at each other for several minutes until the woman went in the rear door of a long shack, made of beaverboard, back off the road.

163

The man followed her later after locking the boy in the vehicle. Little Frank sat quietly inside the truck behind the steering wheel, playing with it. He hummed to himself, caught up in this new game. He had never played with toys and the other children never liked him. In fact, he felt no real affection for anyone. There were feelings he had, sensations that had no names for them. He put his head down into the seat cushion and screamed, enjoying the sound of the muffled shrieking.

Finally he decided he was tired again and nodded off. Just before dark, the man woke him with a kick in the shins. He was smoking another cigarette and the woman, in the same mood, stood behind him.

"He really gave us a nice bunch of collards an' them cukes were real nice size," she said, winding down the window on the driver's side.

"Them cucumbers can't hold a candle to what I got waitin' fuh you," the man joked as he put one of the swollen vegetables in the obvious place.

"You crazy fool," she said, feeling Little Frank between his legs. "Baby, I think he shit on hisself. It that runny kind, not solid turds."

The man looked over her shoulder and studied the boy thoughtfully. "I knowed I should've left that idiot back where we found 'im. Nothin' but bad luck to keep 'im around. You didn't answer mah question, what I ast you earlier. Have you been wit a man since you got out of the penititary?"

She made a sucking sound. "Gettin' a man is the least of mah worries now. We should be worryin' 'bout this boy right here. We can't leave 'im locked up in this hot truck whilst we's inside. He might die in this heat."

The boy moved closer to the open window, near the woman and tossed a bit of crushed turd at her feet. She jumped back and yelled. Her lover pulled her away from the ranting mute and said he'd locked the boy in the truck while they were inside trying to figure out what to do with him. They shared a cigarette as they walked back to the long, gray building. Other trucks and beat-up cars were starting to come into the area, parking and discharging their passengers. Little Frank stared at the headlights, the shadowy moving objects and wanted to get out and run. He was confused and frustrated. This was no good, he couldn't move around. He beat his head, his aching head, against the truck door, opening up the old wound along the cheek. Blood covered his face in no time but he continued to bash his face into the steel, then the plate glass.

Eventually he stopped when he heard the music, the faint stir of voices enjoying themselves, having a good time. The window was opened just a crack, enough to hear a little of the festivities. Soon the woman came in the darkness, smiling at him and thrusting a cup of Coke in his hand. He rocked with the music, hearing it full volume made him happy. The woman let him get out and she stood with him, watching him drink the soda water. In a little while, someone called to the woman and she stroked his head, then left. He was out, free. He tossed down the crumpled cup and ran for the rear of the building.

The moonlight rolled out from underneath a bank of clouds, permitting him to see no one was near the back door. He cried for a moment at the lovely song of the nightbirds because he couldn't see them. The music was coming from inside and he could hear thunderous clapping gathering force as a swell after each number to shake the rafters. Such noise, the mute thought, with a slight sense of shock. He noticed the gas pumps, marked Texaco, through the dark; rusting car bodies piled high, oil cans, stacks of shattered windshield glass. The music began again, followed by loud foot stomping and cheers. He crawled silently through the tall grass, stalking like a tom cat, entranced by the smell of gas. A new, odd smell that clung to the nose. He found himself at the first pump, lifting the long, metal snake, but then he lost interest and laid it down. He could not recall why he had been so fascinated with the pumps in the first place. Then he went silently to the oil cans, smelling their slimy residue, turning them upside down. The outlines of the roadhouse had been briefly illuminated when a car backed into a parking spot between a tractor and a decrepit station wagon. He watched two men leave the car with his chin resting on his hands. They walked toward him.

"I told him to stop the bullshit," one of them said, flicking away a lit cigarette butt. "You owe me cash money an' that's what I want, not a jackass in trade or some smoked pork."

Little Frank touched the bruise on his cheek where a large blue lump had formed. It did not hurt. His eyes, cold and bloodshot, remained fixed on the spot in the grass that sent up gentle cords of smoke and he wanted to get his hands on that discarded butt. A minute or two later, the other man coughed sickly and spat tobacco not far from his hiding place. The mute examined the smoldering cigarette at arm's length, blowing on it, enjoying the wild sparks. Still he did not feel happy. Something was missing. He felt completely alone. Once he thought the men were looking his way and he scooted closer to the pumps, near the alluring odor of the spilled gasoline. The aroma made him tired but he rocked again for comfort.

In that instant, they saw him by the pumps and oil cans, called to him. One of the men put out his hands to the boy. Little Frank paid no attention to their words, words meant nothing at a time like this. They knew him, the crazy Boles boy, knew him capable of just about everything. He was scared of them until the still air suddenly caught afire and blew him back across the gravel lot to the tree line. Screams and panic filled the sky. The wind carried whiffs of dark, choking soot. He was hearing more and more painful shrieks, more windows shattering ... and the whoosh of two lines of golden-orange flames scaling the side of the roadhouse. He cocked his head to get a better view of the crimson brilliance above and the horrible carnage before him. Several people rushed the back door, trying to kick it in, trying to force it open. They were met each time by thick clouds of smoke and dangerous licks of yellow fire, frying timber and flesh. There were choruses of hellish cries now, rising first inside the holocaust and then trailing off to the spectators after a roaring explosion collapsed one side of the building, pushing out windows and hurling showers of red sparks on would-be rescuers. The mute circled the crowd, mumbling, imagining bacon on the grill and the foam returned to the corners of his mouth. He glanced down at himself and saw parts of his clothing were missing, sheared off in the blast. He smiled, he felt no pain or remorse.

A man picked him up, wiped the blood from his face and covered him with a blanket. The front of the burning roadhouse toppled under another explosion, causing the crowd to back off. The man started crying, shaking under the weight of the tragedy, so he wisely put the boy down. It meant nothing to the mute when the woman emerged from the throng, staggering, her hair singed by the heat. She recognized him and called out. Meanwhile the mute looked up at the man beside him, listening to his protector weep softly. Charred bodies were being stacked in a clearing near the smoking ruins. Sirens, then the sheriff's car arrived. The mute crawled up into the flatbed of the pickup. His lady friend walked over and hugged him tightly. She murmured that her man was still in there, sobbing. Her eyes examined him for a second, checking for injuries while she scraped a fleck of caked blood from his cheek. She wet a finger on her tongue and rubbed it on the exposed raw spot.

"Here, take this," someone said from the shadows. He handed a kerosene lamp to the woman and she placed it on the truck's hood. The mute slid over the side, easing toward the light. The flame in the lamp danced to the sighs of a gentle summer wind that blew the remaining smoke in a swirl.

Little Frank turned down the wick, smiling at the woman. She smiled back at him, sitting there like a little angel. "That's a good idea," she said with pride. "If evahbody acted like you, we wouldn't be cryin' tonight." The mute rocked, happy with himself.

Part Three

NO HARM DONE

Part Three

NO HARM DONE

Chapter 23

Frank was jarred out of his preoccupation by the sounds coming from the woods on the bank nearby. There was the light rustle of the summer-dried leaves, the rush of the brackish water, and above it, the chirping of the birds. Farther off, a truck's motor was starting with a husky whine.

He stood motionless. True, the day was sunny and clear, but it was too warm. Standing there, his head tilted as he listened and watched for her. He was a pitiful sight; all of his clothes were worn and patched.

At the top of a ridge directly ahead, Adele emerged from a cluster of pine trees full into the rays of the sun. It bathed her in a wonderous light. He watched her look for him. Her strong features, the curled nose, the nut-brown eyes suggested of a woman with a face that was not a stranger to admiring glances. Presently, her face sparked as anger was replaced by anticipation.

Seeing him, Adele began to run. Holding her skirt high, she raced toward him, waving to him. A grin flashed on her face as she stumbled momentarily, then quickly regained her balance. And finally, in what seemed an eternity, she was in his arms.

Frank laughed softly, bent low in a mocking bow. "Ah, the Mistress of the house has arrived! Better late than sooner. Adele, you can't get nowhere on time. You always makin' peoples wait."

She looked at him quizzically. "You been waitin' long, Clark Gable?"

To her discomfort, she saw Frank look at her as if he had never seen her before. The expression was a puzzled one, his brow wrinkled with a frown. He disliked her phony concern, the fakery in her voice, her calculating words. Only his desire, the idea of holding her close, prevented him from cussing her out.

"Why didn't you tell me them horses were damn near wild?" asked Adele, walking back the way she had come. "And they're stolen to boot."

"Borrowed, not stolen. Where you get that wild shit from? Every one of them animals been gentled." He slowed his steps to let her keep pace.

"Hell yeah." She was fuming at the notion that he had conned her into bringing the stolen horses from Ol' Mister Phil's stable. They wouldn't be missed until later, he said. Or at least that's what she thought he said.

Soon he was riding one horse, a spotted mustang, and leading another one for her. Hers was a spirited beast, a supposed gelding, so he coached her on how to handle it.

"Don't hold him in so tight, honey," Frank said dryly.

She grabbed the reins firmly, forcing the horse to walk slower. Probably the best idea would be to ask the farmer to switch horses with her, she thought. Her mind raced to find a lie to tell, some twist of words to make him do as she wished. Fuck it, she told herself, and patted the horse's thick neck.

"I should've said to you to make sure you got the mare," Frank teased and yelled for his animal to run. She chased him through the woods, leaning forward on her mustang while she shouted at his back for him to stop.

He was waiting for her in a clearing ahead, near a grove of plums, with his mount sweating heavily and panting. "Are you thinkin' 'bout putting me out?"

Adele's anger melted into a catty reply. "What's wrong? Don't you reckon you're up to the task anymore? You couldn't be gettin' tired on me, Frank?"

He pulled his horse around to take a path back toward town. They would drop off the animals first at the stables, that would cover their brief theft, then go home and play. He laughed at her, after telling her that he loved her and would never let her go.

She lapsed into silence and placed her horse into a trot behind him. This was not the time. There would be plenty of opportunity later, before she made her move. Adele had to wait for the right moment. Everything would remain locked away inside her.

Chapter 24

The window was open, probably due to the hot air filling the room. Frank thought he heard the faint whine of a harp filtering up from the street below, but the sound was swift in passing. He must be losing his mind. He was wary of the unbearable weather, the heat seemed endless. A Mississippi summer.

About six minutes passed and his woman came to put a cold, damp towel on his forehead. "You very good for me," Frank said to Adele as she turned to go. "We could be nice together if you didn't act so hinty."

The woman stopped. She was more than repulsed. She was tired of his childish games, his self-pity, and his attempts at manipulating her feelings. His words sickened her.

"What's ailin' you, gal?"

The woman did not answer.

"Have you got another man?" He ran a comb through his

hair a few times. "Or are you up to your ol' tricks again?"

"Why are you tryin' to get my goat?" Adele spoke in such a low voice that Frank could hardly hear her.

"There's somebody else, I know it." Frank knew he was making her mad, so he sat down in a rickety chair near her.

"Frank, stop talkin' like this. Like a damn fool." Adele lit her cigarette after she said it.

"I jes want you to know me better. To be my friend as well as my lover. That ain't bad, is it?" His mood changed too quickly. He was surprised at himself.

"I think I know all I need to know 'bout you." Adele glared at him. She couldn't admit to herself how scared she was. It was not her imagination. Yes, yes, her friends were right about him. He was nuts. A stone fool. Either he moved out or she was going. Her feelings for him had changed, becoming something else other than love. One night she would make her move. His drinking had stopped for a time, a short time, before starting back up stronger than ever.

"You never need makeup like them other gals," Frank flattered her. "You a natural beauty."

She frowned. Some other subject was consuming her mind. "Why don't you ever want me to douche no more? I reckon you done gone plumb crazy now."

He crossed his legs and joked with her. "Honey, I like its fresh fruity taste." His tongue rolled obscenely around his abundant, parted lips.

Adele's eyes narrowed to slits of disgust. "Goddamn idiot! I think the best part of you slid down your papa's thigh. You ignorant bastid!"

"What you mean by that?"

Her answer was frigid. "Nothing, lover."

She was vexed. He swore off drinking for almost three weeks, kept his word just long enough to convince her that he was trying. Presently, he was at it again. Drinking more

176

jake than ever. Sometimes he spent days locked away in the house, drinking. It was taking a toll on him, the liquor and the solitude combined. He looked older than he really was, about ten years older.

"Are you sure you feel alright, Frank?"

"Fit as a fiddle," he boasted.

Adele took a mouthful of smoke, feeling her depression make the room sag and drain her in the process. Her next question left her mouth before she could think about what she was saying: "Are you ever gone go back to your wife an' the kids?"

Frank stared at her. "Don't know. I live here. This is my home now, here with you."

"But don't you think it's shameful that you ain't with them when they may need you the most?" Adele pressed.

"There's no joy back there." Frank closed his eyes and adjusted the towel on his forehead.

It was as if she was really seeing him for the very first time. A selfish, uncaring hick. He looked beat-out, whipped. His back was against the wall for support, and all his nerves seemed raw, exposed. She no longer knew what to expect from him. If she said the wrong thing, he might explode. The man could laugh or weep or turn hostile at any second, and she knew this too well, which compelled her to carefully choose her words whenever they talked.

Frank was looking straight into her eyes. "Oughta join the service, 'least I'd be able to make some money without kissin' them crackers' asses."

"Service, shit," Adele chuckled. "I thought you didn't like takin' orders. You won't last a day in the army, a hard-headed nigger like you. Plus you too old. Frank, you can't keep dodging your problems. You got to face them one day."

"I know I gots to do somethin'," he said it painfully. Everything was coming to the surface. She sensed the depth of his inner torment when he covered his face with his hands, mumbling. "I need a change. I gots to . . . gots to change up what I's doin'."

She watched his rough, trembling hands silently, concentrating on the tobacco stains on the fingertips.

"Do you listen to me at all?" he asked her, grimacing. "Or am I jes' talkin' to myself."

"Naw, I listen," she assured him. Then her face shifted expressions. "Frank, you got to make up your mind to do somethin'. I always say a person who can't make up his mind will be a chile all his life. You's dragging around here like you want someone to feel sorry for you. Well, not me."

Frank smiled a very sweet little-boy smile. "I don't want shit from you. Not a damn thing."

"I can't tell you how to live," Adele said emphatically. She touched his cheek with a tender stroke. "You is grown. But believe me, drinkin' won't help you none." She blinked at the sight of him, the puffiness of his face resembling yeast rising in spots, and the red veins in his eyes which killed whatever sympathy she had for him.

Frank was almost in tears. He didn't like being talked to this way. He didn't know what to say anymore. Exhausted, his head dropped on his arms in front of him.

"What's wrong, Frank?" She didn't understand any of this. "What is it now? Why are you lookin' at me like that, Adele? What is it?"

"Please don't drink no more of that stuff," she answered. "Please, baby. Put it down for me."

"Don't preach at me," Frank said, turning his head like a snapping turtle. He had a drink in his hand now.

"Well, at least don't drink while we're trying to talk 'bout somethin' because it'll all be for nothing. You won't remember a word we said later."

He set the drink down on the floor beside his chair. "Okay,

go head on and speak your piece."

Adele forced a weak smile. "This is what's wrong with you. You walk round all the time harpin' on the same ol' things, day in an' day out. No wonder you act crazy. Always in the same rut. Between this and the liquor, you ain't got a chance. You better do somethin' quick. Frank, put your mind away from this mess 'fore it all take you under."

He spoke to her in a husky, sexy voice. "Why don't you let me put you on my mind?" He was looking at her body in between her legs.

He could pick up a new tone in her words. "Naw, no foolin'. Frank, you should think on what I said." She meant for him to listen, to take heed, but he didn't give a damn about her advice in his present state of mind.

"Oh, I don't do the trick for you no more, huh? Not like I used to."

"That's not what I was talkin' about, Frank."

"I ain't good enough for you no more." He was frightened and suspicious, pleading with her to give him the right answer.

"Not when you drink too much."

"Shit, how can you tell me anything when your life ain't so great? What are you doin' with yourself that's so good that you can tell me what I should be doin'? You ain't nothin' but a slut."

That crushed her. "I's jes trying to help you out, Frank. Don't hurt me."

He drew an imaginary halo over his head, and flapped his arms like wings. "You want me to behave, huh?"

Her lips tightened in rage. "I's not foolin' around with you. Don't make what I said into a joke. Because none of it is funny, none of it."

Frank waited a second, then said, "All right, what you want me to do? I will listen to you. I do listen to you. You know I do."

"Naw, you don't. If you did listen sometime, all this mess wouldn't be goin' on for so long. On an' on. It'll be better, baby. That's all I hear from you. Talk is cheap, Frank, real cheap."

She was on the offensive and he sought some way to put things back in balance. "Adele, do you think I act like I gots good sense?"

"Not all the time."

"Woman, you tryin' to make me mad at you."

She lifted the used towel from his forehead and squeezed it over his face, with a bitchy smirk. "Naw, I'm not. I's jes tryin' to make you stop drinkin' so much."

Then Frank became quiet, sensing that he had lost this round. What could he do? Maybe he could get her to write a letter to one of his relatives for help, some money or a bus ticket. But there were not many of his kin left. One aunt in Detroit, one cousin in Philadelphia and a brother in Gary, Indiana. He hadn't spoke to his brother in years and now was not the time when he was flat broke. In the past, when he asked someone to write a letter for him, he wondered what they put down on paper because he never received any reply mail. He couldn't read or write.

Seizing the opportunity to divert attention away from himself and his drinking, he asked Adele to write a letter to his cousin Peetie in Philly, a few kind words and then the big pitch for a bus ticket or cash. Standing back on his heels, as a rich planter would do, Frank dictated the contents of this most important letter to her. She knew her English, even though you wouldn't know it by listening to her speak.

"Let me see what you wrote. Hurry up."

Adele sounded bothered. "Wait a minute."

He grew impatient with the whole business. "Read it to me." He walked over to the table where she sat, scribbling in a couple of last second revisions.

She put the pencil down and glanced at him. "I don't like this letter. It's not right."

"Why? What's wrong with it? I can't see where I did anything wrong. I ain't gone tell the man all my business. You have to keep some things to yourself."

Adele swallowed hard, visibly trying to regain her composure. "You know what I mean. You know why I don't like this letter. We've talked 'bout it until we both get blue in the face."

"What's wrong with the letter?" Frank repeated.

"The letter sounds like you an' your wife are still together," Adele said sharply. "I don't like that at all."

"Why?" He reached for one of her cigarettes.

She got up from her writing, wiped the hair from near her eyes, and disappeared into another room. But he could still hear her. "So what are we doin' here? Well, I guess we must be playin' house. Answer me. Why are you here? Are you ashamed of me or somethin'? What is it? I want to know now 'fore I put any more time into this. Tell me, Frank."

Somehow Frank was unable to protest much. "Sweetheart, I gots to make it sound that way to get the fool to help me out. If he thinks I ditched Mary an' the kids, he won't do a damn thing for me. He likes my wife a lot." He looked at the letter, which was left on the table with a half glass of Dr. Pepper. "What's all this scratching out right here? Did you change what I told you to write?"

She came back into the room, carrying two glasses of cold water, and gave him one. "Where? Show me."

"Here." Frank pointed to several lines of script that were deleted. "What did-d . . . you do? You must have crossed out the best parts."

"Naw." She didn't want to look at him. "It ain't nothin' but some mistakes I made. You got to give me an answer 'bout you an' your wife. Don't beat around the bush. Tell me the truth."

"I don't know, I don't know," Frank admitted boldly. "What do you want me to tell you? I can't say I'll nevah go back home. I jes don't know now. Am I here now? That's the important question. Answer that. I's with you . . . right? That is what matters, right now. Who am I with right now?"

Adele's mouth quirked ruefully. "You got that wrong. You livin' off me, nigger."

Her answer hit deep on another question, his dependence on her, his dead weight on her dwindling resources, and his reluctance to admit his laziness. Maybe he wasn't crazy after all, Adele thought. Maybe he was crazy like a fox. Sweet Jesus! She watched him, his eyes profoundly sad. Everything now was very difficult for her. Wherever she turned there were too many barriers and problems, most of them her fault. The time wasn't right. She took a shallow breath and smiled. Soon, real soon.

"Read the letter to me," Frank said.

Adele eyed him shrewdly. "Don't try me so much. I can't take too much of your craziness today."

"Adele?" No answer.

Frank drew his legs up and moaned slightly when his knees creaked. "Adele? Baby, I wanted to say what I likes best 'bout you."

"An' what is that?" She pretended to be angry. "I want to hear this one."

"Not until I hears what's in that letter," Frank said firmly. "Please read the letter so I can know what's goin' out of here with my name on it."

"I ain't a great writer, Frank," she said solemnly. "Wasn't even a good teacher."

"Read the letter, Adele." His attention was riveted on her hand that held the letter, and she finally read it aloud in a clear voice:

182

Dear Peetie:

I take this pen in hand to tell you I fine. Ain't no releaf for a pore niga. Even tho you ain't rote me in a wile, nothing has change. I still gots a house full of lil childrens to tak ceare of. You know my baby gurl dead on me a wile back. Suckhole et her up. Throwed me back some. Then Jake dead on me too. Fever. Mary most dead herself hind it. Really took it bad.

Tim Bailey boy went to rob a stor wit a knive. White folk caught him, runned him out. Som way he come back to see his mama an aint nobody seed him since. Want to put him in jail. Did him som dirt, I speck. Bue courtin now. Got a boy sniffin in hind her.

Ef you sen for me an help me. Me an my family mite be ther soon. We ain't sufferin but wants betta. Rite soon. Oh, Capt Dodge the white folks niga got knock in the head. He dead. Color folks glad. Rite soon.

Frank

He took the letter from her. "Did you sign mah name?"

"Yeah, why?"

Why? He thought about what she had said to him earlier, him on her, needing her. He had been a good husband, a good father, a fairly good provider. He kept all the rules of being a man, a real man, until now. His back had never been turned on a problem before nor had he ever let fear get the best of him. Feelings, for the most part, was something he didn't allow to get underfoot. He needed no help, he knew the goddamned answers to all of it. All of it. If you wanted something, you went after it, no matter what it was or what it cost. No crying. No pity. No sympathy. No bending to the will of women, shit he was a man. A real man. He knew it. To make him a man, his father forbid his mama to breastfeed him when he was a wee baby, not a drop. No tit for this boychild; like his daddy always said: A real man had no mush in his heart, rock hard it was.

"I know what I want," Frank joked, ending another silence. "Hair pie. I want to get some of your black, curly hairs in my teeth."

Adele's mouth was set stubbornly. "What you talkin' 'bout now? You drink too much for your own good."

He made his face somber, its smile twitching when he stifled a naughty laugh. "Them short, black curly hairs, them pussy hairs."

"Frank, you should go in there an' lay down for a spell until your head clears some. You ain't makin' no sense at all, you drunk fool."

By now, Frank had stripped and turned around, showing his swollen, throbbing dick to her, in its full state of ascension. He looked down at it, then at her, and smiled wickedly. "You is one beautiful woman. I love hearing you ball me out. An' I love them titties of yourn, jes the prettiest thangs I ever seed. I loves the way you loves me. You loves me 'cause you knows I know how to make a gal feel good. Jes' think if we wasn't colored down here workin' for this white man ... I could take you to a fancy place to eat like them movie stars do, candlelight dinner with lots of food, good food too. An' plenty of wine. Jes me an' you an' we'd talk and kiss. Yak, yak, yak, yak, yak, yak, yak. Then we'd go off dancin' an' maybe to a picture show, Cary Grant an' Mae West. Or the blonde gal with all them titties an' teeth. But anyway, somethin' like that. After that was over, we'd go to a big, fancy hotel an' lay up, jes you an' me. I'd fuck you real slow, make love to you like we jes meet. I'd kiss your feet, lick your toes one by one, suck them soft in my mouth. Soon ... you lay back an' enjoy it all, me kissin' you up your legs, all in between them; along that soft, sweet part of your leg. On up to your juicy pussy. Blow on it for a while an' let it simmer, cook a little bit. It would get real wet, the lips would glow from the sauce, and I would suck it up, lick it real clean . . ."

"You shouldn't be talkin' like this," Adele said, stroking him admirably. "That's the liquor talkin' for sure."

Frank looked down again, prouder still. "Lord, I'd lick it good an' you won't tell me to stop. You jes smilin' like crazy, not a care in the world, an' I'd stick mah tongue deep down in there. You scream with joy an' all of a sudden you push me off an' you take that thing you got your hands on an' you suck like a baby until I 'bout to come. I start pinchin' them big, brown nipples of yourn an' you beg me for more as I work mah tongue around them. Real quick an' I's back at your sugar hole, rootin' around with mah tongue, givin' it long licks, makin' you moan in pleasure, while I put one then two fingers up inside you. Wiggle them back 'an forth. You want that ten inch up in you an' you know that I can eat you out like nobody else can do it. Rock hard, like daddy said mah heart should be. But not for you. Your long dick daddy love you, jes you sweet cakes. If I start ridin' the way I feels right now, shit we'd be in the saddle for three or four hour at least, you know I ain't lyin'."

She was real catty with him. "Is that why you carry my panties around with you sometime? What you be doin'? Is you sniffin' them or somethin'?"

He grinned, walking over to the bed, and Adele came over and joined him. She laid beside him, her breathing more rushed than usual. Despite her rising passion, she grabbed his hand, put a pencil in it and helped him to sign a shaky signature. Afterwards, he playfully corralled her neck with his thick arms and with a semi-graceful motion, he turned her toward him to greet his lips in a blistering kiss. Then he pulled her on top of him and his hand went to that part of her back just before the hips rise. He quickly whispered in her ear: "Gimme some of that hair pie, sweet mama."

185

"Arbee," Mr. Ralph told Peterson. "Your friend sounds kind of bitter hisself. What wrong, boy? You must have female trouble bad. Bet you do. Don't you?"

"Naw, not really. I jes' know they game, that's all."

Shouts and yells came from down the crowded street, and the men glanced in that direction. The blind sage wasn't ready to let the subject drop. "Arbee, tell the boy a thang or two. A gal gots to do somethang. You niggers don't let her have nothing. She really don't own her own body, since most of the time you tell her what to do, what to say, how to dress, who to talk to, when to laugh, when to piss."

"I don't care none about that junk you talkin' there, old fella," MacArthur said, shaking his head disdainfully. " 'Cause I know about them womens that thinks they smarter than the man. They want him to take low from them an' the peckerwood too. Shit, I ain't gone do it."

Mr. Ralph was smug. "Boy got it bad. Son, you married?"

"Was," MacArthur answered after awhile.

Frank was itching to know what happened to make the boy go wild, so he asked.

The stud appeared to think about it before he said anything. "My wife was a real slut, fucking me an' a gang of other mens too. She raised so much hell that I had to leave her. She couldn't change none, she tried. I know 'bout them now. You think they the woman and you riding her, but all the time, she be the one that riding you."

"What you do, catch another nigger there?"

"Naw, Arbee, she jes' changed up on me," MacArthur said, his voice cracking. "You know how they do when there's another mule kicking in the stall an' it gets good to them."

Mr. Ralph mouthed to him, "Son, how you know what made her act like that, what the problem is, if you nevah caught the man there with her? Could have been somethin' else on her mind worryin' her."

"I jes' know. I ain't no fool now."

"You might be one an' not know it." Frank couldn't resist getting a lick in.

"Shut up, Frank." Peterson was sympathetic to the young man's marital problem.

"I's jes' kiddin'."

"You know, Frank—"

Don't start no shit, Frank thought. He asked Peterson what it was he was about to say and stopped. It made him mad to think that the half-wit might be referring to Ellis being in his house, sleeping in his bed with his wife.

Peterson kept his words to himself.

Instead, the old timer put in his two cents. "Frank, it could be this here is the real problem. The Lawd know some mens can only handle one part of a woman at a time, an' that's between their legs. Frank, how many chillun you got?"

He didn't want to think about his children or his family. "Too many. Why?"

The blind man sighed, convinced that Frank was the one that was hiding something, and that the boy Mac hadn't lived long enough to accumulate any real dirt in his life. He moved Frank into the spotlight. "Mary was probably tired of you before you left. Mac here don't know what real life is. Frank, why Ellis over there in your house? You ever stay home with her any? Why you leave? You know, a woman likes a man to stay home with her sometime."

Frank snorted, hoping to cover his anger. "What you saying? Damnit, I's a man. I ain't supposed to stay home like no woman. That's her job. I's the man, she ain't."

Mac and the others agreed with him, and said so.

"Frank, I know that. I can tell you a man, but I don't think you see what I's talkin' about."

Behind the farmer, someone said, "I don't either." Frank didn't turn, deciding instead to watch the blind man.

"You all think 'cause I's blind, I miss everythin'. But you's wrong. I's serious 'bout this. The boy needs help an' if he listens to me, then he'll learn 'bout life. Look at what happened to Frank, an' learn from what was done to him. Frank, we all know you a man, 'cause the man got the seed an' the woman got to come to him for it. Hell, your wife must have come often. But ain't no other way she gone get it unless she come to the man for it. Without the seed, she ain't nothing. She ain't no woman an' she ain't got no balls so she ain't a man. Womens gone always need a man an' vice versa. It's only so much that they can do without each other. They's need each other to be complete."

"So what are you gettin' at?" Frank asked quietly.

"Listen, Frank," Peterson volunteered. "What the old man is tryin' to tell you is to stop jumping the gals so much an' save yourself so you can last longer. So you can still be humpin' away in your old age."

The men all chuckled at his sarcastic remark.

"I ain't saying that at all," Mr. Ralph said glumly. "That don't mean a damn, 'cause some peoples spend their whole lives saving themselves an' still don't have nothing in the end. Shit, look at me. What I's trying to say, if you gives me a chance, is that a man who seeks to downgrade a gal by going after her body, her poontag, is a fool. Unless he jes' buy it outright. But if he jes' likes to mount this one an' that one, that's stupid. If he hates womens that bad, he should keep the hell away from them 'cause when it end up, he'll jes' ruin hisself. Jes' all the scheming that go into it will be enough to kill him, to put him into an early grave. An' it'll kill him on the inside."

MacArthur said immediately that he loved his wife, and that he had done the best he could to stay with her. He didn't think the old man was well anyway, probably was too messed up over his dead son to see anything clearly anymore.

"No," the young man said nastily. "I don't appreciate no mannish woman, no how or no way. An' that's how my wife was."

"Mannish womens come from soft mens an' stupid mens," Mr. Ralph snapped back. "Soft mens with no backbone an' stupid mens with no feelings. Them womens, either 'cause she been hurt so much or not loved enough, make up their mind that they can do a bettah job at being a man than a real man. Mac, you don't have to be no gal-boy or no hen-pecked man, jus' be natural with 'em. Go easy on her sometime an' treat her decent."

MacArthur cried out defiantly, "You talk like this 'cause you blind an' can't get round the gals no more. They only want your money, jes' like Pete here say. You'd sing a different song if you could see."

The blind man stirred and stretched, moaned a little, and moved toward the young buck's virile voice. He cleared his throat, then spoke. "Mebbe so, mebbe so."

As a group of women walked past, talking loudly, the men cut short their debate, and leered at them, carnal thoughts in full bloom.

Mr. Ralph sniffed the air, the fragrance of sweet oil and pungent perfume wafted by his cocked head. Dumbly, he saw a moment to make another point, which would get lost on the others as long as the ladies were in view. "Frank, you especially should listen to what I have to say. Often, the peoples that thinks they have the most freedom are the ones that's toting the biggest chains. Picture this, Mac. This is you: An army always on the attack, never taking the time to secure the ground they done won, will always be whipped. That's how you niggers try to conquer the women folks with your privates. Damn fools."

Of course, the men soon tired of standing along the parade route, watching the folks having fun, so they headed toward the carnival site. They walked in zig-zagging steps among the hastily erected tents on the midway, wading through the alluring siren songs of the barkers, past sweet talking game agents and lines of excited black children waiting in long lines to ride the small, rusty airplanes and boats suspended from chains. Frank recognized a group of church-goers gathered in a herd near the merry-go-round and laughed after a deep swig of jake from Mr. Ralph's bottle.

The young stud noticed the food table, rubbed his strangler's hands together in anticipation, and ambled in that direction. Only two female members of the Junior Usher Board were stationed near the eats to make sure no one tried to be a hog and get more than his portion. Slabs of freshly baked ham, heaps of Southern fried chicken, golden brown, plates of cornbread, wedges of cobbler and pie. Large bowls of precisely seasoned black-eyed peas.

"I think I know that boy's peoples," Frank said to Mr. Ralph. "Did his papa used to stammer a lot and had a bad cataract eye? Always hung around the jukes with singers an' the like."

"Uh-huh. He's a Northern nigger, ain't much for workin'."

Frank smiled. "Yeah, that's what I thought. I hate them Northern niggers. Ain't nothin' to them, ain't nothin' to them but mouth. They can barely stand a good taste of jake and a good woman would kill them."

Both men laughed heartily at the farmer's remark. Frank grabbed the blind man under the elbow to guide him through the mob, pushing passersby out of the way, almost dragging the handicapped man in his wake.

"Frank, you from 'round here originally?"

"I's from all over. Yazoo City, McComb, Itta Bena, Houma, Cleveland, all over. Been up an' down Mississippi an' through Louisiana, all through Madison County an' Sunflower County. Work a while an' move on. I done pulled corn,

195

plowed, cut logs, did road work an' pick cotton. All of it."

"How you feelin' these days, Frank? Adele tells me you been feelin' poorly."

Frank took a deep breath and threw out his chest. "I's fine. Doin' okay. Jes' needed to walk 'round an' suck up some of this here fresh air. An' do a little thinkin'."

"Yeah, walkin's good for that."

"How long you knowed Adele?" Frank was fishing for any information he could get on his woman, if she was that. "Have you knowed her long?"

"Heheheh, Adele," the blind man chuckled. "That gal's been somethin' else as long as I's knowed her. I used to stay up over her when she lived with a nigger name Benny Strong. Some folks say she's a bulldagger, that's what they say."

Frank looked away and let his expression sour. "What do you say? Is she one?"

"I don't know. An' what if she is, she's good to you, right?"

"I guess so, but . . ." Frank broke off his reply, when he saw MacArthur returning, with a drumstick in each hand.

The blind man heard the young man's approach and wisely switched subjects for discussion. "Yah, Frank boy, Lawd jes' dealt you a bad hand. Don't worry 'bout a thang. You know, even Jesus had trouble wit' the bunch he picked, one came up foul on him. But 'member this, somethin' good comes out of evahthin' bad, no matter how bad it seem."

Some men started a fight near one of the games of chance, turning over a table laden with stuffed toys and trinkets. Temporarily distracted, Frank and MacArthur fell silent and watched the commotion. While everyone was concentrating on the minor battle, Frank thought for some unknown reason about Biloxi, about his slain Uncle Jenkins, found dead, laying face down on his front porch, with his soiled bib overalls in an untidy roll around his ashy ankles. Along side his body, the sheriff and his boys found a pair of ripped panties, a

196

bloody comb and a woman's high heel shoe. There was a cane knife broke off in his uncle's punctured back, snapped off at half blade. No one could blame this on the hoogies, this was strictly nigger business over some hussy, he admitted to himself.

"Hank say white folk shot into his house the other night," Frank said to talk about something other than his family and his personal grief. "On Thursday past," he went on, "someone fired into his house while his family was at the supper table. The grandson and Hank's wife took some buckshot in the face and chest. Hank got it in the arm, his shit-shoveling arm, an' the oldest gal, Brenda, had window glass in one of her eyes. Bled like hell. Hank say they all jump to the floor after the first two shots come through, then he run out of the house with his pistol. They was gone that quick. An' the sheriff never did come."

Yessir, colored peoples always could comfort themselves with the knowledge that they knew where they stood, or laid, under Mister Charlie's foot, thought Frank. No guesswork about it. That was fact. The "colored" and "white" signs only drove that point home and there was nowhere colored could go that ol' Jim Crow wasn't strong.

MacArthur's voice snapped him back to the present. "Them pecks gone always hate us 'cause we's black. An' we ain't even black, we brown. The real black folk are back ovah in Africa. I figger that white hate is somethin' they made up to keep us busy so we can't do nothin' wit' our lives."

"We give 'em too much credit," the blind man said. "They ain't that all-powerful or the world wouldn't be in the shape it's in today. Everythin' would be goin' their way an' it ain't."

Frank chortled, "That youngster Martin Luther King Jr. has a trick or two for them. If they don't watch out, he's gone turn thangs 'round on them. God-dog, he's 'nuff to make you want to go back to church."

"If he don't get hisself killed," hissed Mr. Ralph. "They can git one of them shiftless niggers to do it, jes' offer him a little cash money, a shiny new car an' a chance to roll wit' one of them thin-lipped white gals. Any one of 'em would do the deed."

More jake, deep swallows. Finally the liquor hit them full force. Playing the jester, Frank made a funny face at his drinking buddies, growling under his breath, and they looked at each other, summed up their lot and began laughing wildly.

"That Ike an' them other crackpots in Washington smellin' they nuts," Frank added with a smirk. "They wants another war, not like Korea, but a big un. An' they'll git jes' what they wants."

"Look yonder!" yelled a man standing near a ride that flipped people upside down.

"Ain't that the man what say he played wit' Robert Johnson? He play a harp, I thinks."

Frank watched the men and listened to their banter. Never know when you might hear something you can use, he told himself.

"Thass him. Oh, that boy can play one of them thangs, make it talk like peoples."

"Wonder if he gone play somewhar here in town during the carnival?"

"Damn if I know. He tole one time, and this otha fella—Baby Face Davis, that he runned wit' Robert Johnson. Say he played wit' him an' all, but a heap of niggers claim that."

"I heard tell of that Johnson. Folk say he was hell on a box."

"Yessir, young boy too," the other man chimed. "They say he was real skinny an' bright as that pale nigger passin' ovah there. Say he love likker an' pussy. Say a man poisoned him near Greenwood ovah messin' wit' his wife."

"Frank, Frank!"

"What?" He didn't look at MacArthur when he answered

him.

"Frank, how did you git them scars on your arms? Look like a razor did it."

"None of your concern, boy," snapped Frank. "Well, I gotta git home 'fore I gits in trouble with Adele. It was mighty fine talkin' to you, ole timer. Take care of yourself, you hear?"

"Bye, son. 'Member what I say 'bout Adele an' that hearsay. Don't mess up a good thang."

Drunk MacArthur pointed at the sheriff and his deputies putting up wooden horses to regulate the crowd, talking among themselves, hands on their holsters. Ready, always ready. "Look at 'em," the young buck said. "See how them peckerwoods lookin' at us? Like they 'fraid we plannin' some mischief."

When the men turned around, Frank was staggering badly back up the midway, sometimes tripping but never falling.

Chapter 26

The drinking continued at home. Slumping slightly, Frank looked down at his hand and noticed the cigarette was burning his fingers with a sizzling sound. He stubbed it in his outstretched palm, his face completely deadpan. His mind was running crazy, just turning everything over and over in a twisted, odd fashion that he couldn't understand. Maybe it would be alright if he bought some gator shoes, but with what? Spinning, spinning, spinning. He ought to get a job at one of the roadhouses washing dishes 'cause he had to support his family or he would wind up out at the Harvey Allen County Farm right near Clarksdale here. No good, no good at all.

That jake made him think about things that he'd rather leave alone, stirring stuff up, jamming it all in your face. You had to see it, the wife, kids, Little Frank, especially Little Frank.

Just before he left his wife and family, one old woman in

the community came by the house and told them that she, like many of her neighbors, felt Frank and Mary were mistreating the boy. He should be in a home somewhere so he can get the proper care, she said. Bullshit! They loved him and cared for him. Damn those folks! His boss knew a white doctor who would look at him for little or nothing, so he toted the boy over there, let the man run some tests on him and take pictures of his head. Shit, he knew the boy wasn't right in the head, knowed that just by looking at him. There, he said it again. It hurt him to say this, even to himself . . . about his own flesh and blood. And that pain had to quit . . .

He threw the empty liquor bottle against the wall, it shattering into a million slivers of jagged glass, staining where it hit. He couldn't breathe, his lungs ached, from the strain. In fact, the air wasn't as close and stuffy as he imagined it, but other things were affecting him, barechested, out of his mind from too much drink and too little sleep.

He tried to keep his wits about him, holding the worst thoughts closer and tighter to his heart, the pain had to quit. Oh God, help me, he screamed inside himself. He wanted to yell, to holler, to blast out the booming inside his head. Ellis broke up my home, fat pig, she's been seeing him all along, all along when I was working or when I was in town, making excuses to stay at home so she could be with him, always saying it was because of Little Frank but it was Ellis all the time, slaving and breaking his back for her and them children, maybe them children wasn't his either, probably all the mens 'round there be getting her, Ellis didn't have to do that to his home, his woman let the fat pig in his house and bust it up, bust it up, they treated him like a fool, like a plumb fool, a chile, like I ain't got good sense, that's why she say Little Frank his fault, both of them, 'cause both supposed to be fools, uh-huh, both of them fools, no sense . . .

Everyone was against him, hated him, Frank thought, putting his head down on his knees, shaking violently from the strange inner tension. Coiled up in a knot. Maybe they put somethin' in his food, poisoned him, the water too, tryin' to make him lose his mind, servin' him blood in a cup, writin' numbers in his hands whilest he slept, in his cracked palms, to make him afraid of them, to make him afraid of everythin', nothing, nothing was going to hurt him no more, nothing, he'd whup Adele's ass an' Mary's big ass too, Mary, Mary, sweet Mary, his Mary snuggled up in the arms of some fat pig . . .

He got up, walked over to a corner, sat down, facing it. The pain and the grief would not leave him alone. It was there in the room with him, heavy in its mood, overwhelming in its strength. Mary, she afraid of everythin', he tried to convince himself. But she gone . . . take him back, beg him to come back, on her knees, crawling, baby, baby, baby, baby please come back, that's what the heifer gone do, beg him an' he'll jes' stand there an' look at her, please come back . . .

He shifted his position, aching, ignoring his heart's increased pace, closing off as much emotion as he could, but the storm continued to swell inside him. Let yourself go, he reasoned with himself. Don't hold it back, let it come. It has to. All of it so hard to think 'bout. Press it down. Was he sure that he hadn't done somethin' to make that boy the way he is? Was he sure? Womens don't like a good man, they'll dog him everytime, they like somebody to whup their ass. Yeah, treat them mean an' they'll love you for life. A man can't get nowhere by doin' good deeds, only the wicked prosper. Shit, that Ellis' fat belly bouncin' on top of his woman right now, she moanin' an' smilin', give it to me sugah daddy, give it to me, she deserve that fool. Can't nobody tell dooley-squat 'bout no woman, they always plannin' some dirt behind your back. Little Frank must be Ellis' baby. He was probably doin' it to her back then, that's right. Ellis Ellis Ellis

203

did it, probably all them mens doin' it to her, she layin' there with all them bucks. Yeah, all of them done had her by now . . .

His legs seemed paralyzed; he wanted to bite hard on one of his hands to stifle the scream he sensed building in his chest, growing in its power, but again nothing would move. His face, his forehead were warm. He was about to cry again. Maybe he should comb his hair, wash up a bit, and go see the Governor. He would help him if he looked nice and clean. If he covered his ears, they couldn't hurt him no more, no more . . .

His mental torment was unspeakable; he couldn't understand the meaning of what was happening to him, the reason for so much pain. All he knew was that he had sunk to the depths of some new part of himself, had looked into the brilliant fires of Hell itself, and it scared the piss out of him. Again his mind began playing tricks with him, creating more cruel images and conjuring ever more guilt. It was his children, he said to himself, seeing them as plain as day right there before his eyes.

He was so happy to see them, to be able to talk to them. And he did speak to these ghosts that he had created in his own image. Teenie, Jake, you done come to see your papa, uh-huh. Hi y'all. Come and give me a big hug like you used to, oooooh that felt good. You knowed I was up here worried 'bout you both. Are they treatin' you right where you at? If they don't, I know peoples that will get the sapsuckers straight. Come on, rest your feets. Sorry I ain't got nothin' to offer you, but some liquor. An' that's 'bout gone. Besides you too young to fool with it anyway. Tell me 'bout where you stayin'. Uh-huh, uh-huh. No kiddin' . . .

Suddenly, he broke off his dialogue with his ghosts, searched for another bottle. He found it under the bed. He gulped the tart homebrew, but there was no pleasure in it.

204

Yes, they were still there with him, his kids. He blurted out, you know your mama out there actin' a fool, yessuh. Actin' plumb wild, makin' a fool out herself, yeah, with Ellis. He put me out, no, she put me out, say she don't want me 'round no more. I's been feelin' real low lately, hates myself sometimes, hates peoples sometime 'cause they so lowdown an' dirty. I loves you both, I loves all of ya, my flesh an' blood. So much, believe that. I ain't got nobody right now but this gal, Adele. She real nice to me. No, no, no ... where ya goin'? Don't go off an' leave me here. Don't leave your papa. Let me tell you 'bout the mens ridin' your mama an' she's lettin' them. Don't leave me with my head hurting like this, jes' stay. Please. Teenie Teenie ...

There was the sound of footsteps coming to a halt just outside the door, a woman's steps. The urge to scream returned and he jammed his fingers into his mouth, holding it back.

Wearily, he asked who was at the door. He quickly got up and walked toward the door, whispering to the ghosts that they should stay until he found out who it was. However, the panic refused to leave him. Spit had gathered in the corners of his mouth, and the crotch of his overalls was soaked with a drying stain of fresh urine.

Adele walked in, with a bag of vegetables in her arms. She was dressed in that white summer dress that he liked, her hair tied back, gleaming with perspiration. The woman sniffed the air, phew. "Frank, why don't you open a window an' let some fresh air in here. It'll do you some good. Did I hear you talkin' to somebody when I was at the door?"

His appearance worried her greatly. He had not shaved or washed in days, hadn't done anything for that matter, but drink. His eyes were swollen, almost closed. She never knew what to expect from him anymore; kind words or a hard slap; flowers or silence; sometimes all of these things at once. He was definitely losing his mind and there was nothing she could do to help him. Nothing. The memory of that time last week came to her, when he had locked her out, bolted the door from the inside and wouldn't let her in. Damn that Frank, she thought. She had turned the key in the lock and nothing had happened. Her knuckles were raw from banging on the door until a crowd had gathered behind her, watching and waiting for some drama. When the door finally opened after several more minutes, he stood before her as he did now, looking filthy, saying something about being in the next world, wherever that was.

Adele stared at him for a long time. "Frank, I asked you a question. Who were you talkin' to when I came in?"

He was breathing deeply, almost painfully. He didn't answer her immediately. "My kids. Didn't you see them goin' out as you came in? Yeah, they came here to see me."

She looked for her cigarettes, had to get one quick. It was going to be one of those evenings, a nightmare.

Frank continued, "They was here to see their papa. Say they miss the old man."

Adele wondered how far gone he was by now. He needed to see a doctor or somebody, a specialist or something. She couldn't handle him when he was like this, between two worlds, half here and half somewhere else. Madness. More and more she wanted to put him out, throw him in the street, but he had nowhere to go, especially with his wife shacking up with some man.

"What children?" she asked. "I didn't see any children. You better leave that alcohol alone. Let that bottle be. You're messin' up your mind, warpin' it. I done told you too many times to stop drinkin'. But no, you won't listen to me. You got to find out the hard way."

She put the bag down, noticing the broken glass from the smashed liquor bottle on the floor near the bed, the stinking yellow bile running down the wall in long trails. How much more of this could she take? She began sorting out the food. Frank was attempting to clean up the glass, hitting at it with a broom, but his hands were not that steady. He was making a bigger mess.

"Leave it for me," Adele said. "I'll get it."

Frank clenched his teeth, the jaw muscles twitching as more fear went through him. "I's gone visit the Governor an' ask him to help me get back my kids. He knows where they are." The confused man stumbled by her, reeking of liquor and urine, and she held her nose.

"What are you talkin' about now?"

"The Governor will help me. I's got to go to the state capital an' see him. He'll see what he can do to help me."

She cut him short. "Yeah, sure. Wash up before I fix your eats."

His voice was distant and shrinking. "I don't want anything to eat. I got other thangs on my mind."

Adele answered him harshly, her voice as stern as it could get. "You better put something on your stomach with all that liquor you been drinkin'. Go on now. Hey, has Nette been by with the money she owes me?"

He watched her eyes, suspicious. "Naw."

She furrowed her brows, while she examined a head of cabbage. "Nette said she came by yesterday an' you wouldn't let her in. Why you do that, Frank?"

Frank was determined not to show any real emotion, but he snorted to show his contempt for her "friend." He kept watching her from behind. "Naw, ain't nobody here but my kids an' they left when you came."

There was a terrible moment of silence, just staring into each other's eyes. Neither knew what to say next.

Adele turned around abruptly, walked to where his last bottle was stashed, picked it up, uncapped it, and poured it out. Frank didn't say a word.

She tried to humor him, all the while wondering how in the hell did she get herself into this, involved with this crazy man. She felt like an idiot.

His face was contorted, on the verge of tears again.

"Frank, you got me worried. I don't know how to help you except to talk to you when you make sense. You're sufferin', an' if you don't work out this family business, it'll bring you down. It'll destroy you."

"You so lovely, so beautiful," he said, hunched over. "I don't know why you want me." He grinned and wobbled over to Adele to kiss her, his bad breath leading the way. She held up a thin hand before her face, blocking his approach.

His bloodshot eyes fluttered and he appeared to be coming back from wherever he had been, in his head. The fog was lifting.

She was chain-smoking, lighting one cigarette after another. Something he noticed but didn't make a comment about. He was firing up one of his own.

"Can I get a light, baby?" asked Adele.

Unexpectedly, he hissed and flung the book of matches at her feet. "Here, bitch."

In a very gentle voice, icy with sarcasm, Adele replied, "Don't try my patience, Frank. Sometimes you push me too far. I can only take so much an' you're pushin' me to the limit. I don't want to throw you out with nowhere to go, but I will if you keep actin' like a fool."

A coldness came into his eyes. "What do you mean?" He seemed shocked by her threat. Squaring his shoulders, he cleared his throat to let his disapproval be known and stared at her.

She could no longer contain her anger. "I's sick of this drinkin'. You got to put the drinkin' down or get out. I mean it this time. There's so much you could be doin' with yourself if you quit that bottle. Nobody can straighten out your life but you an' you ain't tryin'."

Ignoring her rage, he kissed her tenderly on the back of her neck, as if that would pacify her. He whispered softly in her ear. "I love you, Adele, I need you."

She pushed him away, roughly. "No, no huggin' an' kissin' until you wash up. I can't stand no bear-smellin' nigger pawin' on me."

He could smell the funk bellowing from his underarms and the rest of his body. "Alright. I guess I do smell pretty bad."

"How long has it been now?"

"Since what?" asked Frank, holding her nose for her and laughing between words.

"Since you an' your wife broke up?"

He rubbed his nose against hers. " 'Bout a year an' a half now. It feels a lot longer, a whole lot longer without seein' the kids. That's why I was so happy to see Teenie an' Jake today. It really was nice, really was."

Adele shook her head sadly. "What am I goin' to do with you? What can you do for me? You don't want to make me happy. One day, you'll go back to your shitty wife an' what will I have? You can't offer me nothin' but empty promises. I think this thing we got here is bad for me. Maybe we should stop it."

He didn't take her seriously when she said things like that. "You know you love me." He laid his head on her shoulder, snuggling as close as she would let him get, with his funk. He beamed at her. "I loves you baby more than you could ever love yourself."

Anger seized her again and Frank felt her spine stiffen. Her eyes, in all their nut-brown splendor, narrowed. "I don't want a damn thing from you."

"Bull-hockey," Frank said quietly.

"What?" Adele turned to face him.

He amended his remark, showing his teeth in a snarl.

209

"Bullshit." Then he touched his crotch in an obscene gesture.

She decided to overlook that, because she was afraid to comment about their sex life, about the nights when they grunted and groaned and it was all playacting on her part, about the nights when he'd fuss at her and expect her to be wet when they made love, about the nights when he'd shove his bitter tongue down her throat and jammed himself into her, about the nights when he couldn't even get hard. She could tell him a thing or two. Some things that would set his ears on fire and break his heart in two. Some things he would never understand about her.

Adele softened her eyes and steered the talk onto another track. "Frank, I knows how you feel 'bout your wife an' kids. You're a good man deep down. You mean well. But we got to look at what we doin' here. It can't go on this way. You got to decide what you are goin' to do."

Now it was his turn to get mad. "Or else?"

"Or I might have to do somethin'?" she answered him with a question. What she wanted to say is that she might hurt him if he didn't make his move soon. She needed some good guarantees, not just some dick and shallow kisses.

"An jes' what are you gone do to me?" he asked her in a tone of feigned surprise. He had no idea of what she was talking about.

"I . . . I might hurt you, Frank, if you don't stop what you's doing." She folded her arms, leering evilly at him for a second before catching herself.

"Shut up, woman," Frank said, moving away from her. He realized that something was different with her, but he couldn't figure it out. This was a new mood, a new attitude, and he couldn't decipher it. He felt hurt again and ashamed at what he had become. He was ashamed because he had once been a proud, responsible man, yet look at him now. Her eyes followed him across the room, chiding him more. That hurt.

210

His tears came slowly at first, but soon he was crying hysterically, leaning against the wall, with his back to her.

Somehow he knows he is sick, Adele said to herself. She had never seen a man cry like that, so vulnerable, so utterly helpless. It touched her soul. She couldn't bear to see such agony. She wanted to tell him that she would always love him, would always be with him, yet she couldn't. Unfortunately, there was that other side of her, her dark side, the side she kept from him.

No matter what, she owed him something, because after all, Frank had been with her all during the Nette ordeal, when she needed him. He supported her. Now she felt obliged to stand by him. She moved gracefully toward him, took his weary head in her gentle hands, and pressed him close to her. He wept quietly against her bosom. They held each other tightly, almost in desperation.

"I's sorry this is goin' on with me." He sounded both bitter and apologetic. "I knows it's bad for you."

"Honey, you act like your life is over. It ain't. You can do anything, whatever you want with it. You shape it, don't let it shape you." She smiled inside herself at this advice, for it contained words that she should have applied to her own confused life. "It'll be alright. You watch. Don't cry anymore. Don't cry. I'll help you as best as I can. Please don't cry."

He finally pulled himself away from her, after swiftly putting his open mouth fully on hers. A wet, passionate kiss. Again staggering, he went to the bed, fell across it, and was soon sound asleep in his rank smelling clothes. No doubt he was spent from the crying, its painful release. Adele lit another cigarette and watched him sleep. He snored lightly, tossing a bit in his slumber, eventually rolling over on his stomach, with his hands tucked under him. She brought a quilt from the next room and covered him. Watching him sleep exaggerated what she felt about him and made what she must

211

do that much harder. For some reason, there were tears in her eyes, as she thought about the upcoming argument that would happen when she told him that she forgot to buy grits for his breakfast tomorrow.

Chapter 27

It was light out, but Frank sensed the threat of a coming storm in the thick, muggy air. Some of the townsfolk were already talking about the Blue Norther swooping down through the Delta real hard this year, he thought, watching a flock of low-flying crows sail over. They said satellites and underground A-bomb tests had ruined the weather, tilted the earth in a strange way, and switched the seasons around. Rain more than usual, snow falling in places it never used to.

Midday, Frank was listening to the screened door at Otis' tiny place behind the drugstore slam shut. It seemed that nobody was home, all quiet. Still, Otis would never leave his door wide open unless he was inside, unless he was upfront waiting on customers, helping the old ladies pick out the right aspirin or laxative.

"Don't leave, stranger," he heard as he was about to pull the door closed. "Don't run off so quick, rest your feets a spell."

Otis stood smiling at Frank, dressed in an ironed khaki outfit, polished black wingtip shoes, starched white shirt, a bit worn at the sleeves, black bow tie, and his trademark Mr. Peanut stick pin on his lapel. His black hair retreated back from his high forehead. What he remembered most about Otis was his craving for Old Gold cigarettes, Sugar Babies candy, strong clear whiskey, and dark-skinned gals with high behinds. There were always one or two of those types hanging around the fast talker's house. Today was no exception. Frank could hear her thin voice coming from the direction of Otis' bedroom, telling the tall and skinny man to hurry back, but the woman never came out so Frank could look her over.

"Why the long face, Frank? What ails you?"

"I's okay. Reckon it could be the flu comin' on. I had the runs yestiddy. For while, I was runnin' from both ends."

The truth was that Frank still had a case of the blues, feeling low and all choked up inside. Otis didn't know how to handle his friend's blue moods, no amount of barnyard humor or gal talk could shake that funk. It was hopeless. Otis had been a close buddy of Adele's for years, and when she asked him to talk to Frank about his drinking, he agreed without hesitation. He had suffered the same problem some years back. At that time, during his recovery, he wouldn't go near the stuff or a still, for that matter. Now he drank more or less the same dose of spirits without any conscience or guilt. You gotta die with somethin', he'd say.

The bedroom door opened a crack and Otis' girl friend motioned to him. He laughed and joked to Frank about duty calling and disappeared behind the same door. Muffled moans, feminine giggles, lip smacking sounds, and the squeals of rusty bed springs. About a half hour later, the woman, rough-looking with too much makeup on her face, too much rouge, exited from the room. She seemed sort of cheap looking to Frank, her wiggling walk, her tits jutted out, her ass all fanned out behind her. Real trash, yet the men must love . . . her magic, her effect.

The high-butt woman let Otis kiss her goodbye, hold her tightly against him at the door. "Here," she held a key in her outstretched hand. "Thanks." Wearing a sullen expression, Otis laughed his quiet laugh and palmed the key, then walked the woman to the street. They whispered among themselves, kissed again, and she was gone.

After her departure, two bottles of whiskey were brought out, along with a couple of jelly glasses, and the two men settled down to do some serious drinking. All afternoon they gulped the clear fluid, getting drunk by degrees. It was pitch black outside when both men realized that they were on the verge of passing out, yet neither would stop because of vanity. They had decided to drink each other under the table, until their glasses couldn't be lifted, until neither could see straight. Looking popeyed, Otis reared back in his chair, watching Frank bend over the table, swaying at a bizarre angle.

"You drunk, Frank?" he muttered.

His drinking buddy stiffened his back. "Hell naw. You?"

"I's fine myself. Couldn't be bet-tah."

Frank stopped in the middle of a nod and looked at the top of Otis' head. "You know Timmie, don't you? Well, he fought in the army with the Frenchmens overseas in the last war. Came back home all puffed up like he did somethin', had a chest full of medals. Couldn't get used to them crackers 'round here, couldn't get no job, so he went up North. Chicago, I think. Last I heard, he had him a white wife."

"Uh-huh, pour me some more," Otis drawled.

"Yeah, sure did," Frank said, slapping a mosquito on his arm. "Bugs bad tonight. All inside the house huntin' for you. Who was the fast gal you jes' had here? You thinkin' 'bout

215

gettin' hitched in your old age."

"Yeah, an' then maybe I can leave my wife like you did," Otis said harshly.

Frank gave him his meanest look. "Shut up, Otis."

"I's too old to make babies. That's really the onliest reason to get married. Can't think of any other reason for signing your life over to some gal, for bettah or worse. Shit, Frank, you got enough kids for you an' me both."

"Otis, jes' drink your liquor an' keep your mouth out of my affairs. They ain't none of your concern."

Otis tapped on the table top and smiled a wry smile. "Nigger can't even take a joke. You too serious these days, Frank."

"You ain't funny." Frank grinned coldly. "Hey, you done stopped drinkin'. Don't stop. Fill up again. I dreamt 'bout gettin' married again night before last. Wonder what that mean?"

Otis blinked at Frank, stood unsteadily for a moment, then slid back down into his chair. "That's a bad sign. Dreamin' 'bout weddings is real bad. It means death's lurkin' 'round somewhere. Somebody gone die."

"I don't believe in that hoodoo mess no how," Frank grumbled. "Drink up. Don't wait on me. Did your papa drink lots? Mine did. He drank liquor like it was goin' out of style."

Otis fingered his glass and regarded its contents with a dissatisfied air. "All I 'member 'bout my old man is how he used to whup my ass. He'd beat you with anythin' he could get his hands on. Shoot, you knowed your ass was whupped when he got through. Whup you if you cry. Whup you if you didn't. An' don't run on him. Oh shit. You ever run from a whuppin'."

"Naw, my papa jes' drew back-k-k . . . ," Frank slurred. "Jes' drew back-k-k . . . an' knocked the hell out of you. You didn't get time to run."

"I run once. See, I had this cousin, Chester, on my mama's side. Fool nigger. Told him to keep his black ass off this fence my papa had out back." Otis stopped talking, grimaced, and rubbed his thigh. "The folks used to make me watch him. The fool had to leap up on the fence, trying to walk it like he was in the circus. He slipped an' fell on it. Wasn't no good no more. They all say it was my fault 'cause I was the oldest."

"Smashed balls." Frank sighed deeply. "That's the worsest pain there is."

"Yessir. Dumb fool."

"Great God Almighty!" Frank thought about the injured boy for a moment, then went on. "I knowed . . . I knowed a boy used to come an' eat with us all the time. He'd been in the penitentary over in Kilby, you know, Alabama. He say they caught hell over there, dogs, guards, swamps. Wasn't no way out, work all day. That's all they did, grow rice, cotton, cane an' corn. He was in there for shootin' a boy in the face over some money. Hear tell somebody killed him with a pipe."

Otis held a bottle aloft. "You want another drink?"

"Huh?" Frank was staring at his shoes, a loose lace laying across the top of the right one, staring blankly.

"You drunk yet?" he said after three seconds to Otis.

"Huh?"

"You drunk yet?"

"Huh?"

"You drunk yet?"

"Naw . . ." Following his shaky answer, the intoxicated Otis burped loudly and keeled over on the table. Frank was the perfect victor. He got to his feet, poured down his drink, walked around the table to his unconscious friend, pulled up one of his eyelids, smiled cruelly and swaggered out of the door toward home.

Adele spotted him stumbling down the street, humming to himself, totally oblivious to everything going on around him. She called to him, once, twice. At first, he ignored her shouts,

217

pretending that he had not heard her, and began walking quickly.

"Where you been, Frank?" Adele asked him when she finally caught up with him.

He kept silent, trying to sort out his thoughts in his whiskey-induced state, trying to figure out what to say. She'd raise hell for sure if she knew he was drinking again, he said to himself. He felt ashamed, guilty, for some reason. He felt like a child waiting to be scolded, thinking of the horrible punishment to come.

"Where you been, Frank Boles?"

He answered in a voice that could be barely understood. "Nowhere." He walked a little faster, but she was wise to him and moved right with him.

"How did that liquor get on your breath?" She smiled a sinister smile, a showing of the teeth that had a bullet in it.

"That's cream soda on my breath. You wrong." He could never lie well when he was drunk, his face usually gave him away. But the lie was weak this time and he knew it.

"You lyin'," she said, nudging him in the side.

Frank lifted his fist as if he was about to punch her, then he burst out laughing. "You crazy, woman."

"You like to beat up womens." She held his arm, stopping him just in time to let a speeding panel truck, loaded with crates of cackling chickens, fly past them.

"Depends." He didn't look at her.

"Depends on what?"

He put his fist in his pants pocket, snorted, and kept walking at a brisk pace. "Depends if the woman put me in a bad spot. But I don't like to do it. Ain't no pleasure in hittin' a woman. A man maybe, but not a gal."

Adele stepped in front of him, glaring. "Glad you said that 'cause I don't fool with mens that go 'round hittin' on womens. Something's wrong with them if they do that. Know what

I mean?"

"A gal can make a man hit her. You know that. Some of them like a man to hit her sometimes. I likes my womens soft, don't want no gal I got to fight an' rassle all the time so she-e-e give me respect."

"No woman likes to be hurt, no woman I know."

He remarked sarcastically, "You mighty evil today. What happened? You an' Nette fall out?"

"None of your business. Where did you get the liquor?"

Frank was persistent. "What you two fight about?" He suddenly turned and trotted off into the shadows. He still had one hand in his pocket, holding himself. Adele could see him leaning against a building, relieving himself, keeping his balance with one arm. When he finished and looked behind him, she had left so he walked home alone.

The next day, Frank awoke with an aching head, speaking of hellfire and damnation, denying all his past sins. He denied his loyalty to whiskey not once, but three times, much as the disciple Peter had done when His Lord's accusers confronted him. Maybe no drunk ever admitted he had a problem. He presented his clean, outspread palms to Adele and swore on a stack of Bibles that not a drop of Satan's oil had passed his lips.

"You's a liar," she whispered.

"Not me," he said incredulously.

She frowned at the stench of his faked sincerity. "Frank, you sick. Everytime you take a drink, you become someone else. Let me finish. A drunk'll ruin everythin' an' everybody he touches. If you want the easy out, why don't you take a gun an' jes' blow your head off?"

He smiled, with an excessive amount of grim pleasure. "You don't know me at all. Who am I hurtin' but myself?" He watched the inviting outline of her lovely butt in her panties. She never wore clothes until she had to leave the house.

There was a long pause.

"Won't you listen to me while you still got some good sense left?" Adele asked. "Last Satiddy, my friends came by to play some cards, an' you strolled in, drunk. You broke up our game, badmouthed my guests, an' embarrassed me. When they went home, I asked you 'bout it an' you got mad. Ain't nothin' wrong with a little sip, you said. You said you's tired of me stayin' on your back 'bout drinkin' an' that you can stop anytime you want."

Frank found himself unable to speak at first. He knew she was right, so right.

"Damnit Frank . . . you have to stop drinkin'. I can't take much more of this," said Adele, bristling. "I can't."

"I can stop drinkin' if I want to. I don't need the bottle to live. I rule it, it don't rule me."

"My pistol is missin' from my drawer," she said accusingly, and they exchanged a long, weary look. "Do you know where it is?"

"Adele, Adele, Adele," he mumbled, then he took a quick breath, relaxed, and glanced around the room.

"An' what happened to my red party dress?" inquired Adele.

Frank shook his head slowly and rolled his eyes innocently at her.

She was ready to scream in frustration. He was lying, lying through his big, yellow teeth. "Sorry honey, I don't believe you. You know what you did to my dress. Know how much I paid for that dress? Never mind that. Why did you shoot holes in my dress, why?"

As her indictment of him persisted, Frank recalled the day he put the dress out of its misery, shot the shit out of it. It died a brave soldier's death. He was high that day, between heaven and earth, drunk out of his mind. That red dress had

220

been taunting him for months and he couldn't take it anymore. She wore it to spite him so other men would look at her body. And probably other ladies as well. The night before, he had found her gun where she had hidden it from him and waited to execute the slutty dress. But why was she 'fraid of him? He would never harm her, not for anything in the world.

"Why did you shoot my dress, my best dress?" She wanted to know, no excuses or lies. "You sick son-of-a-bitch! Tell me!"

If she thinks I's crazy, she'll have me put away in the funny farm, he thought. Anything but that. He was too terrified of her response to tell her why and how he stole her red dress, the tight hussy's dress that often rode up her wide hips. He nailed it to the fence out back and pumped five bullets into it, two in the belly and three near the heart. Wisely, he kept his mouth shut.

Finally he said that he knew nothing about her dress or her missing gun. He lit a cigarette, inhaled deeply and started re-lacing his brogans. That signalled the end of talk on the murdered dress incident. Still Adele didn't talk to him for three days and he felt that was just punishment for his deed.

Chapter 28

"Here, use this." Otis handed Frank a clean, white handkerchief to wipe his red-rimmed eyes. Afraid to intervene and maybe make a stupid move, he let the man flog himself with his sorrow and self-pity. When Frank finished dabbing at his puffy face, Otis asked if there was anything he could do for him, if there was any way he could help achieve some kind of relief. Maybe he needed a woman, that sometimes helped to ease the pressure. Frank had his head down on his arms, crying softly. He gave no answer. Otis wanted to assist him in some way but didn't know how.

"How are you an' Adele doin'?" he asked Frank.

"So-so." There was a nervous tic in one of Frank's eyelids that acted up occasionally, and it did so now.

"When is the last time you worked?"

"Four months ago, pumped gas at a place over near Route 1. The paddy fired me, say I moved too slow. An' he smelt

223

liquor on my breath once or twice, so he thought I drunk on the job."

"That may be the problem 'tween you an' Adele," Otis said quietly. "She might want to see you doin' somethin' with yourself, other than layin' 'round an' drinkin' all the time."

"You right." Frank nodded his agreement with Otis' theory.

"What do you want with Adele? Have you thought 'bout that any? Every gal likes to feel that there's some kind of hope for a future with a man she loves."

Frank gave a tired shrug. "I don't know. 'Sides, I don't think she wants that with me anymore anyway. She's fed up with my mess. She wants me to go."

"Do you know this as fact? Has she said this to your face or are you jes' guessin'?"

Frank measured his friend with his eyes. He said glumly, "I can tell she's fed up, I know it in here." He tapped his finger on his chest near his heart. "A man can tell a thang like that without words. I watch how she treats me an' it's different. She loves me different, talks to me different, everythin' different. Oh, I knows what I knows is true."

A loud pounding on the back door ended their conversation, its surprise made both men wonder about who could it be visiting at this time in the afternoon when everybody was at work. Otis walked to the door and opened it, revealing Frank's two sons, Buddy and Mance. They were eager to see their father. Their search for him had taken them all over the town before the blind man told them where they might find him.

"Is my papa here, Mister Gates?" It was the older boy, Buddy, talking. His younger brother stood behind him, off to his left, barely concealing a small paper sack under his arm. Otis beckoned them to come in, which they did timidly because they were in a strange, new place.

"Yeah, he's here. Come an' give your daddy some sugah."

Frank whirled around in his chair, his muscular arms outstretched, with a bright beacon smile. Happy, the two boys ran into his embrace. Their father hugged them tightly, burying his head between them. Buddy immediately noticed the dark rings surrounding his father's deep-set eyes, spotted the new worry lines in the old man's aging face, smelled the stale liquor breath and the raunchy odor of his clothes.

"Howdy, boys," Frank said, pinching their fat cheeks.

"Hey, papa," they chimed back in chorus.

Frank winked at Otis, so proud that his boys were here with him. They did care after all. It had been over a year since he had seen any of his clan, and he was beginning to worry that nobody cared about him anymore. Out of sight, out of mind.

"You sweatin'. You ain't ailin', is you papa?" Mance asked his father about his health with a concerned look as he sat on one of his father's knees. On the other side of the small room, out of their view, Otis' most recent girl friend joined him to watch the tearful reunion.

"Naw, ain't nothin' wrong with me that a good drink couldn't cure. How's your mama?" Frank poked Mance in the belly and the boy's serious mask melted into a laugh.

"She fine," answered Buddy. "We all fine 'cept we miss Jake an' Teenie. An' you papa. When you comin' home? We miss you real bad. Mama, she miss you too."

After a while, Frank asked, "Your mama know you came to see me?"

Both boys lowered their heads. "Naw, suh."

Their father cleared his throat, picked at a wrinkle in his pants and gazed off. Otis and his friend, sensing this was something private, left the room quietly.

"You still love us?" asked Mance.

Frank rubbed his hand along the side of his jaw, then said that they must know that he loved them, all his children. "Sure do. I love you all to death. Why you ask that?"

Mance stared at the ceiling. "Jes' wonderin', suh."

He knew why his sons were thinking this foolishness; after all, he had deserted them, left them with some fat man. He knew the whole story, at least he thought he did, but he skirted the issue. " 'Member all the tall tales I used to tell you kids at night by the stove. 'Member that?"

They said yes, their eyes all lit up at the memory.

Frank pushed his chair back and his sons found places to sit on a nearby table. Their father wiped away a tear, thinking on that past time. "Boy, we had fun then. That Dit an' Teenie ... they loved a good tale. They sure did ..." His voice lost its steam.

His sons took deep swallows, remembering those days too. They watched Frank closely, sharing his grief.

He coughed once and started running his mouth. " 'Member the one I told you 'bout how the dog got his name. Must have told that thang at least eight hundred times. I still 'member how it went ..." He hesitated for an instant. "When the Maker come to the woods to give the animals some blessings, all the animals were there. Rabbit, squirrel, possum, deer, all there. Everybody 'cept the dog. That ole dog took his sweet time. Supposed to get there at two, he got there at four ..."

"Yeah, we 'member." They answered together.

Both boys had heard the dog story too many times, but, nevertheless, it was the song in the rich, dark tones of their father's voices that captured their attention, that compelled them to listen to the tale as if it was the very first time. They loved how he breathed life and vitality into the words, making the old sound new. And also, his husky talk was much more pleasing than Ellis' high-pitched squealy voice.

"But what happens?" he asked them. But before they could answer, he went on with the tale. "That lazy ol' dog stopped somewhere for a meal along the road, picked up a soup bone. When he got to the meeting place, all the crowd done got their blessings. God looked at the dog and that mutt was all bent over, chewin' an' smackin' on that bone all loud." Frank loved to stretch the end of the story, to play all the parts and raise his small voice to match that of the Almighty.

He pointed his finger at the two of them. "God told that dog, he say since you have gone off an' don't listen to nobody ... I's gone name you dog an' you gone have to eat bones all your live-long days."

He paused, then smiled at Buddy. "What did that dog tell God?"

Buddy, honored to have been chosen, straightened his back. He considered himself to be the example for his younger brother, just as his father was for him. He replied by rote, "The dog talked back to God. He say, you gived everybody else somethin' an' you ain't got nothin' for me. But I don't care. I's gone find my own blessings."

His father nodded that he was correct, and then he asked Mance: "He right 'bout that part. Well, everythang gots a message. The birds gots one. The sun brings one every morning. What's the message in this story?"

Anxious to please, Mance rattled his answer off fast, almost without taking a breath. "The story mean lotta folk think we dogs 'cause we poor an' we ain't been to school, but we can't be what they think we is or what they even want us to be. Or we gone alway be eatin' table scraps like the dog."

Buddy added, "Be on time, right?"

"I got two smart sons." Frank palmed their heads, smiling with pride, a father's smile. But he knew they weren't finished with him. He must give them some answers about what he was going to do. They wanted to know.

"Are you ever goin' to come back to us, papa?" Buddy finally asked the expected question, refusing to be sidetracked.

227

Frank looked away, alarmed. He didn't know what to say at first.

"We miss you bad," said the younger boy.

Their father was pondering his reply, one that would give them hope without being an out-and-out lie. "When I say I still loves you, I mean it. I will alway love you all. But, you see, your mama an' me gots problems. She don't want me 'round there no more. I ain't her kind. She gots a new feller. I did right by you all. I left you all the house 'cause you all needs it more than me." He knew that wasn't enough. That answer wouldn't satisfy a child. Nervously, Frank watched a few cobwebs in the far corner of the room. He hated doing this but he had to do something.

Mance moved closer to his father and hugged him around the neck. "We don't want Ellis there. You . . . our papa an' you should be there with mama an' us."

What could he say to that? The boy was right again. His kids were . . . his responsibility. Frank's eyes lowered for a minute and a vein twitched at his temples. "That fat fool really livin' in my house?"

The boys didn't speak. They only looked at each other.

"Well, is he really there in my house?" asked Frank gravely.

"He don't stay there but he be 'round lots," volunteered Mance. "He was there when Jake died. He stayed for the night." The boy put some emphasis on Ellis spending the night, waiting for his father's jealous response.

"Damn him." Frank grunted, balling up his fists until the skin on them was tight across the knuckles.

"Little Frank stabbed Mister Sam's cow," Mance blurted out. His father's mind was focused elsewhere so he asked the boy to repeat it and he did.

"An' he burned the baby with a hot skillet," Mance continued. "Mama say somethin' really wrong with him now. Know what he done? After he stabbed the cow, he came home

228

with blood all over him. He took a swipe at Buddy with the knife. An' me too. Didn't he, Buddy? Mama came out an' took it away from him but he acted like he wanted to take a cut at her too. He growled at her kinda like."

Frank put his arms around the both of them and asked for more details. "Has he done anythin' since?" They shook their heads in unison.

"What 'bout Bue? Is she behavin' herself?" He turned his despairing glance on the boys.

Buddy's face was impassive. "We's watchin' her an' she ain't did nothin'."

"Now you ask me some questions?" Their father's voice was deep but gentle.

The boys watched him pull a bottle of jake from under the table, mumbling to himself. Their father sighed, sagged a little. Then he closed his yellowed eyes, held them shut for a time, then opened them wide. Great God Almighty, that boy was a constant thorn in his side, but he was here in town and Mary was getting the full blunt of the problem. Little Frank, the idiot. How much was it his fault about the retarded boy? These were thoughts he didn't want to enter his head, like that time in Vicksburg. The boy seemed alright sometimes. The Lord knew he tried to treat the youngun like the others, like he had good sense, like he was a regular child. Normal. But then sometimes the boy would even act up with him, even strike him, hit his big legs with his tiny fists, then scratch and bite anything near his mouth.

"You had bettah straighten out, boy, or that's your ass," Frank had told Little Frank with piercing eyes. "I knows you ain't crazy, you jes' play crazy. You gots them other folks fooled but not me. I knows bettah."

He would scoop the boy up and give him a ride on his back, even though Little Frank was getting too old for that kind of horseplay. Hell, the boy was a wonder, a freak or maybe

229

an idiot. No one could convince him that something was loose in his son's head, not Mary, not Adele, no one. What had his old boss Mister Walters said to him once: "Niggers are the merriest animals on the Lawd's sweet earth. Any coon anywhere, they jes' want the basics. They don't want nothin' much, jes' enough to get by. If they get more than that, they go crazy." Frank thought about that for an instant and attempted to see how those ideas fit his boy's sorry plight. They had nothing to do with the boy. He was another matter. Sometimes he'd just sit there, blank faced and staring at the walls. Sometimes he'd whoop like he was cut or something. For hours, he would crawl on the floor, getting in things, and if Mary tried to pick him up, the boy would curl up like a possum. He would lay on the floor, either dead-still or rocking back or forth. That drove Frank nuts. Yeah, something was wrong with him but no one could tell him that his son, his namesake, was dangerous crazy. He was harmless, just a little bit slow.

"What does the Holy Ghost look like, papa?" asked Mance scratching his head.

"I don't know, boy," his father answered shortly.

"Where does the rain come from?" Mance, again.

"I don't know."

"Why do white peoples have different skin color?" asked Mance, with the studious look of a mule trader.

"I don't know, son." He regretted starting this quiz.

"Did mama ever have a wee-wee?" Mance put his hand in his pocket, afraid to look his father in the face.

He suppressed a wise, amused grin, because he knew the boy didn't mean anything nasty by his question. It was only curiosity, yet he shook a warning finger at the fearful boy. "Boy, I don't want to hear that kind of talk."

Mance ignored his father's rebuke. "What 'bout Grandma Martha?"

"Shut your mouth," Frank said angrily. "You know too much already. That other stuff you'll know soon enough. Stay a kid as long as you can, 'cause bein' an adult ain't no picnic."

The older boy felt left out. "Daddy, mama say it wrong to play with yourself down there. Say you won't grow up normal if you do it. Is she right? Did you ever play with yourself?"

Frank lit a cigarette and reminded himself that he shouldn't drink in front of the boys. But damn, he wanted one right now. "Naw, your mama knows what she's talkin' 'bout. I never touched myself down there an' look how I turned out."

The boys chuckled gaily, so much so that Mance dropped the bag with the peaches, spilling the fruit across the wooden floor. They were on their hands and knees in no time, crawling after the rolling golden spheres. It was supposed to be a surprise, it was.

Frank squatted so he'd see the boys in action. "Who gived the fruit to you? Huh?"

"Some ole white lady on the street near the feed store say we could have 'em for free whilst we's on our way over here," answered Buddy from underneath a rickety chair. "She say we 'mind her of her dead nanny's two little nappy-head boys."

"Did she say nappy-head? Did she say that?" Their father's voice was almost comical.

"Yessuh!" The boys were glad to reply this time.

Frank grabbed his oldest son's arm firmly, not knowing what else to do. "Nevah, nevah, nevah take anythin' from some peck stranger," he warned them with his sternest stare. "An' 'specially somethin' to eat. I mean that. You don't know them peoples, could put a hex or chopped up glass or anythin' in it an' make you sick. Or kill you. Nevah do that. Do you understand me?"

"Yessuh!" Both answered with repentance on their tongues.

"What's gone happen to us now, papa?" asked a tearful

Mance. "Since you been 'way, we 'fraid mama gone leave too. Is she gone leave us too?"

"Naw, she better not." Frank sat solidly on his chair.

"But she might, with Ellis there handlin' stuff," Buddy said, hinting that he knew more than he was saying.

"Would it be better if your mama an' me had stayed together even if we didn't get along?" asked their father. He didn't want them to think that he had runned out on them in their time of need.

"Naw, papa," Buddy said. "But . . ."

"You didn't like all that fussin' an' fightin' goin' on right there 'fore I left, did you boy?" This was the hardest part of the whole affair, leaving away from his kids and not really knowing what was going on back at home, he thought. Probably if he came around there, they could make some arrangement so he could visit once and a while. He knew her. She'd probably leave the house before he would arrive, to avoid harsh talk, so he would have to deal with chubby Ellis. Damn that.

"You didn't have to leave, did you papa?" asked Buddy.

Frank tried several answers on himself but none of them were any good. The room became silent. He regarded them vaguely and let the question go by unanswered.

"I hurt myself." Mance held out his injured hand for his father to see. A minor diversion.

His father took the wounded hand in his own and winced in mock pain. "Oh Lawd, we gone have to get you a new one." And this lightened the mood. Everyone laughed and Otis nudged his girl friend in the next room. He thought the laughter was a good sign.

"You boys oughta get back home 'fore your mama have a fit." Frank walked to the door between the boys. "Don't worry. I's be home real soon. Won't y'all like that?"

Buddy and Mance agreed.

232

He held the door for them and watched their horseplay as they trotted down the street. When he closed the door, he turned around to face Otis and his high-butt girl friend standing there. The woman wore a little less make-up than before. She was giving Frank a hard look while she slid her arm around Otis' roly-poly waist.

"The perfect daddy," she joked and covered her rouged lips. "Jes' pitiful, jes' pitiful."

Frank froze, anger rising in him. But he remembered where he was and who she was, so he behaved himself. Very deliberately, he stepped around her, smiled a Cheshire cat smile, and sat in the same chair as before. Otis offered him a cigarette and he puffed for several seconds in silence, his hands beginning to shake.

"Jes' pitiful, jes' pitiful," the woman repeated.

That was getting to Frank and Otis noticed it. He asked the woman to get him the jar of Vicks to put in his stuffy nose for his head cold. It was buried in a box, he knew she wouldn't find it in a month but he gave specific directions anyway. And off she went.

"Them boys of yourn look like good boys," Otis said.

Frank was staring at the ceiling again. "Yeah, I reckon so. Mebbe I shouldn't have taken a wife. Hell, I messed it all up. Yessiree. I should have knowed I ain't no family man, but I knocked her up, Mary, so that was that." He looked at Otis for a hot second, then glanced back to the ceiling.

"What your chirren like?"

"Alright, they mostly good kids," Frank boasted. "My baby Lincoln, too early to tell 'bout him. Dit's too soft, a follower, but he knows it so he uses his head instead. He lets the others do the hard work. He's the kind of man end up runnin' somethin', you know like a straw boss. Now, Buddy 'bout the best out of the bunch. He's the type who would get up every day an' do what must be done. He takes thangs as they is an' don't want no more than he already got. Mance a fighter. He gone stick up for what he thinks is his an' what he thinks should be his. But he lies too much."

"Ain't there another boy?"

Frank blew out a plume of smoke and glared at Otis through it.

Otis pursued his question. "I heard the boys mention . . . a Little Frank. You don't talk 'bout him much."

"Parents nevah knows which of their younguns gone make it an' which ones jes' ain't got it," Frank began. "I told you 'bout him. Somethin' happened to his head somewhere along the line. He's a little off. An' I gots a gal too, Bue. She gone make a fine wife for some man. She makes me think of Mary when she was younger, act hard but soft as fresh butter on the inside. You knows she'll be there when her man needs her."

Otis shook his head. "How the hell do you know how they'll turn out? You can't predict nothin' with no child."

"Too much doggone responsibility," Frank said it in a flat, lifeless voice.

Otis' woman came back into the room, holding a dark-colored bottle in her hand. She smelled like talcum powder. "Honey, I can't find that Vicks for the life o' me. But mebbe you could put some of this Heet stuff up your nose, that'll chase the cold out of your head for sure." During the entire time of her Heet sales pitch, she stood by Otis' side, hands on hips, but her eyes were on Frank.

The men laughed and Otis asked her if she was crazy. Frank said she should let him put a dab of it up her nose, might loosen her mind a tiny bit.

"The perfect daddy," she teased him. "Jes' pitiful, jes' pitiful."

Chapter 29

Frank hurried to the big, brown house, Matt's jook joint, looked around, up and down the street, then went upstairs. The man with the gimp leg checked him in the main door with a dour expression, and led him up another set of stairs. Frank could hear the rocking sound of music through the wall, good down home blues. A few people standing at the entrance moved aside to let him pass. After a brief survey of the dance floor, he decided that he didn't know anyone there, not even the sad-faced man standing by the window dispensing the paper cups full of corn whiskey. The head of a light-skinned man bobbed as he pounded a piano into joyous submission, accompanied by another man playing a harmonica and a tricky-fingered guitarist, who looked sleepy. Stationed in front of the musicians were two singers, a man and a woman, slickly dressed. Frank laughed to himself, noting how the lights caught the glimmer of the male singer's head. Both entertainers seemed drunk or close to it. In between numbers and the hurrah of the crowd, the two would down a few gulps.

The music never stopped. Everybody was talking, singing, and dancing all at once. The place was jumping! Among the revelers, Frank spotted a few of the Holiness people, the back-sliders, several drifters, two or three medicine men from the Dixie road show parked just outside of town. He searched the mob for a glimpse of "Pine Top" Hawkins, the best piano player in the area, checking each face, but the well-known basher of the ivories was not to be found.

Every tune sounded faster than the one before it. He loved to watch people dance. One woman, with a low-cut dress, was snapping her fingers over her head as she shook her wide ass to the steady beat. Many of the old heads there did a dated shuffle, nothing to work up a sweat though. Once and a while, someone would step out from the group, do some spins and twists to leave the others wanting more. Lovers were snuggled up, belly to belly, whispering heatedly in each other's ear.

He stood safely off to the side, watching. Often in the mid-dle of a tune, some bad bucks would start cussing bad, push-ing and shoving, or going for their pistols. He wanted no part of that, so he preferred to watch. Most of the players that worked at Matt's knew its rowdy reputation and usually set up the stage near a door or a window, insuring their escape if the crowd got out of hand. Word was out about the gun-play and knife-throwing that sometimes took place here. According to the veterans, it was a tradition carried over from slavery times, the wild and raunchy Saturday rumble. Onliest thing he ever did exciting on a Saturday night before he came to Clarksdale was throwing a brick at a guy who cheated him at cards, Frank mused. That was funny.

The male singer swept a couple strands of processed hair back from his glassy eyes and sauntered across the stage, wiggling his hips to the ladies' delight. This happened only after the band had been playing a lazy, simmering blues at a breakneck clip for about three minutes. The singer paused, feeling out his audience. He knew them well. Just then a shout from the back of the room sent heads spinning, but he ignored it, and went on with his slow introduction to the next song, a suggestive ditty from Tampa Red named "She Loves So Good." By the volume of noise from the cheers, Frank could tell it was a favorite of the house.

More stragglers were coming in the door, pointing at a square-headed man, his shirt open to his navel, doing splits in a corner of the dance floor. On the stage, paper cups were making the rounds again. Laughing between lyrics, the male singer sang the bass part of the song, rocking back on his heels, while the woman did the falsetto. They cut up something awful, bumping and grinding against each other. Frank surmised that the mean-looking crooner was slipping it to her when they weren't doing the shows, probably a nice roll too. People on the floor loved their insinuating antics and singing, clapping and stomping in tune to the heated words of the song:

"I've got a gal, she's low and squatty,
I mean boys, she'll suit anybody.
She loves so good,
She loves so good,
And everybody likes her, 'cause she loves so good.

Last night she loved me for a while,
You could hear me holler MMMMMM! for a mile,
She was loving me good,
Aw, she loves me so good,
And everybody loves her, 'cause she loves so good.

Sometimes she makes me sneeze, sometimes she makes me cough,

237

Lawd, you ought to see her when she starts me off,
Aw, so good,
Aw, she loves me so boogie-woogishly,
And everybody wants her, 'cause she loves so
peculiar.

Last night, while I was sound asleep,
I felt a funny feeling from my head to my feet,
Well, she was loving me so good,
Aw, she was loving me so differently,
And everybody wants her 'cause she treat me so
kind."

Then the woman broke in moaning, singing, twisting and wringing her hands, feeling all over the man, then all over herself. That excited the crowd. She gapped her legs while whimpering, panting, hissing:

"Aw yes . . . honey baby . . . yes lover . . . jump
me . . . daddy anythin' you want . . . kiss me now
. . . oh right there . . . yes right there . . . that's
the spot . . . jes' the tip . . . oh oh oh so so good
. . . so so so good . . . yessssss yessssss . . ."

After she ended her turbulent storm of emotion, he came back to wrap it up, beckoning to her with his lewd movements, hair flying behind him, singing wantonly:

"She was born in Kentucky, raised in Tennessee,
Come all the way from Dixie to put that Thang on
me . . ."

Still in perpetual motion, he turned to the crowd, saying in a roguish way, ". . . not the best in the world, but the best

I ever had." Suddenly he spinned in his tracks, dropped to one knee, holding out his hand to the audience, singing in a hair-raising voice that made the folks squeal:

" 'Cause everybody wants her,
Lawd, she loves so, oh, so goooood."

With that, he hit a nerve, and everybody clapped, shouting encouragement. Fine applause. Maybe these singers were not originals, the real McCoys, but the crowd there at Matt's was crazy about them, and for good reason. They sang along, whooping and hollering. Chuckling at the lyrics as if it was their first time hearing them, when it was not. It was the feeling and spirit of the place that Frank liked the most, the knack for letting anybody be at ease and kick up their heels. But at your own risk. Still, he thought, it was worth it.

On through the night, the singers and their musicians worked the audience to a fever pitch, so rough, so free and easy. No let-up. The big women lost their minds, imagining the men's fingers caressing their hot flesh, screaming and tossing their hefty arms and legs. Two were carried out, one of them sporting a deep gash on her cheek. Another split her dress in the heat of the moment. The whole crew was jerking, prancing, much like a seizure or a fit, under the spell of the wailers throwing their souls and hearts into each torrid note.

When a couple would get away, get fancy, people crowded around them, cheering. Boy, they'd strut then! With the man rocking and rolling his pelvis, his female partner took center-stage, enthusiastically shimmying, mumbling phrases, humping the air, to the appreciative roar of the onlookers. Then she threw her head back, gyrating her belly like the demon spirit was upon her, hair all sweated out and yellow grease running down her tortured face. The man, cool and calm, adjusted his stingy brim at a rakish angle, popped his fingers, and put that extra bend in his knees.

Frank continued to look around for someone he knew, even walking around the dance floor five times, only stopping to have a few drinks. He danced twice with a slick-haired woman, very closely cut, who whispered to him: "I got somethin' for you if your health can stand it." He turned it down, choosing to make one more sweep around the floor. Onstage, the man on the harp and the piano player were fighting it out in a battle royal, adding some thunder to a Memphis Minnie blues song, with the woman vocalist sounding again in fine form. He had had enough. He left the noise, the liquor, the funk, the laughter behind him, and started down the stairs for home. Upon arriving, he discovered Adele was not there, her bed had not been slept in, so he walked the streets for the remainder of the night, restless and angry at her betrayal.

Chapter 30

Adele gunned the motor of the sputtering Chrysler, weaving in and out of the flow of traffic on the highway, glancing up at the rear view mirror as she pulled onto a shoulder alongside a drainage ditch. She wanted to get out to stretch her cramped legs. Her heart beat faster when she remembered her destination. Nette, Nette, get out of my mind! she cursed to herself. There was a lukewarm Coke stashed under the front seat that would provide her with a brief lift, just in case. Why did that gal have to come all the way out here to this hell-hole? What was she running from? What had she done now? A thick, dry lump rose in her parched throat, causing a vile taste to rush into her mouth, and she spat it out on the road. She got out, walked around to the other side of the car, and sat on the fender, with her legs dangling. She stayed there for a few minutes while she wept quietly. What was she going to do with Frank? He had to go, but how?

241

Like clockwork, the 2:30 Greyhound local went speeding past on the blacktop, enroute to Vicksburg, and overhead, the sun heated up. She thought of Alligator, and what Nette would be doing in a small, out-of-the-way place like that. That puzzled her to no end. She'd know the answer soon enough. She reached inside the car and flicked the radio on for any kind of music. Even hillbilly songs would be better than nothing, something to let her know that she was still in the land of the living.

The radio crackled, sounded off with a pop, and static. Eventually, a redneck's voice drifted to her through the electrically induced soup: ". . . Those big spending liberal communists in Washington want us to turn the country over to the niggers. Look at Little Rock, Birmingham, Montgomery, all through our beloved South. Our traditional values and beliefs are bein' destroyed by those reds and their puppets, Martin Luther Coon and that SCLC and NAACP. We better wake up 'fore it's too late. Up North, nigger hoodlums are runnin' the cities, terrorizing decent white folk, good God-fearin' white folk who have to lock themselves in their houses to stay alive. The commie unions are pattin' the nigger criminals on the backs, yelling Go-Go-Go! We, America, need a new sense of direction, need to look back to the glory of our honorable past, and return to the old basic values that made this nation great. What's wrong with turning the clock back to the way thangs used to be? Who can tell me that the way thangs are now are better than they were before? They would be a liar. Women need to turn back to the Scripture and take God to their bosoms. They need to take off all that make-up, stop wearin' pants. Men wear pants, not women. They need to go back to the kitchen where they belong. We need to get government off our backs, tellin' us what to do with our women and children. Do you want a nigger riding on a bus or train with your wife or daughter, sittin' there beside them? Or in the same school? Wake up, America! If you agree with me and believe that this country is in a moral crisis, a spiritual crisis, write me. Let me know what you think. And if you can, send a dollar or two so we can continue to get the word out to those who believe in democracy and the American way ..."

Adele laughed to herself, turning the dial again. That was the angle, selling fear to make money. The cracker probably was raking it in, scaring the shit out of these good Christian people, the Russians and niggers are coming. Watch out! Oh, the Southern way of life. Some of them still fighting the Civil War, damn Yankees to hell was the motto. She had other things to think about, Nette for one, and how to kick Frank out was the other.

Back on the road. It was another steamy twenty minutes of finding her way through a network of twisting dirt lanes before she arrived at Nette's Alligator hide-out; a small, tin-roofed shanty down a long, muddy path. She parked the car under a group of pecan trees, mindful of the hot plastic seats, and took the crumpled paper sack, full of her clothes, from the trunk. She was burning up.

"Anybody home?" yelled Adele.

A new, improved Nette was swatting at a threatening bumblebee, swinging and missing, hopping around the room elf-style. Her back was to Adele when she entered. "I see you got my message," she told her visitor. "Have a seat." Piles of freshly washed clothes covered every available resting place, including the much abused plaid couch and crippled table near the front door. Nothing much on the walls but a Clapper Girl calendar and a snapshot of a young black girl having her high cheekbones licked by a bloodhound. So, Adele stood watching her friend chase the elusive insect in the suffocating space of the tiny room, slashing the air with crumpled newspaper, growing more frenzied with each attack.

243

The bee dived at her head and she ducked, a close call.

"Why did you decide to come back to me now?" Nette asked, looking over her shoulder. "Why do you want me now, Adele? Is he tired of you? Is that it?"

"Who said I was comin' back, Nette? Maybe I jes' want to talk to someone else, jes' want to talk to someone who might know what I's talkin' 'bout. Honey, don't pat yourself on the back yet."

"But what have I done to you?" Nette was genuinely shocked at her friend's attitude. She walked to a far corner of the room, propped herself against the brickpaper wall, staring at Adele in disbelief.

Adele pretended to be happier than she actually was, on the aloof side. However, it was a poor act. Her fortunes had not been this low since she married a weight-lifter from Natchez, an ill-fated union that lasted every bit of three years until she became fed up of his wide-open affairs with anything wearing a dress. Yes, three years in hell. At that time, she earned her keep as a warden for second-graders in a third rate, make-shift school outside of Tallulah, wasting most of her classes shouting over their shrill yells. Her muscle-bound husband played baseball, left field, for a dairy sponsored team in the colored leagues. The scoop on him was his weakness for a fastball, missed it every time. He struck out in the bedroom, too. No peter there at all. Somewhere along the way, she discovered the forbidden love of women, the gentler sex, experimenting, dabbled in it on occasion. She needed relief from sexless nights, empty bed nights, punched-in-the face nights, and the best remedy for a long time was the safe harbor of another woman's arms. Nette, unfortunately, had been her first real relationship, romance with a butch-sheik, and it bothered her that this Florida woman still had such a grip on her.

"Why ain't you back in Clarksdale with the baby maker?"

244

Nette asked, with venom in each word.

"I don't want to talk 'bout that mess right now." Adele flashed a fake grin that wouldn't have lit up a small matchbox. "I ain't here to cry on your shoulder, I don't want no pity or sympathy. Naw, no thank you."

"Why are you here?"

"I need a friend," Adele whispered finally.

Nette stood up. "When you wanna talk 'bout the bastid, we will. Take your time."

Adele cleared a place for herself on the worn out couch, sobbing, her breath catching in her throat. Her ex-lover stood looking down at her now, waiting for the proper time to provide comfort. When Adele finally quieted, Nette lifted her and stood her on her feet. The soul-weary woman swayed briefly and Nette put her arms around her, holding her up. Adele wrinkled her nose at the sight of her yellow fingertips, from burning that nicotine. Plus Nette was loud, gambled with the best of them, cracked jokes, and was very allergic to bras. She always smiled, it seemed. They joked about her collection of bow ties, loved bow ties, all colors, all sizes. While they were close, her eyes looked into Adele's, and familiar sensations shot through the divorced woman's body, bittersweet waves of hot sensuality.

Adele wrenched herself free, leaving only one of her hands captive. "Let's jaw some. I don't feel like no huffin'-puffin' today. Alright?"

"What you give me is deep an' satisfyin'," Nette murmured. "Alway feel like I's meltin' or somethin'. I never felt that before or since." A long pause, then the plea. "Don't take that away."

Adele waited a cold second more, then she withdrew her hand. "But you use me, baby. You used me like a man would use you, beat me up an' put me through more hell than this hick farmer could ever think up. I's your fatted calf, but no more. It can't ever be that way again."

"So why do you have that cotton picker livin' at your house?" Nette was furious. "What the fuck is he doin' for you? Huh? You knows he ain't nothin' but dead weight."

"Wait a damn minute!" Adele came forward a step and fronted Nette. "An' what did you ever do for me but kick my ass? You an' my first husband would've been a top-rate team, two jackasses!"

"You ever love me, Adele?" Her aggressive stare played on her foe's breasts, then on her belly and thighs. Nette quelled an urge to touch Adele's breasts, to move her hands over them, lightly caressing their soft roundness. The bitch is crazy as hell, Nette told herself.

Adele said nothing. She saw Nette's expression change to bewilderment, surprise, then to barely restrained anger.

"Is his dick that big?" Nette asked.

"leave Frank out of this!" snapped Adele.

"You's right . . . you's right . . . ," Nette stopped in mid-sentence. "I meant no offense. I don't know why I said that trash, jes' upset, I reckon. Upset that I can't have you the way I want you. All mine."

"You got any cigarettes? No menthol, please."

"Here." Nette took a cigarette from her battered pocketbook, which hung limply over the head of the fold-up bed, almost totally hidden by clothes. The flap on the purse laid back like an open wound. She handed the cigarette to Adele and lit it for her. "Come, lay on the bed with me."

"No tricks, gal."

"What tricks?" Nette asked in a tone of feigned shock.

"You knows what I mean." Adele was not softening.

"No funny stuff, alright." She glared at Adele when she sat on the bed beside her, making the bed sag and groan. She spent several seconds doing this before she put fire to the rolled tobacco stick in her hand. Was this the end? Was

246

it all over? Still she wanted this woman badly, to hold her again and make love to her. Once she was closer to her former lover, she tried to kiss her but Adele turned her head at the last moment, and the kiss missed its mark. She attempted to stroke her arm but Adele pulled away. She imagined that Adele let her do as she pleased, sucking and licking her nipples to a throbbing hardness, finger-touching her smooth thighs. And when she thrust her fingers into Adele's wetness, between her legs, Adele spread her legs and surrendered. In the old days, Adele could never get enough.

"If I let you, you'd have me back where I was," Adele panted hoarsely, feeling the heat. "You'd have me crazy . . . crazy, but I can't go backwards. I can't do that."

"Why? Why don't you want me no more?"

"Thangs have changed. I's changed." Adele smoked her cigarette and moved farther away from Nette on the bed. "I ain't here for lovin'. I want your friendship."

Nette pursed her full lips. "Did you ever feel anythin' for that cotton picker? Be truthful."

A silence followed, and the husky, raucous talk of field-hands walking to a roadhouse for a night of free-wheeling drinking wafted to them through the wall from the outside, drifting over the two women sprawled on the bed.

"Do you love him?" Nette asked again.

"Naw, I did 'fore," answered Adele, lying, staring into space. For a moment, she couldn't bear to have Nette so close to her, couldn't stand her touch, her mannish clothes, hair-cut, and ways. The tears came again, backed by strong sobs. Nette cupped her gently around the nape of the neck, press-ing her friend's face to her breast, muting her cries with her body.

"Ain't you gone answer my question 'fore you go home?" Nette asked. "Or are you gone keep me guessin'. That ain't no good."

247

"You'll have an answer 'fore I leave. Count on that. Let it ride for now." It was neither a request or a demand, but a mixture of both.

Taking her cue, Nette went on to something else, another subject. "Gal, I's done thangs my mama only dreamt of. You know somethin', I believe my mama went for womens, too. I really believe that."

"Why?" That revelation aroused Adele's curiosity.

"Queenie." That was Nette's name for Adele when she was feeling good about her friend, an endearing label. "Queenie, my mama never let another man set foot in our house after daddy left. Left mama for a New Orleans coochie-coo gal. A stripper. Mama had no men friends, but plenty of gals spent the night."

Both women laughed heartily.

"You know what I always wanted to do, but nevah had the chance?" Adele asked, stubbing out the cigarette on a snuff can top. "Bet you'll nevah guess."

"What? Tell me."

"Don't laugh. It's silly, but I always wanted to hold a man's half-hard dick while he pissed. Foolish, ain't it?"

Nette almost laughed but caught herself. "Once I had a terrible longing for my father to hold me, to hug me, but he never did. Real mens don't hug their daughters. Folks might talk." Her words trailed off. The tightening of her jaw and the quiver in her throat made talking difficult for her. "I wanted that real bad. Daddy went to his grave nevah havin' touched me, nevah havin' hugged me or said a kind word to me. A Christian man, yes Lawd. One thang folks can't say is that he lusted after me, that cold cucumber."

"Is that why you lust after womens, Nette?" Adele loved the really rare times when Nette revealed herself, talked about her past and let her guard down. "Tell me your secret."

"That ain't it," Nette said a little later, in a choked voice.

248

"Looka here. I didn't even cry when daddy died, but I did when you left me. You hurt me so bad."

Nette never stopped smoking, one cigarette after the other. Sometimes Adele made sense, she thought, when she went to the heart of things. But today was not one of those times, she was cloaking something.

"Do you have any quinine in the house?" Adele asked, totally at ease now.

"Naw. Why do you need quinine?"

"Never mind."

"Is you sick? What ails you?"

"Nothin'. I's alright."

"Now tell me why you became a bulldagger." Adele was sitting up, with her arms draped around her knees.

"Don't use that word in this house," Nette said, gritting her teeth.

"Tell me why you gave up mens. You promised to tell me long time ago, you never did."

"Not now."

Nette measured her friend's body with her eyes, examining every hill and valley of it in adoring glances. So different from her. Hers was strangely masculine, fleshy, full figured with wide shoulders, large breasts, and the face of a riverboat pilot.

"What you thinkin' 'bout so hard, Adele?"

"Nothin'. Jes' thinkin'."

Adele sighed as her friend's plump lips touched hers, and their eyes met again for an instant. And suddenly, the woman reached under her, feeling her breasts through her blouse, and their bodies came together in the roaring flame of passion.

"Don't." Adele held a hand between them, pushing Nette away from her.

"What can he do for you that I can't?" asked Nette, playfully pinching her friend's arm.

"What do you think?"

"Well, he can't touch what we had. We had somethin' special, an' you knows that."

"The past is past." Adele sat back, watching Nette.

Adele caught Nette's hand in hers. "Like Grandma used to say, 'all that rollin' 'round an' nothin' goin' in. She had a point."

Nette didn't want to hear anything like this. "She can't say nothin' 'bout it unless she's tried it. My mama used to say that too, but she changed her mind. I knows she did. Damn, she threw out all her dresses an' stayed in pants. Unladylike, huh? The ole biddy told me I'd be punished for pussylickin', as she called it, an' the wrath of God would surely send me to hell. I'd fry forever." Nette watched her hands for a time. "Adele, Frank's a dumb bastid."

"That ain't true," Adele said. "Frank's a damn sight better than my ex-husband. My husband wanted a mother, a nurse, a whore, all in one. I jes' wanted to be his wife. But he nevah let me. The fool didn't like to have sex normal, he was always tryin' to put hisself in my behind. I can't stand that."

"Mens is a waste of time," advised Nette. She considered giving Adele a brief lecture on the evil of Men, the deadly trap of Family, the curse of Children, and the agony of keeping up a "happy" Home. But she decided against it.

"Ain't I right, Queenie?" Nette asked, folding her arms.

Adele leaned forward, making a face. "There's more to mens than what's 'tween their legs. I learnt that with Frank. He can be decent sometimes. I took him in 'cause he needed help."

"How you give that help, on your back?" Nette got nasty.

"What are you 'fraid of, Nette?" taunted Adele. "What is it? You 'fraid of bein' hurt by a man, you 'fraid of gettin' a disease, you 'fraid of givin' in to a man, you 'fraid of bein' used an' throwed away, you 'fraid of bein' not sexy enough to hold a man, you 'fraid of bein' a mother, you 'fraid to stop hatin' yourself, you 'fraid to stop feelin' like shit. What is it?"

"You a doctor now with all them damn questions? Tell me this, tell me that."

Adele plucked the smoldering cigarette from Nette's grasp and puffed it. "What are you hidin' from me? Ain't no reason why you can't answer my question? Nobody gone hear what you tell me here."

"I knows that," Nette began slowly. "I don't want to talk 'bout it. What's this? You havin' second thoughts 'bout how you live, gal? Well, why you like gals?"

"I was born that way," answered Adele. It sounded like a bad joke, but nobody laughed.

"Okay." Nette moved closer to Adele on the bed, arms behind her head. "I was the boy my papa never had. He never had one, but he wanted one real bad, so he raised me like one until he left. For a long time, I never felt like I was any sex, didn't know what I was. That's until I first had sex with a woman. Ain't no man ever touched me that way. I never let them get that close. I knowed early on that I's a woman that a man's body couldn't satisfy, that I was different, that what was unnatural for others was natural for me." She was talking a mile a minute, saying things that she hadn't told anyone before.

"Doggone." Adele muttered to herself, noticing Nette's broad shoulders and absent hips, stunned at how odd she suddenly felt. Something about all of this bothered her in a way it had never done previously.

Nette scratched her cheek. Quietly, she got up and kneeled on the floor and reached under the bed, pulling out a small tin box. She opened it, rolled three reefer sticks, and they smoked them slowly, one after another. By the time the women had finished the second stick, they were giggling like schoolgirls, feeling high and mellow. Nette eased back on the bed, licking her lips, moving her long red tongue sideways in quick, teasing flicks. She regarded herself to be the finest female lover in those parts, no big feat, for her kind were few in number.

"What you thinkin'?" asked Adele.

"Nothin'." Nette blinked, holding the reefer between her fingers. Her teeth were on edge.

"What is it, Nette? Tell me."

Adele inhaled the sweet, pungent marijuana smoke deeply, feeling it go straight to her head. It relaxed her and the ill sensation she felt earlier passed as quickly as it had come upon her. "What's botherin' you, woman?"

"I'd like to knock the hell out of you right now." Nette smiled coldly. Whether she was joking or not, her words carried a hard, true edge to them.

Adele turned angrily. "Don't threaten me. I don't scare so easily no mo'. You jes' went too far an' you won't use me again, ever. I mean that."

That narcotic stick was handed to Nette, who immediately put it to her lips. "Tell me 'bout the baby maker."

"Tell me 'bout them young gals. Which one you sleepin' with now?"

"Who you kiddin'? You ain't no angel. You left me for that stupid cotton picker. You did that to me. You hurt me, hurt me bad."

"Hush up!" Adele cut her eyes at Nette. "I said what I had to say. You reap what you sow. Who made life hell for me? Who gave me heartache? Who made me eat a yard of her shit? You, you ... I tried to hold on, you stomped on what I felt for you, pissed on it. You want to hear the truth, that's it."

Unable to meet Adele's searing glance, Nette flipped over on the bed, face down, and cried. Her words were tangled in the soft down of the quilt. "My ass has been draggin' 'round for weeks since you left. I don't want to hear any of this. You was the best damn thang that ever happened in my life. Don't hurt me like this."

"You disgust me," snarled Adele. "You ain't cried 'fore. I ain't moved by it. It won't work, Nette."

"So what happens now?" yelled Nette. "Say it, goddamn it. Get it over with."

Adele's voice was emotionless, matter-of-fact. "I don't want to see you again after today, Nette. Never. It's over 'tween us, through. Finished."

"What you mean?"

"I ain't comin' back to you. It's over."

Nette wiped her eyes with the back of her hand and tried to steady herself, but the rage was still there. "I don't care what you do. You jes' a snappin' pussy, some bitch I helped out once."

"Watch what you call me, watch your mouth," Adele said tonelessly, smoking the last of the stick.

"I don't need nothin' from you or nobody else." Nette sucked her teeth and rolled her puffy eyes.

The tears ran down her face, sour tears, down onto her neck and hands and she made no attempt to wipe them away this time. She was full of pain, depressed and ashamed, because she realized she was responsible for the end of their relationship. She had abused her power over Adele, becoming ridiculous in her demands. She messed it all up. Everything had come full circle, her reduced to tears and begging for another chance, and Adele in complete command. The irony of the situation was not lost on her. Never had she been so stricken, so defenseless.

"You ain't liable for my pain. It's me, my own doin'." Nette shuddered, and a choked cry came from somewhere inside her. She sniffled and tried to regain control of herself. "I don't want it to be like this, jes' over. It hurts, Adele, it hurts."

"It hurts me too," Adele said tonelessly.

An instant later, Nette sighed and slumped against her former lover. She wanted reassurance, some consolation, something. But there was nothing there. Adele didn't move away from her nor did she hug her, no resistance was offered nor comfort.

Finally she sat up and Nette grabbed her arm. Adele told her in her most frosty voice that she had to go and that she should think about what happened between them so it would never occur again, so no one else would get hurt. She lit a cigarette, blew a few nonchalant smoke rings, and started toward the door, with Nette still hooked on her arm.

Adele stroked her former sweetheart's agonized face lovingly and said icily, "Bye, baby. 'Member what I said an' don't come 'round my house. I don't want to see you."

Nette appeared puzzled, shocked, her eyes still brimming with tears. "Naw, Adele, naw . . . you can't . . . I love you, gal. I can change. Wait an' see. I can do bettah."

"I *loved* you. That's over." Adele forcibly removed the weeping woman's hand from her arm and shoved her away. She didn't like this scene at all. It was against everything in her character and upbringing, this coldness, yet it had to be done. Undaunted, Nette grabbed her hand and began kissing it, with her eyes pleading for another chance. A detached expression settled on Adele's face as she jerked away from the nearly hysterical woman, raising her own hand as if she wanted to strike Nette, and after a long moment of tension, she went outside.

Chapter 31

Sometime well after three that next morning, Frank stumbled along a vacant street, coming once again from Matt's jook joint, eyes bloodshot and glazed. He ignored a group of young rowdies that passed him, with girls on their burly arms. All drunk, desperately seeking excitement. Thrills. They brushed against him, shoving him a bit as they walked by, and one of them spat at him. He ignored the insult and pressed on toward home, wobbling. The biggest of the bunch, a wiry-haired brute dressed in khaki work clothes, followed the intoxicated man, imitating his faulty steps while the others laughed and mocked him.

"What you-u-u . . . you's got in mind, good peoples?" Frank slurred, jerking his head around to look at them.

"Your mama gone kick your ass when you get home," one teased, seizing the drunk by the shoulder. This set his friends off again, cackling in loud guffaws.

255

"Got any money, nigger!" The big guy said, approaching Frank with fists poised for action.

"Look in his pockets," yelled another one. "Country niggers loves to tote all they money 'round with them. Dumb bastids."

Somebody tripped Frank, sending him crashing to the ground, but he snatched one of the girls down with him. He felt shoes kick him in the side, the stomach, and the back, as they struggled with him. He caught two or three punches in his face but kept his feet this time, turned and hit the man nearest to him, a nice chopping blow. Colored against colored, he thought while he tried to shield his face with his forearms. One of the man's friends dived at Frank, who dropped to his knees, letting his attacker sail over him, and suddenly he lunged at the brute. Frank hit the big man twice and the man went down heavily on his side. In the darkness, he recognized two of the men as loafers that hung out at a roadhouse just outside of town, two really rough customers. One grabbed him by the throat and forced his bleeding head toward the ground as the others threw powerful punches at his body, sometimes jerking his head from side to side with their impact. Frank jumped one of his assailants, getting a handful of his face and bending him backwards. The loafers rushed him, one high and the other low, and they pinned him. Out of nowhere, a sharp blow carrying the sock of a billy-club smashed into Frank's forehead, opening it up, blurring his vision. Intense pain swelled behind his eyes and a flash of white light engulfed him and then everything went soundlessly dark.

The first thing he heard when he revived was the squeals of the girls, and the gumbo voice of the brute saying something about Nette not wanting him killed, just roughed plenty good so he'd get the message. What was the message? Somebody should tell him, he thought as he lay watching their shoes step near his dirt-smeared face. One attacker came and kneeled next to him. He didn't expect the vicious uppercut Frank shot into his unprotected chin, and an instant later, blood spurt out from his nose and mouth onto the farmer underneath him. Frank scrambled to his feet, swinging wildly, cursing. He heard someone behind him and tried to sidestep whatever blow was coming, but not fast enough. He felt a hot prick of pain surge through his skull and he collapsed.

"Don't let him up!" someone shouted.

With much effort, Frank crawled forward on all fours, trying to pull himself, aching so badly, knowing that he was about to lose consciousness. He loathed them, hated them without understanding. Why him? Why did Nette suddenly want to see him hurt? Why? Why?

They surrounded him quickly, kicked him, and spat on his sprawled body which bounced and jerked with each lick. Realizing that the assault was not about to let up for a second, Frank protected his blood-covered face the best he could, shielding it with his injured hand. He fought back, throwing roundhouse rights and lefts, attempting to beat them off. Their punches came faster, in waves. His split head snapped back, then whipped to the side, strings of fresh blood flying off in a thick spray.

"Kill him! Kill the hick bastid!" someone yelled.

"Kick him in the balls! Kick him 'tween the legs!" He heard a whiny female voice cry out.

When Frank tried to get up again, one of them popped him in the mouth, solid, but he didn't pass out again. The pain, instead, doubled him over. One of the loafers came closer, so he could go in Frank's pockets. There was more blood oozing from the side of Frank's torn mouth, not a lot, not enough to make him give in. He hurled a straight right at the man, catching him high on the cheekbone, clicking his teeth together so hard that he almost bit his tongue off. Soon the man's legs gave out under him and he fell on his ass.

"Spread his legs, hold his hands!" It was the brute's voice, sounding tight and hurt. They handled Frank's arms, twisting them back cruelly, his head hung forward, limply, and he felt shoes thud savagely into his groin. Again, again, and again. His scream sperished in his throat as the dull, consuming pain ripped through him, causing him to spew more blood and vomit from his cracked lips. Kick him, kick him, he heard in a fading echo.

Chapter 32

The ice man discovered his unconscious body two hours later, sent for the sheriff, and they loaded Frank Boles into the patrol car and delivered him to his home. Adele knew what had happened immediately. She quickly linked the attack on Frank to her break-up with Nette, knowing this was her former lover's way of warning her that there would be no peace for her until they reunited. The swelling between his legs, especially around his privates, seemed to take forever to subside, and it was a good three weeks before he could leave the bed for even short walks.

When Frank was feeling better, Adele suggested that they take a drive so he could get some fresh air and stretch his legs. He was reluctant at first, arguing and complaining that he had not recovered fully. She protested loudly and he finally submitted to her wishes.

Limping badly, he walked to the car and got in on the passengers' side. He wore his blue checkered shirt buttoned at the neck and brown cotton pants. Adele, seated to his left, was dressed in a simple light green gingham affair which flared over her legs while she drove the car with both hands on the wheel. She rolled down the window on her side, just a hair, then halfway. The breeze was tame and soft on their faces, going through the car like a cottonmouth. After a brief coughing fit, Frank inhaled and let the air out slowly. One of Adele's hands wandered from the steering wheel and touched his knee, the one closest to her. He kept his eyes straight ahead. A car, full of young white boys, flew past them and back into their lane and down a street to their left. They drove on, out beyond the town's outskirts, and eventually they turned onto a gravel road.

Adele sped up, and the car rounded a bend in the road, going full tilt. Frank looked at her nervously but she didn't pay him any mind. In the distance, Frank spotted pecan groves, farmers toiling behind mules and hand plows, sawmills, packing plants, snuff factories, dry creek beds, and low flat land. Then came a small rise by a levee and a lake beyond that, and he decided that this was the perfect place to stop. She agreed, pulled the car up on the embankment, and rolled down her window, all the way. Sticking out her slender arm, she yanked the door open and got out. The door had been broken for months and Cephus, the car's owner, really didn't care if it ever got fixed, as long as the car ran. They walked to the levee's edge, saying nothing, only peering into the brackish water. For a lake this size, the water was unusually deep, maybe eight men deep. Birds played in the cypress and willow trees across on the far bank, darting from branch to branch. The silent couple listened to the sound of the water polishing the rocks, rippling slightly, as it flowed past. Adele sat on the car's bumper, smoking another cigarette, watching the water come and go.

The solitude of the spot pleased Frank, and he tossed looks back and forth between the depths of the murky lake and Adele's wasp waist, her brown kinky-curl hair, her better-than-average sized breasts, and her finely tapered legs. Yes, the woman was a honey. He loved her, couldn't hurt her for the world.

"It sure was nice of that man to let you use his car," Frank said, feeling good to be outside. "What you call him?"

Adele was distracted but answered anyway. "Who? Oh, Cephus. Yeah, he's real nice."

"What he do for a livin'?" He limped over to her.

"Can't tell you. Ain't none of your business no how."

His eyes narrowed, then he laughed. "Must be doin' dirt for the peckerwoods."

"Naw, it ain't nothin' like that. Frank, have you stopped drinkin' altogether? You ain't still drinkin' on the sly, is you?"

"Nope, stopped cold." Frank fidgeted with his hands, his face very solemn. "That stuff ain't no good for me, I knows that now. Makes me act a fool so I don't need it. Anythin' that be on your mind all the time ain't no good, gotta have a drink, gotta have a drink. Naw, it can't be no good. No matter what it is, ain't no good. That's why I put liquor down."

"What's on your mind, Frank?" asked Adele. "Your face went blank like you was thinkin' hard 'bout somethin'."

He was staring across the water at three fishermen wading on the other side, with their gear held high above the swirling wetness. "I decided not to put the boy away."

She exhaled smoke and asked why. "Frank, if the boy need treatment, you should do it. Ain't nothin' shameful in admittin' a true fact. The boy might need special care an' you can't give him that."

"I believe that I can handle him. He ain't that crazy. Shit, ain't nobody in our family ever needed to be locked in some funny farm. We take care of our own."

Adele fumed, "That ain't no reason to keep him from gettin' the help he need. If you love him, that's what you told me, then you should let him get help."

His face was almost serene. "Baby, was you out to see Nette? You want that bitch back even after she treated you like you was lower than snake shit. Yeah, I's a hick whatever you call me but I knows when somethin' ain't right. That gal's wicked."

Adele laughed shortly. "Ain't so. Her an' me are over, finished. We been for a long time an' you can't bring back the dead. Damn it, Frank, you always been jealous of her."

A blackbird swooped low over their heads and they watched it glide over the lake circle, and plane gracefully to the ground near the willows. Frank rubbed his crotch, wincing, and complained about the pain.

"No mo' poontang for you, big boy," joked Adele, pointing to the wounded area.

"You ain't funny. You gone answer my question. Did you go out to Nette? An' for what? Did y'all sniff pussies for ole times' sake?"

Her eyes got very cold and deadly. "Frank, don't try me. I could tell you a thang or two that's liable to make you really go crazy. You country fool."

"Did you go out there? Answer my question."

"Ain't none of your business if I did. That's my personal affairs an' this here is somethin' else. You should be worried where you gone stay. Don't take me for granted, Frank."

"Why you say a thang like that?" he demanded of Adele. "You knows how I feels 'bout you, care 'bout you. Gal, you been there whenever I needed you. I thanks you for what you done while I was laid up."

Adele broke in, "I's tired of bein' there when you need me. What the fuck have you done for me? Not a damn thang. I clean them damn white folks' houses, fix they food, wipe they

262

kids' behind an' I come home every night to see your big black ass sprawled out on the floor. I's tired of cleanin' up after you, tired of cleanin' up your puke."

"You loves Nette, don't you?" Frank was baffled by her calm voice, its vague hostility. "Adele, ain't I changed? I ain't touched a drop of liquor in weeks. You loves Nette, not me. Right or wrong?"

"Naw. I don't love her or you no more." She said it flatly and picked nervously with her earlobe. "You was sick an' still is. I's tired of your shit. Won't stand for it for no more."

He was puzzled, amazed at this sudden transformation in her attitude toward him. " 'Fore you say I was better, now you say I ain't. Make up your mind."

"Better but not cured. There's a difference, a big difference."

"You the craziest talkin' woman I ever knowed," said Frank. "I ain't no fool. You tryin' to make it look like I used you. Well, I didn't."

Adele corrected him. "I ain't said nothin' like that. I didn't say you used me. I ain't never thought that way. You brought it up. Well, is that what you thinks you're doin'?"

He snapped back, "Ugly bitch. You loves her. Ain't that it? You knows it is. The rest of this mess you talkin' here ain't nothin' but bullshit. You don't know what you talkin' 'bout. I thinks you jes' talks most of the time jes' to hear yourself talk."

She walked closer to the water's edge, a few steps ahead of him. "Nette's so right 'bout you farmers. Say she wouldn't love one of you if they paid her. Too much trouble."

Frank smiled his little angel smile. "Baby, what you gettin' all mad 'bout?"

That phony smile was a constant source of aggravation for her. "You's a real ignorant nigger." She was thinking of his love of yard dogs, cream poured hotly over hominy grits, fried pig brains, slightly curled buttermilk, and chow-chow on greens. Or the time he stepped in a pile of stinking dog plop and tracked it into the house, all over the front room and near the bed. He ranted like a madman when she told him to clean it up, as if she had to wait on him hand and foot like a servant. Or a slave. Presently, Frank put his arm around her waist, tried to pull her closer, but she moved away.

"Don't come over here with that kissin' mess," she said evilly. "Get away from me, get away. You don't know how to act."

"I still don't know why you all mad. What did I do now? You treat me like I did somethin' wrong. An' you won't tell me what."

She bumped against him and felt the hard muscle in his pants press against her leg. "Watch it, Frank Boles. I wish your head worked as good as that thang there. You'd be a man worth knowin' then."

As if he had read her mind, Frank said, "You never expect me to get back on my feets, did you? That's what you 'fraid of, me gettin' strong again. We ain't got a future together as long as you loves womens, runnin' with them pussy-sniffers. Like that Nette. She's still in your system an' that would never let you love me or any man."

She mused, "You goin' home soon. I knowed it all along. I want you to go." From the instant those words left her lips, she held an image of her sleeping with the pillow between her legs and the quilt pulled tightly over her head. Alone. With some uneasiness, she went on, "You finally accept the truth, we can't make it together. Too much has happened. When you started straightening out, I figgered you was doin' it for somethin' an' all you been talkin' 'bout is your family an' your children. I knowed you was plannin' to go back there soon."

"You don't like that." He raised an eyebrow.

264

"Yes an' no." She glanced at him quickly, then walked back toward the trees on the bank. "Mebbe your wife ain't gone want you back, now that she got a new man an' a new life. What then? Some folks don't like to go backwards if they can help it."

Frank smashed his fist into his open palm and gritted his teeth. She would take him back, he said, because he planned to chase Ellis out of his house. That's all. Kick his butt, if need be. "Her an' me was happy until he come 'round there, tippin' 'round like some snake," he added.

"Why blame him? He didn't bust up your family, you did. You don't care 'bout nobody but yourself."

"How the hell do you know? You wasn't there. You don't know a durn thang 'bout it."

He regarded her coldly, "Adele, if it don't work out, I can't come back. You won't let me come back. This is it. How can you do that? Why can't we end up as friends so I can come an' see you sometimes?"

"Naw. I can't do that. I don't want my love to come that way. Friends, shit. I have had enough of that in my life."

He pretended that he thought she was joking even though her voice gave away nothing. "Aw, baby ... baby ... you don't mean that. What is this? What are you doin'?"

"I's cleanin' house," she said, completely relaxed. Often in the old days, they made love in the dark, unable to see each other. They were only shapes to the other, voices, moans, sighs, and shadows. She let herself be held, cuddled, stroked, as she cursed herself for succumbing to the artificial feelings of comfort, love, and security. Now she would be free of all bonds; nothing would ever imprison her again, especially love.

"But ... baby," he protested.

Adele was standing firm on her decision, a clean break. "Frank, you heard what I said. I meant it." Adele slowly shrugged her shoulders. The image of her hands squeezing Frank's thick neck flashed through her mind and she smiled at him.

His smile faded. He was fighting a losing cause, he decided, but maybe later he could persuade her to let him stay another two weeks or a month. Now was not the time to force anything. "Hey, look here. I meant to show you this letter from Peetie. Came today while you was out."

" 'Bout time. Did he send any money?"

She held out her hand. "Lemme see it. I'll read it to you. Where's the letter he sent?" She was suppressing laughter for fear of angering Frank.

He pointed at the sheet of paper in the envelope. "This is it here. You lookin' at it."

Adele burst out laughing. "You kiddin' me."

His voice rose in pitch. "What's so funny? Let me in on it. What you laughin' at?" Just then a soft wind swept over the pastures, swaying the heavy branches of the willows.

"Is this what he sent you after you asked him for help?" Adele started laughing again, uncontrollably, gasping for breath.

His jaw was set hard. "Adele, tell me what's wrong with the letter. Don't play now. What is it?"

"What kin is this man to you?"

"My cousin," answered Frank nervously. "Why?"

She chuckled to herself and said, "You ought to disown his black ass. Listen to this." The letter read as follows:

Keep on asking and it will be given you; keep on seeking and you will find; keep on knocking reverently and the door will be opened to you.

—St. Matthew 7:7

This letter is your prayer, your hymn for good luck and

many blessings for both this world and the next. The original came from Jerusalem. It has been sent to you. You have been chosen. You are to receive good luck and the first of many blessings within four days of receiving this letter. This is no joke.

Send twenty copies of this letter to people you think need some good luck. Do not send money. Do not keep this letter. It must leave your hands within 96 hours after you receive it.

Evelyn Mills received $40,000 and a baby after being barren for ten years. Brenda Jackson received $25,000 but lost it because she misplaced the letter.

Please send twenty copies and see what happens on the fourth day after. Add your name to the bottom of the list and leave the top name off.

Walter Nichols
Sarah Lucas
Jather Johnson
Willie Mae Rodgers
Peetie Tate

Bewildered, he exclaimed, *"What!"*

Adele gave him a mischievous grin, balled up the letter and tossed it in the water. Frank grabbed at her hand, almost knocking her over, but it was already gone. All his good luck. The current carried it swiftly downstream.

"When do I have to get out?"

"As soon as possible, tomorrow if you can."

He put his hands on his hips, his defiant pose. "Why you throw my letter away? It wasn't yours."

"Don't get mad," she explained. "I did it for you, Frank. You got enough on your mind without that junk."

They walked on in the soft, gentle air. Adele though about contacting an old friend, her brother's ex-wife, to see if the woman would let her come to Los Angeles and stay with her until she got situated. The couple said nothing to each other during their walk along the levee and back to the car. In a panic, Frank tried to recall the name of a woman he had met two days before at Matt's, the red-haired gal who fooled around with the white men at the post office. She said she'd put him up if anything went wrong. Little did he know that she was drunk when she said it, and that she would later even deny knowing him when they met again.

Chapter 33

At the start of dusk, about the time when the bugs fire up their nightly hymns, Frank Boles left the red-haired woman's shotgun house with a hang-dog look, bags in hand, and a growling stomach. The morning with Adele had ended in a big argument, her yelling at him for being alive, and him shouting that she was a heartless bulldagger. Both of them played their parts well, bringing up old slights, opening ancient wounds, and rubbing the other's face in their most intimate, shameful secrets. He was glad to be out of there. It was a good traveling day. There were numerous flat clouds overhead, clear pockets of blue sky, and no wind stirring. Day, soon evening. Sure he hated to leave that gal, he mused, but he had to do more than just lay around and he couldn't let those lust feelings get the best of him, reduce him to being a stud or run himself in the ground. Yeah, there was his home, his family to think about. Still, Adele had been a good woman

269

before everything went bad. It was good to have a woman tell you that you had some red-hot loving and he, besides, had cut the drinking loose. No more liquor. That was the best part of it.

Frank reflected on the old times when he had made Mary feel that way, made her sweet with his loving. She was never the type to say anything about how good it was, but he could tell if he did a good job by the way she treated him afterward. Back then when she needed him. Would she need him now? He was afraid to consider what he would do if her answer was no, if she turned him away. She had every right to do that. No reason at all for her to take him back after all he put her through. He failed them, her and the children, in the past. But no more.

No more lies, no more alcohol. No more, no more, he thought, walking alongside the big state highway, holding out his thumb, with traffic zipping by. Frank Boles. He pondered on his history, on the flesh and blood that went into making up his heritage, all the way to him. And how lust and the lure of that velvet pocket could make you forget all of that. When he returned home, he would carry the load again, just like he used to, before he became sick. His mind rambled on and he listened to it for once. All them years, all them babies, and he still didn't know who Mary was. Truth was, he didn't know her feelings. She was probably a whole other person inside, completely different from what he had seen.

From what he had seen, Frank repeated several times to himself. Mary was probably afraid to show him what she was, afraid he didn't want to know. Or, that if he did, the stupid and stubborn part of him would try to destroy her with that new, terrible knowledge. He decided he wouldn't treat her like that anymore. But how many men listen to their women anyhow? They felt like he did: the more you listen to them, the less you are a man. You would be on their level then.

Maybe so, maybe not. Maybe it took a bigger man to listen, to understand what they were feeling and talking about. Hell, he was not by himself. Plenty men did what he had done. But that was no excuse. No more, no more.

He looked down at his extended thumb and spread his legs wider so that his weight was more evenly distributed. Inside, his mind exploded in thought. All them excuses help mark time, make the days pass without too much strain. It was like being half asleep, nothing could harm you then. Oh yeah, the strain would still be there, working and tunneling underneath like moles and woodchucks. Why so many women? What was he looking for that he didn't have right there? Sometimes he felt like two or three people, all at once. It was the other one that gave him so much grief. That one told him that he was afraid of putting in time to anything other than himself, that he was afraid that he'd miss out on something somewhere else. Why not be able to roam at will? Why should anybody have to answer to anybody else? That was all a lie. You had to belong, you had to be a part of something, you had to be a part of somebody. He knew that now, because you are whether you want to be or not. He took the argument one step further. People are afraid to stick and stay because they don't know how it will all come out. They want to be at the reins all the time. Nobody is at the reins all the time in this life.

The cars and trucks kept on coming. No one would stop for him and it was getting darker, colder. A panel truck with two white men in it honked at him and slowed but didn't stop. He breathed a sigh of relief. The truck drove on for a short distance, braked suddenly, and pulled off the road. Frank didn't look up, continued walking and prepared himself for any possibility. Luckily, the truck started up again and drove back on the roadway, blending into the traffic. No telling what's on these peoples' minds, Frank told himself, listening to the sound of his feet hitting the ground.

He walked and walked, ignoring offers of a ride with cars packed with whites since it wasn't safe at that time of evening. Anything could happen. Behind him, another horn sounded. Some of our race, he said to himself, a couple. Their car had out-of-state license plates, a liability he noted immediately. It glided to a stop just ahead of him and Frank ran to it, jumped in.

He sat back on the car seat, saying nothing. The man's wife scooted closer to her husband. He yanked his leg inside the car as they rocketed off, tires smoking on the road's surface. He was amazed by the black man's custom-fitted Italian business suit, white shirt, horn-rimmed glasses, and thin black tie. Frank stared at the couple, trying to figure them out.

"Where are you headed?" The colored woman was talking to him. She was dressed like the white women in the movie magazines, all made up, hair flipped up on her head.

"A no-name place outside of Pinetop," he answered after a few seconds. "It ain't but a hour's ride from here. Where you peoples from?"

"Cleveland." The couple answered in unison and laughed softly at their timing.

"Cleveland, Mississippi? I ain't seed no colored dress like you folks there." Frank sat open-mouthed, dazzled by their smart attire and cultured manners.

"No, Cleveland, Ohio," the woman said in a soothing, friendly voice. She was smoking and sometimes she tapped the cigarette ashes into the tray under the dashboard with a graceful movement of her finger. Very stylish.

"Ohio? Where's that?" Frank was watching the husband's driving, concluding that the man wouldn't last three minutes at the wheel of a tractor. Too nervous.

The wife sniffed, not looking directly at their guest. "Ohio, in case you really don't know, is north of here, near a lake.

Lake Erie, in fact."

Frank didn't like her tone of voice, too snooty for colored. "What do you do with yourselves up north?"

"I'm a housewife," the woman said grandly. "I belong to several social clubs and we sponsor Negro children to colleges, worthy colleges, with scholarships. We give parties and the like. Have you ever heard of Jack and Jill?"

Her husband interrupted her with a wave of his hand. "Darling, I'm sure that these people don't have time for that sort of thing down here." He paused, thinking for a moment. "We forgot to introduce ourselves. How impolite. I'm Cuthbert Walker and this is my wife, Edith."

"Frank Boles' the name," the farmer said. "Glad to meet you both."

"Same here, Frank." The husband said it as if he was a salesman of some sort.

Mrs. Walker exhaled a long breath, looked in her purse, took out a lace handkerchief, and wiped the back of her sweating neck. "Hon, ask him if he knows where there's any good restaurants in this area. I'm famished. You know, some place where we can sit down for a while, because riding in this car all day just wears you out. It's so dreadful, confined in this hot car."

"Are there any decent eating places around here, Frank," asked her husband, glancing quickly in his direction.

"Well, ma'am, there be a place down the road a piece where you can eat," Frank said quietly. "Mahalia's, a little place for colored. Nice peoples run it an' they ain't stingy with the eats either."

"Honey . . . honey, excuse me." She was powdering her nose.

"Yes, dear, what is it now?"

"Ask him if there's any place where we can get postcards and souvenirs. I've got to send something to my mother and your aunt or they'll be totally put out."

The man did not ask Frank anything so he remained mute, taking his cue from the husband. For several minutes, an awkward silence filled the car, with everyone pretending to be preoccupied.

"I'm burning up," Mrs. Walker moaned, wiping the sweat from her forehead, then she unbuttoned her blouse to reveal the swelling tops of her golden breasts. Frank stole a peek and looked down at his hands laying in his lap.

"A lot of our race up there in Cleveland?" asked Frank.

"Quite a few, Frank." Mr. Walker talked in a white voice that annoyed him. "Frank, I'm from Kentucky originally, moved to Cleveland with my family when I was three, and my wife's parents are from Boston. One of the older black families in that city. Right, darling?"

"Definitely," she assured her mate in a soft tone.

Frank knew he would sound dumb but he had to ask. "Jes' where is this place, Boston?"

Mrs. Walker assumed a patient, benevolent posture on the seat. "Boston is in the state of Massachusetts, north of New York, near the ocean. Frank, you do know where New York City is?"

"Yeah, Noo Yawk City. I got peoples up there somewhere."

The wife fanned herself, talking right over Frank's reply. "Anyway, I think that's why this unbearable heat is just devastating me. I don't see how you people can stand this hot weather all the time. So much heat must do something to the brain, always so steamy. I tell you, I can't stand it. I couldn't stand it. I would just die."

Frank brushed at a grease stain on his pants. "Ma'am, it ain't so bad once you get used to it. We been livin' here all our lives so it don't bother us none. Shoot, I hear tell it gets real cold up there. I hate the cold."

Mr. Walker smirked, "My wife complains when it does

that too."

She was still fanning, faster than before. "Don't tease me, sweetheart. This heat's killing me . . . really it's a bit much."

"To tell the truth, this kinda weather is poor folks' weather," the farmer hung his arm out of the window. "I bet up there where you live, you got to keep a fire lit in the house all the time. An' that cold most likely cut down on you movin' 'round when it sets in bad. Down here, you jes' up an' go anywhere you want."

"I saw the most beautiful cocktail dress at Halle's before we left," Mrs. Walker chirped. "Absolutely stunning. Gee darling, I can't wait to have a house full of people over, put out my best china and crystal, and show the lovely slides of our trip below the Mason-Dixon line. Can't you just see it, Cuthbert?"

Her husband nodded sheepishly. "That'd be awfully nice, dear."

"Sweetheart, you think we could stop somewhere so I can touch up my face?" Mrs. Walker fingered her long, fake eyelashes elegantly, barely stroking them.

Meanwhile her husband was speeding on a Mississippi highway, passing cars and trucks as if they were standing still, only occasionally scouting for the police in his rear view mirror. "Of course, dear. No problem."

"Don't be silly, honey. If you think we should go straight through to your relatives' house, that's alright with me. After all, you're the boss. But I'm sure that you don't want to arrive there looking like a slob."

Frank sat quietly, unable to understand the two of them. He had never seen colored people act like this, putting on airs for one of their own kind. It was tiring for him to watch it too long. He couldn't wait for them to get where he could get out.

Mr. Walker kept his eyes on the road. "I guess you're right, darling. As usual."

"Of course, sweetheart, I'm always right." She turned slightly toward Frank and winked impishly. "What time will we get there with this new stop added?" Her thumb jerked at Frank.

"Around eleven-thirty." Mr. Walker maneuvered his car, an enormous Lincoln Continental, around a stalled station wagon, stepping on the brake, then accelerating. "Frank, I didn't want to stop for you but my wife insisted," he said snidely. "So you have her to thank for your good fortune. This is my good deed for the day."

"Thank you, ma'am." Frank acknowledged his debt.

She smiled insincerely and said don't mention it. Then, for no reason, she kissed her husband's cheek lightly and whispered aloud. "Sweetheart, should I tell Frank why we are down this way?" Mrs. Walker faced their guest and proceeded to tell him sordid details of their failing marriage. "See, we are vacationing in an attempt to rekindle our marriage, trying to revive it before it's too late. Nothing like being away from hearth and home to put the fire back into a fading romance. Isn't that so, darling?"

Her husband frowned and made a sudden turn of the wheel to avoid a car coming up fast on his blind side. Mrs. Walker slammed against Frank and apologized. "If you say so, honey," her husband replied tersely.

"Guess what?!" she exclaimed. "I forgot my suntan lotion. Fiddlesticks! Oh, sweetheart, you know how much I love a good tan. It would have been great to return home with my skin fried a golden brown. Like a bronze color."

"Bright-skinned folk usually do," interjected Frank.

Mrs. Walker stopped chattering for a moment, and looked at him, slightly annoyed. "I can see you don't have to worry about getting a tan, not with that gorgeous smoky black skin of yours. I bet you almost live in the sun with a skin like that. Almost purple. You must be awfully proud of it."

"Proud of what?" asked Frank.

"Of that dark and lovely skin of yours," answered Mrs. Walker, stroking his bare arm near the elbow.

"Most colored peoples' proud of the color of their skin so they don't make a big thang of it. It's a part of life. All 'cept them wantin' to pass or be white."

"I'm a race man, too," her husband said, in an artificially hip voice. "Just like yourself, Frank. I was so glad when Madison Avenue began using Negroes in their print ad campaigns. Did you see that beautiful one with Maxine Sullivan pitching Chesterfield cigarettes?" He assumed the manner of a bogus radio announcer. "Yes, ladies and gentlemen, Maxine says always buy Chesterfields, they're really good to you."

Frank rolled his eyes at the man as if he was completely crazy. "Sir, can I ask you somethin'? What do you do for a livin'?"

Mrs. Walker fished in her oversized purse and brought out a handful of hard candy, all cherry. "Want one, Frank? Don't pay him any attention. He's a fanatic for commercials, any kind of commercials, radio, television, magazines, even newspapers. You name it, he knows it. He's nutty that way."

"Oh," Frank said and shot a probing look at her husband. He was starting to worry about this ride, these crazy folks, maybe his chances would have been better with the crackers.

Their car almost sideswiped another car going past, its horn on full blast. Without warning, Mr. Walker chimed up in song, singing another television commercial. "Brush-a, brush-a, brush-a, new . . . toothpaste . . ." Frank guessed that the two of them were supposed to fill in the blank, pick out the product, and sing the jingle. What kind of fools are these folks? He was wondering about that when the man's wife tugged his arm and asked him if he knew the answer.

"Naw, ma'am, I ain't got a teevee." He kept his eye on the both of them.

The wife shouted suddenly, "Brush-a, brush-a, brush-a, new Ipana toothpaste! Right, sweetheart?"

Mr. Walker was all smiles. "Right, you are! Yes, folks, avoid 'tell-tale' mouth with Ipana toothpaste. Use Ipana for a cleaner, sweeter, more sparkling smile!" He made a sound similar to a royal fanfare of trumpets. "Okay, dear, that was pretty good. How about this? This product helps hair grow, makes it more attractive, longer and healthier looking. A woman's product, gives her hair that's soft and shining with natural lustre. What is it? You've got sixty seconds. Beat the clock."

"I don't know," Frank said, playing along. "Does colored use it?"

"Be quiet, please," Mrs. Walker snapped. "I'm thinking. This is a toughie, Cuthbert. Is it print, television or radio? Help me narrow it down."

"You folks must be drunk," Frank observed drily.

"Neither of us touch the stuff," the wife said with a haughty air. "Sweetheart, give me a clue. Is it an ad from Ebony or Tan or Sepia? It doesn't sound like Redbook, Life, Look or the Saturday Evening Post. Help me out."

Her husband honked the horn for emphasis, once, loud. "Shucks, I was sure you'd get it. Sulphur-8, dummy. Alright, one more and that's it. Let's see if you can get two out of three. Who was Negro America's Golden Skin girl? The most famous one. And what was the product she represented? You've got thirty seconds. Go!"

"What year?" she asked.

"No clues."

"I got it," yelled Frank. "Lena Horne!"

Mr. Walker turned up his nose. "Wrong. Next contestant, please."

His wife was stumped. "I don't know that one, sweetheart."

This gave Mr. Walker the opportunity to break into another radio spot, using that white voice Frank loathed so much. "Since we have drawn a blank from our listening audience, it was the glorious, glamorous, glowing Miss Mildred Thomas, Negro America's Golden Skin girl. Known to millions. The product . . ." A long pause here for maximum dramatic effect. "The product was Mercolized Wax Cream, a widely used beauty product for over 40 years. Get Mercolized! Yes indeedy, Mercolized Wax Cream, the modern miracle works on rough, darkened skin to reveal a more golden *you*! Makes your skin look lovelier than ever seemed possible."

"Is you on the radio up north, Mr. Walker?" Frank asked.

The man's wife shook her head, smiling with glee. "No, he isn't, but he sure has the voice for it. His voice is one of the reasons I married him. So smooth, so deep."

Mr. Walker craned his neck, looking for road signs. "The good old days. I was so young and had so many dreams. I miss those times. Remember Lena Horne singing 'I Feel So Smoochie.' I don't know if you ever heard it, Frank, but if you had, you'd remember it. A great song. What about the poodle haircut? You had one of those, didn't you, dear?"

"I hated it." She didn't want to think about it.

"Remember that winter in New York City when I played that Hattie Noel party record over and over. Boy, I loved to hear her do 'If I Can't Sell It' and 'Hot Nuts.' She's funnier than Moms Mabley. You didn't like that record too much. You said it was too dirty, remember?"

"Yes, I remember all too well." She grinned uncomfortably.

"My father lived in Texas and Kentucky all his life," Mr. Walker said sullenly. "Frank, you remind me a lot of him. He was a man of few words, all action."

Mrs. Walker didn't want to be left out. "When I was

younger, I had two horses but then my family had to sell them. I love horses, they're such big, magnificent beasts. So big and powerful." She squirmed in the seat for an instant and Frank wondered if that had anything to do with the horses. She caught her breath and continued talking. "I love to ride them, I always feel so free."

Frank sat quietly and watched the woman suspiciously.

A freight truck almost ran them off the road, causing the car to rock as it whizzed by, and Mr. Walker slowed down. He looked over at Frank. "Listen to this. I took my wife to my father' splace before he died, in Kentucky, and she couldn't stay away from the stables. Day and night. She was always on them. Sometimes I'd come out to the stables, and she would be there, just staring at them. She's just crazy about horses and big dogs. We've got two Great Danes at home."

Frank felt a little befuddled by their revelations about each other. Surprisingly, his laugh was somewhat high and mocking. They noticed it and the mood changed in the car.

"Why did you laugh, Frank?" Her husband was seeking a challenge of some kind from the farmer, a veiled threat, anything. "Is it that funny?"

"Naw, it ain't really. Somethin' else struck me funny. Tell me, where y'all goin'?"

Mrs. Walker tossed her head, swinging her long black wig over the back of the seat. It didn't impress Frank in the least. He was thinking about asking them to pull over and let him out when she answered for her husband. "We're on our way to visit *his* relatives in Biloxi, some people on his father's side of the family. It was his idea to come down here. Believe me when I say that I don't like it at all in this part of the south; you know, the race problem and all. I'd rather be in Europe or Puerto Rico or Hong Kong. Anywhere but here. There, I've said it at last!"

"Why did you come if you hate it that bad?" Frank asked

meekly.

"Because she's such a dear," Mr. Walker interrupted the farmer impatiently. "She's afraid we might get lynched."

"White folks the same all over," Frank said with a chuckle. "Ain't no different down here from nowhere else. If you jes' mind your business, they won't mess with you."

"That's exactly what I was telling her before we left home. There's no damn difference. By the way, do you have any little ones?"

"Little what?" Frank played dumb.

"Children, my man." That hip voice again.

"Yessuh, got seven. Had nine, two died."

"Nine children!" Mrs. Walker screamed as if she had been stabbed. "Is your wife still living? Good God, if I had eight children, I'd just die. I couldn't take it."

"We get along alright." Frank was quick to point out. "How many do you have?"

"Three children," the husband boasted. "Two grown, one is still at home. He's with my sister while we're on the road. My oldest, Cuthbert Junior, is attending Howard, and my girl just married a criminal lawyer. Great guy, really knows his way around a courtroom."

Mrs. Walker frowned and said, "I told my husband that three is enough for me, no more kids. I can't handle any more than that because the three we have almost drove me up the wall. They'll drive you batty if you let them. But nine? How do you manage it? But then you people always have a lot of children anyway since you don't practice any kind of birth control, so I guess you're used to it."

"There ain't nothin' wrong with chirren," said Frank proudly. "I loves mines."

The woman placed a finger beside her nose and sniffed twice. "I just love the way he talks, don't you Cuthbert?"

Her husband ignored her, but Frank kept on talking. "The

other day, a reporter from the Atlanta Journal asked me what I thought about Reverend Martin Luther King's house bein' shot into and I tole him that somebody must not have liked him. Probably some evil peckerwood. I say I ain't reckon no colored person in his right mind would want to hurt their own peoples like that. 'Specially somebody doin' what he's doin'. That's like a man shootin' hisself in the balls to spite his wife 'cause she's got another mule kickin' in her stall. You know what I mean?"

Mr. Walker laughed quickly, but his wife didn't. She looked at the road ahead, staring at the miles and miles of blacktop in the distance.

He spotted his drop-off point and motioned to her husband, who was cutting off another car with a fancy move. "Mister Walker, you can let me off over yonder near that turn-off," said Frank eagerly. "Now 'member, the eat place ain't but ten minutes up the road. Jes' ask for Swanky. Tell him that Frank sent you an' he gone treat you right. Y'all have a safe trip. Missus Walker, you don't have to worry 'bout these white folks. They ain't studyin' us, don't worry."

"Look out, sweetheart!" Mrs. Walker yelled suddenly. "That car's trying to get by." Her husband braked too fast, the car skidded sideways, and he floored the gas pedal, spinning the vehicle in the opposite direction. When he jammed on the brakes, it was too late to stop the car from making a full revolution and a Mac truck loomed in front of them. He cut the wheel sharply to the left. The car jetted off the road, crashing into a gulley, making Mrs. Walker and Frank smash their foreheads on the dashboard. Both were bloodied, but uninjured otherwise.

It was not as bad as it had seemed at first. With the help of some passing motorists, the car wa spulled from the ditch, and the Walkers again wished Frank Boles well and were on their way. He still had a long way to go, about three hours of walking to do. The couple had been pretty nice people for northern niggers, he thought, walking away from the highway. A little crazy, though. He wanted to find a place to rest up before heading out for the last part of his journey, anywhere he could stretch out for a time.

Frank Boles knew he was frightened. "Mebe it ain't the same, mebbe it's changed for the worser," he whispered to himself.

Chapter 34

Minutes later, Frank knelt beneath a large willow tree in the all-encompassing darkness. His head was killing him, shooting pains traveling from the base of his neck to the crown of his skull. Searing, knifing pains. It was quite apparent to him that he might not make it home that night, unable to stumble through the nothingness, forehead throbbing, and sharp thuds between the legs. He stumbled, he couldn't see a foot in front of himself. His eyes ached, signaling his fatigue, calling to him to sleep, to leave this world for the next.

Drifting, floating through the emptiness. The light was coming from behind him, outlining her shape, or his shape, forming a silhouette. What attracted his stare was the silvery glow around the figure, the pulsating center of it. A voice called to him from somewhere out there, luring him, and a paralysis crept over him, rooting him to that spot. The voice faded back into the blackness where it had come from, the luminous face of a man dressed in a white suit, gray shirt, with a scarf of jagged, angled designs knotted at the throat. Something about him attracts you, what you can't say but you feel forced to speak to him. You imagine him to have a deep, rich voice to match his round face and stocky body, built so close to the ground. It gets lighter, dims, gets clearer. You try to cry out, your lips move but nothing comes out. Words grow louder, louder, spell them out, clear. You don't understand them, tractor talk, machine blabber, white noise. You cover your ears with your hands, blotting it out, you think. It penetrates the flesh, ruthless, all-powerful. Nothing can stop this flow, the enchantment, under a spell. Your face is putty, ever-changing, the trance embraces you, wraps you in its arms. All sensations invade you and anybody could look at you and know that you weren't all there.

He trembled, shook to the very core of himself, sensing the images' grip on his mind. He clawed the fertile earth, handfuls of moist, black soil. Any effort to control his body was futile, against the will of the invisible thing that spoke to him from the outside. The buzzing in his ears, his chest, and other hidden cavities. Lost in the sleep, the sailing over golden clouds, weightless.

You watch a wee ball of light bounce back and forth, pivoting your head like you were watching a fist fight, you can't rise to your feet. Then you can, but you can only crawl toward the boom of a voice, the blinding light, it felt your eyes on it and it knew you would come sooner or later. It knows who you are. You can't resist it, can't. Who can tell you that the only reason you die is because your heart stops, there are other ways, there are other deaths. The rumbling talks to you, without sound, and you decide not to give an answer too soon. Make it wait.

Frank Boles snored and talked in his slumber, not fully realizing what was happening to him while he lay helpless, unguarded, without walls. He was afraid of waking up, of returning to the real world, the land of jim crow. That could be the end, something he didn't want. He needed hope.

This ritual, this spirit has not looked at you the entire time it has been talking, before you could speak. The voice comes at you again, and you notice how the face never changes, not a blemish, no maybe a slight smile now and then. At first, you feel like your body is covered head to toe with countless running sores, blisters. Itching. You feel like a thief surprised by the sheriff, you feel strange right now. There is something about the man deserving trust, what. You feel he has something to say, something you should hear. A terror sweeps through you, a terror for which you have no words. An echo, the scratchy music of birds' wings beating fast. Different colored lights flash around the man, the emptiness surrounding his shape peels back with a deafening roar. For a moment, the man and his yellow glow stand behind you and you cannot see his face, yet you know what it or he is thinking. A wave of his hand and the silence opens without a sound; warmth, tingling through your limbs, and you turn. The ball of brightness is so near you that it could kiss you, it is that close. You can stare at it, there is no talking now. Maybe you are not there, maybe. The man smiles and at the same time, you do the same. You laugh, alone. It is a laugh of discomfort, a laugh to relieve tension. You stare as if it is against your will.

He curled up in a knot, sheltering his cold arms with his hands. His body felt alive, energized, full of an unusual voltage. This power held him captive, imprisoning his mind in the vise of an other-life freedom. He lacked the strength to break loose from its hold, to flee if it was worth the effort.

You recognize that smell: it is the scent that comes after a rain, you feel your heart stop then continue. The man in white sits motionless, like stone, shutting his eyes until there is only the fluttering of the lids. Jacob and the angel, Moses and the burning bush, the two angels at Sodom and Gomorrah. A warning, and you watch him produce two large green seeds in the palms of his hands, his fingers outstretched and flat. He smiles, knowingly. You move your eyes back to his hands, the seeds have taken root into his dark flesh; and large, leafy flowers—light orange with gold trim—push up toward the ceiling. You can hear the song of their sprouting and you know that you only understand life to a point. Anything can happen, your mouth drops open in surprise. You must calm yourself, your hair itches, your neck itches. Your ears feel like something is stuck in them, and sweat pours from under your arms and between your legs.

He shivered again and again, unable to resurrect himself. His sleep resembled death; if only he could tame this world, control what awaited him in this life. That would be like asking the earth to stop moving, to halt to let him catch up. Lord God, the pain. More than anything, he wanted to give his life order and set the pace. There was no way he could hold the reins.

The Devil is everywhere in this world, in you, probably in your boy. The man has seen the growing terror, the mushrooming suspicion in you, the way you scowl at him when he talks to you. The voice comes from above you now. It is all-knowing. You are frightened as well; the man, the spirit can tell by the weakness of your breathing. The flowers are gone from his hands, vanished in air, and he understands how you want so much to be somewhere else other than here. You talk at a rapid clip, much as an excited schoolgirl would, asking more and more questions. You point at the man, his eyebrows lift. He watches you for a moment, expecting strength. You give him nothing, you are empty. You feel nothing but fear, a selfish fear mixed with a spark of a prayer that this night will help you in some way.

He tossed and turned in the throes of nocturnal bliss, the smugness of this Delta nightmare, the tug of a father's conscience. He wanted to find his wife, his children, sweep them up and give them a hug that would make them gasp. No one could tell him that he didn't see the situation more clearly, with a more calculating eye. But there were still questions he didn't bother to answer.

It is all-knowing. He knows your arm aches, pestering you from when you broke it years back falling from a truck. Remember? Remember how afraid your wife was. Remember how odd your arm felt after you fell. You let your spine stiffen, you let your head shake in disbelief. Your lips say silently how could he know all of these things. How could he? Things stashed away in the back of your memory, things you never told anyone about. How could he know? He is doing this to your mind. You peer at his hands for they now clutch wiggling light beams of different colors; power, moving, rushing. The golden, blue, red beams flow in a triangle, then each color separates, collecting in a cube shape, dividing in half and finally swirling in a circle, splitting again and again. The hair on the back of your neck rises, the man leans back and laughs a hearty laugh.

It wasn't the first time this had happened to him, this panic, this fear. Suppose this was how his Little Frank felt, locked away inside his mind, trapped. He knew what it was like now. Trapped. Still he shouldn't think on that too much. Perhaps his warning had come that day Sailor Gibbs' little girl stepped out in front of a car by the Baptist church in the Brickyard. Killed her dead. Suppose this was the same hant that got Sailor Gibbs, made him scream and run in circles. They tried to grab him but he broke free; one straddled him, rolling on the ground. Sailor started to kick and howl, and they held his arms and legs.

A blue-white beam of light arcs from the man, seizes you,

289

again and again, absorbing more of your strength each time. Resistance is useless. You want to say something to the man, but before you can, you are thrown against a wall of cold air, with your arms spread like wings. The air takes on a silver sheen, bright enough for you to shield your eyes. The air pushes itself at you so hard that it feels like a sharp blade. You fight for breath, then the air is no more. All is calm. The voice again, from the ball of light. Evil must have a way to enter this world, through lost souls and the weak. You must be redeemed, your family must be redeemed, washed in the blood. For what you must do, there will surely be forgiveness. The voice now seems to come from you, familiar but strange. The sound inside you was like that of a drum beating, in the core of your brain, now closer and louder. You must rid the boy of the serpent. The whole of wickedness. This evil was not real, fortified with no magic but that which he gave it. Could the demons in the boy be traced back to you? Or Mary? No good could come from evil. To hell with waiting on God!! Evil had no soul. His son, his family were evil.

For what he was thinking at that second was sinful, regardless of why he believed in God or not. He would have rather driven a dull knife through his heart or sent it in a crimson crease across his throat. The sleep departed from him just as it was getting light, his head whipped back weirdly as if it was broken. Suddenly his body went stiff and bitter tears came to his eyes. His ranting could almost be heard in the next country, possessed, his eyes rolling back in his head. Staggering, Frank Boles hoisted himself up with the aid of the willow tree, had a coughing fit, and wiped the foam from his lips. A tinge of shock surged through him. Across the clearing, he saw something ethereal floating, like vapors, in the open space; a disembodied thing. Worms and other underground parasites had taken their toll; the weightless corpse was a torn and tattered mess with its burial clothes trailing behind. It was his father, his dead father, hovering above the ground like the body of a woman he had seen defy gravity in a magic show near Baton Rouge. The face of the apparition had a whitish-blue hue to it, part of the skull was gone, along with the eyes and many teeth. He stood transfixed by the horrible sight. Slowly it vanished, and he ran screaming into the black, his mouth agape.

Chapter 35

"What you doin' here?" Mary asked Frank with an edge of rebuke in her voice. Her temper flared to its limits at the sight of her prodigal husband, the wandering good timer who finally decided to come home after he had used himself up. Now he came to her beaten and bruised, just a shell of his former self. She left the rocker and crossed the porch to look beyond Frank at the woods teeming with shadowy sycamores, pines, and oaks.

"I came home," Frank announced, taking leaden steps toward her. "You want me to go away. I won't cause no trouble."

She glared harshly at him. "Frank, you jes' can't walk back in here when you get good an' ready. It don't work that way. I won't let you mess over me again." Her words stopped, then started again. "Why you limpin'? Must have been fightin' again. Look at that gash on your forehead. One day you gone

293

get yourself killed."

"I knows you been gettin' your face rubbed in the mud out here," he said, pleading. "Most of that was my doin'. I was wrong."

Her voice was a hoarse whisper. "I never hurt you, Frank. You left us, your family, when we needed you. It wasn't right. If I let you come back, you gone do it again. I know that for a fact."

"Naw, I ain't," Frank begged, feeling his stomach turn to jelly. "I ain't pullin' your leg. Folks change. I had a vision, Mary. My dead daddy came back from the grave an' tole me what I had to do to put thangs right. You ain't gone get treated bad ever again, never again."

Mary shrugged her shoulders, assuming her wildcat stance. "You can't do nothin' for me now. What you gone do for work? Mister Jesse ain't high on lettin' you come back to work for him." Her rage broke free and she struck at him, but he dodged the blow. "You lazy bastid! I hate you. You shamed me."

"Can I say anythin' that might make you look at my side of everythin'?" asked Frank.

When her husband walked to the steps of the porch, pausing there dramatically, Mary averted her gaze. She pondered her answer carefully. But it eventually came as a question. "An' how do you intend to explain your sudden return to them chirren? How do you figger to make thangs right?"

He asked her a second time if she wanted him to go. She shook her head slowly, sleepily, deciding then to be as hard on him as possible. Why did Frank feel that he could do this? How come he could do whatever he wanted and she had to go along with it? Why couldn't she just send him away?

"I hurt, baby," he moaned. "An' I ain't got nowhere else to go 'cept here. Thangs gone get better 'round here 'cause I's changed. A new man. You'll see."

"Stop lyin' to me. What you want, Frank?"

"What you want from me? That's the question."

"I got what I want," she replied. "I got them chirren an' they all I need."

"What 'bout a man? Have you got one of them, too?" He pressed her.

She smiled politely. "I got a man."

"You talkin' 'bout Mister Fat-Ass? He ain't no man. He ain't man enough to run this house or to be your husband. All Chubby knows how to do is to feed his face an' break up families. Say I's lyin' 'bout that."

She was almost too mad to talk. "Don't try that with me. Ellis ain't done nothin' but help out. He gives an' gives, askin' nothin' in return. Where were you when I needed you? Answer that."

"Sorry." He lowered his eyes to the floor.

That apology didn't satisfy her desire to punish him, to get revenge for putting her in a position where she was at the mercy of other people. Nothing he could say or do would lessen that feeling.

"I want to set thangs right," he said. "Let me do that much."

She retreated to the doorway, weighing his proposal against her disgust for him. It was a draw. "You make me cuss, you jackass," she frowned. "Come in. You got till morning to change my mind, but right now, I reckon I hate you as much as I ever could. Mebbe I should tell you to go an' never show your damn face here again."

He assured her. "I won't let you down."

"How you get that wound on your forehead? Bet it was over a woman."

Frank put his fingers to the stinging gash, tracing its length tenderly, checking to see if a scab had formed. "No gal involved. It was a car wreck."

She went by him in a rush. "Stay there. Let me get a wet

cloth an' some alcohol. It needs cleanin'." In her mind, she rejoiced to see him again, to have him at home once more. Not just for her sake, but for the children. She could feel his muscular arms encircling her body, pressing their stomachs together; her mind pictured her knees going up under the pile-driving rhythms of his pump and thrust, ramming between her thighs. No more out-of-breath fat man bouncing on her. And she would begin to cry at the force and beauty of it all. Frank and her together. Why she doin' this to herself? This was all something she made up. What really happened night after night was that she would wait until the children were asleep and the house was silent, before she stripped away her clothes and laid down on the sweat-stained mattress. For hours, she would keep her eyes closed, praying for sleep. If her need was too great, she permitted Ellis to stay the night, but she always regretted it afterwards. But there was another way to quiet her inner hunger. She had faced too many nights alone and afraid. Thinking of Frank and where he was not, where he might be, touched her in a way that drove her crazy, and she opened her fleshy thighs. Her stubby fingers slid over the mound of her belly to enter what she called "the wound between her legs." With her other hand, she tweaked and caressed her nipples, working them to a sensual hardness. She hated doing this, pleasuring herself, her finger wiggling inside her, and then she would always linger for an instant, imagining her errant husband's lips on her privates. She could feel him holding her close, his tongue flicking at her ear, and his free hand busy down there. Oh, yes Lawd! At the very second that she was totally losing herself in the fantasy, a glass would shatter somewhere in the house or footsteps would sound from another room or a cough, but it was too hard to stop. Too difficult to stop. And her fingers would maintain their furious dance to the instant—her release came. She would shiver for a while, letting the waves of ecstasy run their course, and finally the sleep would come.

"Mary, Mary," he was calling her for some time before she acknowledged him. "Mary, have you stopped lovin' me?"

Her face tightened in a brief storm of annoyance. "Don't ask me that now. You ain't got the right to ask me anythin' like that. Hush!"

"I jes' want to know," he said weakly, with a baleful look. "Everythin' else is small next to that. If you don't love me, we wastin' our time."

"Why you never sent us no money? I had to scuffle an' scrap to get by, beggin' my neighbors an' Ellis for food to put on the table. You stingy son-of-a-bitch! Selfish nigger!"

Frank jumped like he had been slapped across the face. "You knows I care 'bout you an' them babies. I couldn't get no work nowhere." Her dress fell open momentarily, revealing skin, and he could see her bare leg. That shut him up.

"You never sent word where you was," she said. "You let me worry myself to death."

He didn't sound surprised. "I was wrong, I was wrong. Ain't got no mother-wit. But I never forgot y'all."

After that remark, she shot him a look that made his blood run cold. Trying to hold back tears, she said icily, "Frank, I forgive you, but I won't forget none of this. You go hogwild out there whilst I slave here, tryin' to keep this house runnin'. That white man never stopped messin' with me. He ain't forgot what you did to him."

"What I do?" he feigned innocence. " 'Sides, baby, I had a vision. I won't stray from the path no more."

Her warm nearness aroused him, swelling the snake in his pants. He quickly squeezed her bottom, smiling wolfishly. "Ain't you missed that good loivn'?"

Mary said no, but he silenced her protests with a heartfelt kiss, covering her mouth with his. She yanked away from him, saying, "Frank, don't get too hot now. Wait a minute whilst I fix you a pallet on the floor in the front room."

Chapter 36

At the start of the day, Frank Boles awoke, washed quickly, and prepared himself a pot of coffee. He fell into a thoughtful silence. At first, he appeared out of place, uneasy, and slightly depressed. The house was quiet, with everyone gone outdoors, probably his wife had forbidden anyone to disturb him. His homecoming brought a warmth to him that he hadn't expected. It took about a half hour for the farmer to steel himself for his encounter with the children, his mouth dry, and insecurity running through his innards like laxative. How would they react? Would they shun him? When he later walked into the yard, those questions were answered the moment he came into their view. The young ones jumped up and down on the porch hollering, and the older children ran to touch him, to get a hug. In that instant, Frank appreciated his decision to return home. But he noticed that all of them were not there.

He saw a figure near the tool shed point at something, then a shot rang out. Ellis and Mary came running from among the chinaberry trees across the yard, and the children scattered, screaming that Little Frank had a gun. On cue, the mute materialized from behind the house, aimed the gun at Buddy fleeing for cover, the trigger jerked once, and his older brother was knocked down to the ground by a bullet in the leg. His knee twisted underneath him as he struck the dust. Then he shouted and didn't move anymore.

Little Frank scowled and backed into the house, holding the pistol in front of him. Temporarily fearless, Frank followed the boy inside, as did Mary and Ellis. The three of them had no idea of what to do. The mute had backed all the way to a wall, so there was little chance of rushing him. Little Frank crouched, looking up at them. The adults spread out along the wall on both sides of the door, Ellis and Mary on one side and Frank on the other. What kept them from jumping the boy, despite their fear and anger at the helplessness of their situation, was the gun which served as an equalizer. They could see the boy meant business.

For a time, the three of them stared at each other, then at the boy, who stood there with the face of a crazed animal on him and a gun in his unsteady grasp. His finger played with pressure on the trigger, a little more, a little more.

A frightened Ellis was the first to speak. "So, you came back, huh? The big man, big nigger in the field, big nigger in the bed. Let's see how big you gone be here." By the way the fat man's voice quivered, Frank could tell he was the most fearful in the room.

"Frank ... do somethin'." Mary began to stammer. Ellis touched her lips with his forefinger, silencing her.

"Don't talk crazy." Frank was determined not to get killed.

"You nothin' but bad luck, Frank," Ellis said petulantly and glanced from the farmer to the mute.

300

Frank ignored him, still trying to size up the situation. He had to get the gun from the boy without someone getting killed. The family must survive, the family must survive, he chanted to himself. Little Frank growled and glared at his father as if he was going to shoot him first, maybe in the head or the chest. Then the mute looked at Ellis the same way, then at his mother, with the same tormented expression.

"Will you give me the gun, Little Frank?" Frank asked his son with sweetness in his words. The mute raised the gun a bit, lining up Frank for a full blast in the heart.

Frank heard Ellis whimper. "That fool gone kill us all. Do somethin'. Do somethin' Frank."

"Can't you make him put it down, Frank?" asked Mary, her face eloquent with horror. It was a stand-off, and the tension increased by the second, gathering strength as the terrifying event dragged on and on.

Ellis rubbed the back of his hand across his heavily sweating face and laughed drily. "Rush the dumb cluck, you stupid son-of-a-bitch."

Frank's head was pounding, about to burst. Too much pressure, he thought. What could he do? You can't reason with a kid with no sense, no way to talk to him at all. He saw his beloved wife slide one of her hands onto one of Ellis' fleshy arms at the elbow, seeking support. It sickened him. Now her tinny voice came from behind the fat man, who appeared to be shielding her with his girth: "Two big mens an' you can't take a pistol from a boy. Sissies, that's what you is." The house was suddenly hotter for some reason, and more sweat surfaced in beads on everyone's faces, flowing in rivulets down their necks, wetting their chests, staining their underarms. They waited, plotting. No one stirred, and the boy maintained his ground, the pistol making an arc to include all three adults. A continuous low growl came from him, from deep in his throat.

"I's sure your lover boy has a plan," Frank said gruffly. He willed his legs not to shake.

Ellis had no answer for that. Neither did Mary.

Time passed slowly, creeping with a nerve-racking pace.

Ellis' patience was exhausted and he said so in no uncertain terms. "Big man, you go for bad. There's your boy, make him mind. Shit, you can't, 'cause he's touched in the head jes' like you." Fortunately, Mary said nothing, just watched her boy there in front of them, keeping them at bay, with that damn gun. She knew all her fears had been confirmed; the boy was out of his mind and something should have been done about him a long time ago.

Which was exactly what Frank was thinking, how he had let things get to this point, how he could have stopped it, if he had put the strap to the boy then all of this wouldn't be happening. He should have heated the boy's ass like he did with the others. But then what good would that have done if the boy didn't understand anything. Whereas the big boys started to cry even before he hit them, Little Frank never showed any emotion. He whupped the boy one time and it had hurt him more than Little Frank. The boy never shed one tear, instead he watched his father like an injured animal betrayed by his master. He had flipped the mute across his lap, pulled down his pants, and thrashed his tiny, naked behind. The strokes slashed quick across the young flesh, stinging it, and leaving long, red welts across the hind cheeks.

"Ellis, why don't you hush up so a person can think some?" said Frank, wanting to go over to the man and drive his fist down his mouth.

Sensing Frank's irritation, the corpulent man taunted him with barbs. "You ain't got no right in this house. If you had been any kind of man all along, you'd have knowed what was goin' on with your chirren. You leave your wife, your kids, to run off and chase pussy. An' let somebody else do your duty. You leave them here with this idiot." Ellis never sounded better, even his voice was picking up a little depth.

Ellis was right, Frank admitted to himself. He had walked away at a bad time, completely selfish. The chickens had, indeed, come home to roost. He figured there was more at stake here for him, Frank Boles, and his family, than taking the gun away from the boy. Other things were involved, such as his manhood and his right to respect from the folks in this house; that was on the line.

Mary seethed at him, from behind Ellis' protective bulk. "Doggone it, Frank, it's your chile. You got to do somethin'. You got to take that gun from him. That's your job." Her remarks made Frank smile knowingly. Maybe she was hoping the boy would blow his damn head off, he reasoned. That would save Ellis and her some time and trouble. Put him right out of the picture with no problem.

The boy coughed and the gun moved somewhat. Everyone became quiet. From his position, Frank could see his son had wet on himself. His eyes went again to Mary's bear-hug on the fat man's arm; maybe they were in love, maybe he had been foolish to have come back.

Surprisingly, there was no anger in his voice when he made a suggestion to Ellis. "Chubby, you reckon you could move in on him from that way whilst I run at him from here. One of us might get shot, but that's a chance we got to take. I need your help to do this."

"Hell naw. You do it yourself." The answer was firm and brief.

Frank glued his attention on the gun; he took two steps forward, inching his way toward his son, opening his hands in a silent plea. He was scared as hell, never had he faced death like this. Nobody said anything. The boy hissed like a snake would do and pointed the gun right at his head and he retreated a step.

303

Damn, damn, damn, he berated himself. Could this have been avoided? If he had married someone else, maybe he wouldn't have been in this fix now. His father had given him some advice on getting hitched, wise advice, but he hadn't listened. What had he said? "Boy," the old man had told him, "if you want to keep your marriage on the right path, there's some thangs you got to do. Nevah go to bed without makin' up after a quarrel. Don't forget to laugh at your mistakes an' then learn from them. Make sure you knows what each other is doin'. Talk 'bout thangs. Set some time aside for her an' you alone, 'way from the kids. Don't try to change the woman 'cause you won't. Nevah argue in front of the chirren. Keep away from ruts. Stay 'tween her thighs as much as you can an' you won't have no trouble keepin' her. Anythin' you want to ask me, son? Do it now 'cause I ain't goin' over this twice." Good advice, and he hadn't listened to a word of it.

He was wrong and had been wrong from the very start of his marriage. Now it was too late. He had to tell Mary that he knew it was his fault and let her know that most of what he had said the night before was true but there was more. "Mary, I knows I been slack in my duties," Frank said. "I figger you don't want to hear this all over again. But I got to say it. If Ellis been the man to you like you say, then I ain't got no place here. I won't stay." As a final touch, he gestured for Ellis to wrestle the gun from the boy, but the man disregarded the signal.

"Well, you fat dandy, what you gone do?" Frank drove his point home.

"After we settle this, I's gone throw your ass out," the fat man said. "You don't deserve this woman."

"Mary, is he talkin' for you? Tell me."

"Don't make me say anythin' right now. Frank, I won't give you an answer till we clear this up." She squeezed Ellis' arm and he smiled sheepishly.

Frank saw red. "What the hell you gone do, Chubby? We can't stay like this all day."

"The boy will make that decision for me. He's gone shoot your balls off." He laughed, too loudly, and the mute shifted his feet nervously.

"Shut up, Ellis," Frank said calmly. "Shut up 'fore I help you lose some weight. Nigger, you ain't nothin' but talk. Go 'head an' take the pistol for your woman, if you reckon she's yours. Go 'head. See, you knows I's the onliest man here. I've come back to get what's rightfully mines. This is *my* house, this is *my* wife, an' these is *my* chirren. If you feels like I ain't tellin' the truth, then you got to be willin' to die for it. Take the pistol from the boy, Ellis." Frank put his hands on his hips, slowly and deliberately as to not to rile the boy.

"Fuck you," answered Ellis.

"I will 'member that, Chubby."

Little Frank began rocking, indicating he was going to do something soon.

"You came back but it's too late. Frank, did she tell you how she hates you? Did she tell you how she loves me? Did she tell you how she can't stand for you to touch her? Did she tell you how we used to lay in bed an' think up ways to kill you? Did she tell you any of that?"

Those words hit Frank in the heart and rage temporarily blinded him. He couldn't believe what he was hearing. There had been a coldness to her when he had arrived but he didn't want to believe the worst. "Is he tellin' the truth, Mary?"

"Nobody asked you to leave. You did that on your own an' you expect me to wait on you to come back when you's good an' ready. I hated you an' I hated myself. I hated you for turnin' your back on us an' I hated myself for lettin' you do it. You bastid!" Then she rebuked the both of them. "Neither one of you willin' to back up what you say. That's what wrong with colored folk, all mouth, no show. Jes' talk, talk, talk.

305

Goddamnit, that boy ain't gone walk up an' give you the gun."

"Now I get it," Frank said with resignation. "She's your gal. I ain't got no rights here."

Ellis swallowed hard; he'd never planned on any of this. He wasn't getting killed over some woman, over some bitch with a houseful of kids that wasn't even his. "I ain't gone get myself shot, messin' with that fool boy. For what? Ain't nothin' under this roof worth my life, 'specially this bitch. I can always get me some poontang, it's a dime a dozen 'round here, but I can't get my life back. To hell with both of you!" Mary had tears in her eyes. Frank could see she was both startled and hurt by the fat man's words. She watched the floor, full of remorse, as the farmer, her husband, went forward toward the boy. He moved cautiously and carefully, not making a sound. The entire time, he talked to Little Frank very, very softly. "Son ... son, gimme the pistol." He continued walking, placing one foot easy over the other. "Gimme the gun, son. Don't be 'fraid." The mute had a confused look on his face, which transformed into a hideous snarl, his lips pulled back over his teeth. Now both Ellis and Mary were scared, peering at Frank, almost hypnotized by his brave act. There was a growing tension in the room. The gun was still pointed at Frank's head and he kept coming. Little Frank's finger worried the trigger, pressing it slowly. Ellis threw up his hands, turning to the door, and started to run. Just as Frank closed in on his son, a shot sliced the air and splinters of wood ripped off the door. The mute fired a second time, grimaced, and shot Ellis, blowing away a side of the man's face. He shot Ellis twice, shot him, maybe because he moved or maybe it was something else. Something deeper. The third shot burned its way through Frank's right arm, clean through it, went through him and punctured Ellis' chest. The fat man screamed shrilly much like a young schoolgirl, stumbled but did not fall. Mary ran to his side while her husband tackled

306

the mute, his good hand gripping the gun as it fired again, and they both rolled on the floor. The boy was underneath, attempting to put the gun to Frank's neck, struggling with all his might. His head was near his father's leg and he sank his teeth in the man's thigh, making Frank howl in pain. The wall on the other side of the room was splashed with blood and brain matter. The first shot had lifted Ellis' head with a swift jerk, leaving the ugliest wound, and the third bullet had opened him up above the belly-button. Blood was gushing from both wounds as Ellis staggered away from Mary's horrified embrace, staggered back against the wall as if he was learning to walk again. He tried to hold himself up with one arm, tangled words fought with blood in his mouth for space, and he finally collapsed on his face. Mary leaned over him, crying onto his chest. Ellis' eyes bugged, his foot kicked out, and his head nodded for a final time. Meanwhile, Frank was still wrestling with his son and he socked him one when he lifted his twisted face to growl again. He yanked the boy off him with one hand, seized him by the collar, and threw him against the wall. The pistol sailed across the floor; the boy scrambled for it, but his father kicked it away. Frank then knocked the boy down with two powerful punches to the side of the face. The boy laid on his stomach, motionless, watching them. Frank sat down on the wood floor, bleeding profusely, watching his wife weep over the body of her dead lover.

Frank crawled to her through the smell of gunpowder in the room, reaching out his hand to touch her. She jerked his hand from her shoulder, glaring at him. "Frank, he's dead . . . Ellis is dead," she said, fully realizing what Little Frank had done.

"I know," answered her husband, tying a rag around his bloody arm to stem the flow. She didn't help him. He fought against the shock and pain to stay clearheaded.

She looked at him woefully. "We can't leave him there. It

307

ain't right." After what had occurred, she was slightly surprised at herself for not being hysterical, for not losing control. This man dead at her feet had been her lover. Her child had killed him. Frank couldn't leave her now, not like this. He couldn't leave. With her lips moving soundlessly, she looked up from the body to where Frank was standing over Little Frank, cleaning the gun quietly. A box of bullets was on the floor between his legs. Curiously, he managed to reload the weapon.

The mute sat still, humming to himself, and playing in a puddle of blood near him.

"Frank, I knows what you thinkin'," Mary exclaimed, very serious. "If you do this thang, you gone have to kill me too. I mean that."

He looked at his wife with disagreeable eyes. "I might jes' do that. I should shoot you, too." The memory of her with Ellis besieged him with force, making him bitter toward her. He beckoned her to him with the hand holding the gun and she went to him, taking shaky steps. He smiled at her, saying, "Mary, I been livin' for myself too long. Now I see what it can come to. This is my fault. I will make thangs right."

She looked deeply into his eyes. "Ain't there nothin' else we can do other than this? This will make thangs worser. Think, Frank, think hard. This is wrong."

"What you think I's gone do? I ain't gone do anythin' wrong. Least I don't think this is wrong. Life is wrong sometimes. You can't always do right in a wrong world. Ain't possible. Damnit, this family comes first an' I will do anythin' to keep it together. It must be saved. The boy will be in good hands, the Lawd's hands. Don't worry."

"What you mean, Frank?"

"I ain't goin' away no more."

Mary made it across the floor into his arms and they hugged, his blood staining her clothes. "What you mean?

308

What you gone do with that gun?"

He didn't answer her.

Mary reached down into the open wound on her man's arm, rubbed her finger in the crimson tide, and brought the red digit up to her face. Suddenly she took the red finger and smeared it along her husband's cheek. "There. This blood is on your head. You did this. This didn't have to be. It's your doin', 'member that." Then the children appeared in the doorway with big eyes and their mouths open. They were crying and the baby made noise in the backroom.

"Told you it wasn't papa that got shot," said Mance.

"Hush, Mance. Is he dead, papa?" Bue stared at the body on the floor.

"Yeah," answered Frank in a matter-of-fact tone. His work shirt was covered with blood.

"I thought you got shot," Bue told him. "I was so scared."

"I's okay, gal. Stop cryin'. It won't do him no good now. Get the kids into the backroom. They don't need to be seein' this."

"You heard papa. Move." Bue herded the others past the corpse.

"How's Buddy?" Frank talked from a kneeling position near Ellis' body, after closing the man's lifeless eyes. He stood up, stepped over the body, and walked to the porch, where his oldest boy leaned against the rocker, clutching his injured leg. His cheeks were bathed in tears. The wound looked worse than it was, the bullet had gone straight through.

Buddy smiled feebly. "Glad you home, papa."

His father bent down over him and kissed his hair. "Glad to be back. Here, hunch forward so I can get my arm under you." The boy did as he was asked, and the man scooped him up, then carried the limp body inside to deposit him on the bed. "Bue, tend to him. Heat up some water an' clean that wound."

309

Mary was on her knees, wiping blood from the floor with a wet rag, wringing it out in a bucket. Her husband squatted beside her, kissed her neck and told her to worry about that later. "We can send for the doctor when we get back. Buddy'll make it okay."

"When we get back from where, Frank?"

"You know what we have to do." His face was grave.

"What 'bout the body? We can't leave him there."

The note of anxiety in her voice did not escape him. "Naw, I got that all figgered out. Can't leave him here. He'll bleed all over the floor. I had a vision 'bout what jes' happened to us. I knows what to do."

"An' what are you gone do?" Mary embraced him in sadness.

Frank kept quiet, but Mary later asked him the same question when they were in the room alone. He did not reply, still thinking of how they could get rid of the body, how they would tell everybody that asked that Ellis went off to parts unknown when he heard Frank was coming back, how they would drill those lies into the children's heads. Drill it until it stuck. Tell them what to say and how to say it.

Not hearing any sound coming in the room, thinking his parents were gone, Mance came out and went over to the body and stared Ellis in the face to see if he was really dead. He winced at the sight of the ghastly head wound.

His father snapped his fingers and said calmly, "Boy, if you don't get your ass in that room . . ." He gave the boy a hard look. "Mary, brin' me somethin' to wrap him up in. Somethin' thick, an old quilt or somethin' like that."

Mance reached in a box and brought out a worn blanket. His father reared back his hand and warned him again, as he took the blanket from him. "Don't let me have to tell you again."

"I was jes' tryin' to help, papa."

Meanwhile, Little Frank rocked back and forth, smacking his leg and watching all of the activity in the room. Mance patted him on the head during his hasty departure. After Mance left, Frank glanced at the mute. No, he could not put the boy away. And he could not leave him around here, not the way he acted. He was capable of anything.

"Help me," he called to Mary, who was fiddling with a length of rope. "Push the blanket under his feet when I lift them up. Yeah, there." His wife moved as if she was in a trance. When that was done, Frank dropped the dead man's feet. Together they wrapped the blanket around the body, talking quietly while they worked. There was some blood on the floor, not much now.

"Where we takin' him?" asked Mary.

"Away from here." Frank was checking the gun again. He reached down and found the box of cartridges and put three more bullets into the weapon.

He lifted Little Frank to his feet, careful of his hurt arm. The wild look was gone from the mute's face, replaced by a blank expression. This was his peoples, his family, and he was responsible for them, Frank thought. Frank Boles and no one else, not some outsider. And if he truly loved them, he must do whatever was necessary to protect them.

Mary asked again, "Where we takin' Ellis?"

He effected his most serious expression. " 'Member where Teenie went down . . . there."

She was frightened of him and his dead, crazy eyes. She nodded. "Frank, we ought to go off some place. Somewhere like California. I got peoples there, kin folk, an' I hear tell there's plenty work for colored."

"I don't want to pick oranges." He didn't like the idea.

"We can't stay here an' you know that."

"I don't like California. I wouldn't go there to see Adam an' Eve." He lit a cigarette, inhaled, and let the smoke go

311

in a trickle. He checked the blankets twice for leaks. "Grab that end an' let's see if we can lift this hunk of blubber."

"I can't. I can't do this." She cried and her body shook. All of her insides were aflame, burning and raw. She shrank back from the body, wiping her eyes.

"Mary . . . you got to help me. You must."

"Naw, I can't."

Frank watched her tremble and spoke in a gentle voice. "Do you reckon I want to do this? Don't you understand why we gotta do this? We gotta save our family. This family comes first."

Mary sank pitifully into a chair, covering her face with her hands. Her husband straightened and told her to get Ellis' feet again, this time he was angry with her. Ellis was pretty heavy, but they could make it. His arm hurt like hell. He patted the sore spot and prayed no one would see them with the corpse.

Frank said irritably, "Quit cryin'. There'll be plenty of time for that later." He put on his coat, dropping the gun into his pocket. He hated to do this but it had to be done. A tainted son meant failure.

"Son," he told the mute softly. "I gone give you some relief. Never forget that I love you." He stopped and looked at his namesake, slobbering, staring into space. "You understand me. Now hold on to your papa's arm. You gone come with me." He did not look in his wife's direction when he said it to the sullen boy, who grabbed his coatsleeve.

"You hate him, you always have," snapped Mary. "The whole thang is wrong, Frank. We can't do this."

"I don't hate the boy. What else can we do with him?"

She was almost begging again. "Send him away to my kinfolk. Have one of Sarah's peoples hide him in Arkansas. Anythin' but this. This don't make sense. Not at all."

"Don't argue with me, woman." He glared at her with killing eyes. "Do as you're told an' everythin' will work out."

He felt love for his boy, Little Frank, but the Lord had somehow turned his back on him and his kind. Once again. It was no time to bite his tongue. "Hush up, Mary. It too late to ask why us? The boy is sick, tainted, an' we have to save him 'cause other folks ain't gone be as kind to him as we are. We can't wait on God to lift his burden. Ain't no other way but this way. I had a vision, I knows what I must do. Be strong. I need your help, not your tears."

They hoisted the shrouded body and started out. Words were lost at a time like this, worthless. This is the fate of the diseased limb that no healer can cure, Frank thought. Whatever it was that was rotten in his seed surfaced in this child with his name. The grass was not so loud as they stole quickly across the field. That was what was rotten in his seed, that which would pain them no more. With the disease cut away, the body would be spared and the future assured.

THE MELROSE SQUARE BLACK AMERICAN SERIES
PRESENTS A NEW ILLUSTRATED BIOGRAPHY OF

OPRAH WINFREY
ENTERTAINER
By Marianne Ruuth

Oprah. The name is known throughout the world. In the 1990s, she became perhaps the most famous woman in America, certainly the most famous black woman. Yet hers is not an empty fame; it is the result of hard work and accomplishments. Oprah overcame a troubled childhood and payed her dues in broadcasting before she went on to become America's favorite talk-show host. Inspired by her father "to do her best" at whatever she attempted, she rose to host her hit show in Chicago, and in taking roles in such films as *The Color Purple* and *The Women of Brewster Place,* and *Beloved*, which she developed and produced. As other talk shows have moved increasingly toward sleaze, Oprah has done the opposite, emphasizing quality and humanity on her programs. For your own copy of this fascinating life story of a remarkable woman, send $6.50 (includes postage and handling) to Melrose Square Publishing Company, 8060 Melrose Ave., Los Angeles, CA 90046. California residents add $0.40 for state sales tax.

THE MELROSE SQUARE BLACK AMERICAN SERIES
PRESENTS
A NEW ILLUSTRATED BIOGRAPHY OF

JAMES BECKWOURTH, MOUNTAIN MAN
By RAYMOND FRIDAY LOCKE

"Jim Beckwith" was the name he was called by friends and fans. The more fanciful tag was given him by a tipsy writer from Boston who spent a

few weeks with Jim in a California cabin and went back east to write the *"true"* story of Jim's life, and virtually ruined his reputation with his fictions. Actually, Jim was born to a son of the British/Irish aristocracy and a light-skinned slave woman in 1800. The family moved to Missouri and Jim was placed in school in St. Louis. His exploits, the actual true ones, are legendary, and include adventures with Kit Carson and Jim Bridger as Rocky Mountain trappers, and General Sherman of Civil War fame. Order your copy by sending $6.50 (includes shipping and postage), to Melrose Square, 8060 Melrose Avenue, Los Angeles, CA 90046. Calif. residents add $0.40 State Tax.

THE MELROSE SQUARE BLACK AMERICAN SERIES
PRESENTS
A NEW ILLUSTRATED BIOGRAPHY OF
ALVIN AILEY
DANCER & CHOREOGRAPHER
By ROBERT FLEMING

No one could have imagined Alvin Ailey would become the internationally renowned dancer and choreographer that he did. Alvin was a large man, six feet tall, with big shoulders and large hands. Some often joked that he resembled a bear with his massive frame. However, when he took to the dance floor, his movements could be startlingly graceful, elegant, powerful. Born January 5th, 1931, he would become world famous while still in his twenties, conquering Broadway in two dramatic plays, then the world of dance which, with his Dance Theatre, changed that art form forever. Order your copy by sending $6.50 which includes shipping and postage to **MELROSE SQUARE BOOKS**, 8060 Melrose Avenue, Los Angeles, California 90046. California residents add $0.40 state sales tax.

THE MELROSE SQUARE BLACK AMERICAN SERIES
PRESENTS A NEW ILLUSTRATED BIOGRAPHY OF
Ida B. Wells
ACTIVIST
By Joe Nazel

With the end of Reconstruction, reactionary whites in the South sought, through the creation of Jim Crow laws, to take away the rights only recently won by African Americans. One woman, a schoolteacher named Ida B. Wells,

stood up to fight for her rights, refusing to leave a first-class railway seat for which she had paid. When she sued the railroad and took her case to the U S. Supreme Court, she gained the attention and respect of black journalists. Soon she herself began writing for newspapers and fighting not only the new concept of segregation but also a rising tide of lynching that was sweeping the nation. When her newspaper office in Memphis was destroyed, she moved north and helped found the NAACP and spent most of the rest of her life in efforts to end injustice. Order your copy by sending $6.50 (includes shipping and handling) to Melrose Square, 8060 Melrose, Los Angeles, California, 90046. California residents, please add $0.40 tax.

THE MELROSE SQUARE BLACK AMERICAN SERIES
PRESENTS NEW ILLUSTRATED BIOGRAPHY OF

ROBERT CHURCH
ENTREPRENEUR
By Cookie Lommel

The first African-American millionaire in the South, Robert Reed Church began life as a slave, at least technically, property of his father, a Mississippi River steamboat owner, who entrusted him with the responsibility for supplying his boats. After the Civil War, he settled in Memphis and gradually established a series of businesses--saloons, hotels, theaters, and, eventually, banks. After the devastating yellow fever epidemics of the 1870's Church expressed his confidence in the city by purchasing the first of the municipal bonds issued to rebuild Memphis. Leaders in the Southern branch of the Republican Party, his family continued to have considerable influence in Memphis and Washington political affairs well into the middle of the 20th Century. Order your copy by sending $6.50 (includes shipping and postage) to MELROSE SQUARE, 8060 Melrose Avenue, Los Angeles, CA 90046. California residents please add $0.40 state sales tax.

PREMIERE TRADE EDITIONS PRESENTS

A NEW MYSTERY BY
NORA DeLOACH

Mama, of the famous mother/daughter detective team, is charming, ingratiating, intuitive and shrewd. But when she is accused of stealing food stamps by one of  her welfare patients, an ill-tempered and alcoholic woman who has the backing of one of Mama's co-workers, she becomes furious. And especially when her sister Agnes indicates she also suspects Mama! But not for long. Agnes very quickly turns up murdered and the two prime suspects are her long suffering husband, and Mama. Of course Nora DeLoach works it all out by uncovering long forgotten secrets, and comes up with an ending that is both a surprise and a shocker. This fourth book in the Mama series is *a stunner!* Order your copy of **MAMA STANDS ACCUSED** from **Premiere Trade Editions,** 8060 Melrose Avenue, Los Angeles, CA 90046. $14.50 includes postage and handling. California residents add $0.90 Sales Tax.

THE MELROSE SQUARE BLACK AMERICAN SERIES
PRESENTS A NEW ILLUSTRATED BIOGRAPHY OF

B. B. KING

By Joe Nazel

Born near the little town of Itta Bena, Mississippi, Riley B. King (his birth name) became the charge of his mother's family (and later that of a white family) in the hill town of Kilmichael, eighty miles

to the east. From the beginning he showed signs of being a musical prodigy, first discovered by his uncle, singing in church. Not much later he took up the guitar, formed his own gospel group, and eventually moved to Memphis where his cousin Bukka White lived--and where Beale Street beckoned to every aspiring blues man in the deep South. From Memphis, King traveled an endless road to become what he is today: "The Emperor of the Blues." Order your copy of this compelling book. Send $6.50 (for handling, postage) to Melrose Square, 8060 Melrose, LA, CA 90046. CA residents add $0.40 state taxes.